FOURTH DOWN

FOURTH DOWN
A BEAUMONT SERIES NEXT GENERATION SPIN-OFF
HEIDI MCLAUGHLIN
© 2021

COVER DESIGN: Sarah Hansen: OkayCreations.
PHOTOGRAPHY: RplusMphoto
MODELS: Michael Scanlon / Elizabeth Babcock
EDITING: Edits by Amy / Briggs Consulting

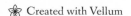 Created with Vellum

THE PORTLAND PIONEERS:
A BEAUMONT SERIES NEXT GENERATION
SPIN-OFF

Fourth Down

Fair Catch

False Start

THE BEAUMONT SERIES READING ORDER

ONE

AUTUMN

As soon as the production assistant motions we're clear, I allow my shoulders to sag, my face relaxes, and I don't hesitate to pull my earpiece out. I exit the stage and head toward my dressing room, which in reality is a closet with a desk and a pocket door. I added a do-it-yourself vanity mirror so I could do my make-up with some decent lighting and managed to change the overhead light to something better. Honestly, anything is better than what was in here when I took the job as *Channel 3's Weather Girl,* a nickname if you will, that some jackass producer branded me with during the promos the station ran before I started. I've tried many times over the past couple of years to get rid of it, but sadly, this is how people know me in Dickinson, North Dakota.

"Great show this afternoon, Autumn," my assistant Parker says as I walk toward her. Her arms are full, and she's balancing two bottles of water and two cups of what I'm assuming to be coffee on her clipboard, which is stacked on top of files filled with paper. I share Parker with three other anchors and have tried my best to make her job easy.

"Thank you," I say, reaching for one of the waters. I don't want her to try and give it to me because I'm fearful she'll spill the contents of what she's holding all over the floor. Parker smiles softly and then sighs. She has a tough job, a demanding one. One of the anchors is a diva with an ego larger than Texas. A few of us wonder why she's still here, broadcasting the news to some twenty-two thousand people. For me, this is a stepping-stone to something bigger and better.

I step into my pint-sized dressing room and pull the metal hook to slide my pocket door closed. It wobbles, sticks, and I'm forced to give it a hard yank. I finally sit down, and I swear my body sighs from exhaustion. I've been up since before the sun to cover for our morning meteorologist, who called out sick at the very last possible moment. Then, I had to hurry across town to an elementary school for an assembly. My neighbor is in third grade and asked if I would speak at career day. There was no way I'd pass up the opportunity. Afterward, I rushed back to the studio for my afternoon slot to tell the fine people watching that the sun is shining, but it's chilly, and a sweater might come in handy.

Slowly, I pull my right leg up to rest on my left knee, and as gently as possible, slip my high-heeled shoe off. If toes could scream, mine would holler from the highest peak in pure relief. I do the same to my other foot, and as I lean back in my chair, I wiggle the digits that I'm so mean to. Heels are a necessary evil, a must. They elongate the legs and force us to stand tall. As much as I appreciate the good posture in front of the camera, it doesn't mean I enjoy standing on the pointed spikes for hours on end.

I've been known to walk around the studio in my slippers. But as of late, I prefer my Birkenstocks. They're comfortable, yet not fashionable at all. They're also a major turn off to the single men who work here. I love it. I'm not looking for an office romance or a quickie against my vanity. I want something meaningful. I want a relationship that grows up from the bottom with dates and old-fashioned wooing. Where, if the guy is a gentleman, maybe he gets a kiss at night. As much as I hate to admit it, I want to be courted. Nowadays, it's all about swiping right and people wanting to "Netflix and chill."

My phone rings, and I groan. Not because I don't want to answer it, but because doing so requires me to move. I hate feeling this way and sense that it's my unhappiness at my job that is bringing me down. Usually, I'm cheery—the life of the party. I'm the one who can have a meaningful conversation with a wall and feel satisfied at the end of the night. As of late, though, I'm a Debbie Downer, and I think it's because every job I apply for, I'm either passed over because someone is more qualified or I'm not the right fit. Still, I'm pushing the send button on my resume and highlight reel for every job that opens up at a new station.

My ex's name and picture take up the screen of my phone. We're friends, better friends than we were lovers. I click to answer and press the speakerphone button. I'm too tired to put in the effort right now.

"If you're somewhere tropical, I'm going to hate you forever," I tell Camden as I close my eyes. We went to school together, both majoring in broadcast journalism. When we first started dating, I was smitten with him and decided to follow his path, minoring in meteorology. The weather was never really on my radar until I met Cam. There have been times over the past couple of years that I wish I had listened to my parents and minored in sports or something else. Don't get me wrong, I love what I do, just not where I do it.

"Okay, I won't tell you I'm in the Florida Keys."

"Ugh, I hate you."

"I know you do. Any luck yet?"

"No," I say. I keep my eyes closed. "I'm giving up hope."

"The right job will come along."

"And the right market. I'm not saying I want to be the next Willard Scott."

"No, that would be impossible. First, you're not a man . . . thank god. Second, you want to be the first Autumn LaRosa. You don't want to follow in someone's footsteps but blaze your own path, which I fully believe you can do."

"You know when you say things like this, I ask myself why we ever broke up."

Camden chuckles. "Because we both want careers, and right now, they're taking us in different directions."

"You're right." I hate that he is, but he is. We've just always been better friends. The type who are very supportive of one another.

"Damn, woman, you have no idea what those words do to me."

"Shut up," I tell him, rolling my eyes. I sit up and glance into the mirror. At least I don't look as hideous as I feel. "All right, I'm going to go. I had to cover this morning, and now I either need a nap or an early bedtime."

"Keep your head up, Autumn. The right job for you is out there. You'll find it."

"Thanks, Cam."

We hang up, and instead of changing back into my street clothes, I decide to check my email. Most of the notices are from the listserv I belong to. Numerous conferences are happening, some of which I'd love to attend, but it's near impossible at the moment. I see one for Florida and mentally flip Camden off for being down there right now. I realize I never asked him why he's there and make a mental note to check for any hurricanes or tropical storms forming in the ocean.

The one email that catches my eye is a job I interviewed for about six months ago. When I didn't hear back—not even a "we're not interested" response—I figured they were looking for someone with more qualifications than what I had to offer.

For some reason, I hesitate before opening the email. Knowing my luck, it's spam, or they're inviting me to their next cocktail event, not realizing I don't work for them. My thumb hovers over the email as I look at the sender's name. "This is stupid," I say to myself. "It's not like I'm waiting for test results or something life-changing."

Hello Autumn,

We're excited to offer you employment with our station, MCAX.

The rest of the email is a blur, and I have to read it repeatedly to make sure my eyes aren't deceiving me. I get to the last line, the second most important line of the entire email. There's a number to call if I want to accept this job offer. My thumb, the hesitant one from earlier, presses the phone number lightning fast.

"Leon Woolworth's office. Sherry speaking."

"Um, yes, hi. This is Autumn LaRosa calling in regard to the email I received."

"Hello, Autumn," Sherry says as she types. "Mr. Woolworth is expecting your call. Hold please."

As if I'd hang up.

"Autumn, Leon here. How are you?"

"I'm well, and you?"

"I'll be better if I know whether or not you're bringing your talents to my station."

"I am. I can't thank you enough for this opportunity." Holy crap, did I just say yes to a new job? Not just any job but one in a much larger market where I know I can thrive? My heart is pounding so much right now. I don't know if I should close my eyes and practice some deep breathing or get up and dance until I can't move anymore.

"Perfect." It sounds like he's clapped his hands or slapped his desk. "The evening team is excited to have you."

Surely, I didn't hear him correctly. "I'm sorry, but can you repeat what you just said?"

Leon laughs. "Autumn, we want you for our evening news. We think you'll be a great addition to the crew. You'll work with Aiden Marchetti, who does sports, and Selena Rich and Arthur Brentwood, who do the news. Lisette Maver is your assistant; she'll reach out to you tomorrow to introduce herself. Once we're done talking, Sherry will send your contract over. When can you start?"

"Two weeks?" I squeak out.

"Looking forward to having you on staff."

"Not as much as I am," I tell him before we hang up. I stare at my phone, dumbfounded. Did this really happen? I go back to my recent calls and press Camden's name. He answers with a laugh.

"Did you know?"

"I had a feeling but didn't want to say anything. I heard it through the grapevine that Leon kept putting your tape in front of the board. Originally, they went with someone else, and the public didn't respond well, and Leon pushed for the okay to hire you."

"Why didn't you tell me?"

"Because." He sighs. "In this industry, minds change like the wind speeds. If I had said something and you didn't get the call, you'd hate me even more than you do now.

Besides, you needed the excitement of speaking to Leon. I hear he's one hell of a producer. You'll do well in the Portland market."

"Thanks, Cam."

"Don't mention it. Now, go give your notice, pack up that tiny dressing room, tell your roommate you're leaving and get your ass to Portland."

"This is the only order I will ever take from you. Thanks again."

"You've earned it, now slay it."

As soon as we hang up, I squeal and kick my feet up in the air. Unfortunately for me, my chair falls back, and so do I, hitting the ground with a thud. "This is par for the course," I mutter as I lay there looking at the ceiling. "Holy shit, I got a new job!"

I bring myself to a sitting position and slowly get up, mindful of my now sore backside. I search the ground for my phone, finding it near the door. I don't know whether I should tell my boss I'm leaving face-to-face or type something up. Maybe, I should do both. I go to put on my heels but think better of it and slip my aching feet into my Birks and head down the hall. The station is quiet. The lull happens between shifts where the afternoon team is in their rooms either finishing work from earlier or napping, and the evening crew is staggering in. I make my way down the hall to my boss's office. I knock, but no answer.

"Letter it is," I say aloud as I make my way back to my dressing room. I don't even want to imagine what kind of space I'll have in Portland. I just know it *has* to be better than this.

I STOP at the hardware store for a stack of boxes, packing tape, and some bubble wrap on my way home. I also reserve a box trailer that I can pull behind my car. When I get home, I find my roommate curled up on the couch with a blanket.

"Hey," I say as I walk in.

"Hey, what's with the boxes?"

"I got offered a job. It's in Portland and I start in two weeks."

Her eyes go wide. She doesn't move from the couch, not that I expect her to. The apartment is hers; I lease the bedroom. When I first moved in, we did a lot of things together. We hung out, had people over, but she's been distant over the last year or so. She doesn't know I know she put the moves on Camden. He told me when it happened. At first, I was going to confront her but then figured nothing good would come from it. When this happened, she knew Cam was an ex. I never bothered to tell her that we hooked up occasionally when we'd visit each other. I suppose I could've told her, but I also never expected her to do what she did.

"I'll pay for rent next month to give you time to find someone else."

"Sure," she says, never taking her eyes off the television, leaving me no choice but to retreat to my room.

Packing will be easy. Moving to a new place will be exciting.

Starting a new job—well, that's downright terrifying.

TWO

JULIUS

Everything in the room is white. The couch. The rug. The walls. Even the television has a white border around it. The mantel over the fireplace—white. Same with the picture frames. Everywhere I look, it's all I see. The living room is supposed to be inviting, welcoming, and yet it feels stressful. I've never been the type of person who asks their friends to take off their shoes when they come into their home. I find it rude, but I also respect it if my friends ask me. When you come into my house—well, my soon to be *former* home—your shoes must be off. Not only off but left outside.

I sit on the couch, with its white pillows, and rest my ankle on my knee. My shoes are on because I'm bitter and angry at the world, the situation I'm in, and my wife. Mostly her, which probably isn't fair, but her actions have put us in this position.

Elena comes into the room and sighs heavily. I know why and I don't care. I continue to stare out the window at the blue sky. Elena and I met in college. I was on a full scholarship at the University of Alabama, playing wide receiver, and she worked for my favorite clothing store. I wish I could say it was love at first sight, but it was fear that brought us together. I had been in her store when a tornado warning sounded. Everyone in the store took shelter, except Elena. She stood in the middle of the room with nothing but sheer panic on her face. Her co-workers tried to coax her into the back room, but she was frozen. I went to her, scooped her up, and carried her to the back. She clung to me until the warning was over. The entire time I just talked to her about my life, football, my hopes, and dreams. She told me she moved to Alabama to go to school, but her financial aid fell through, and she was too embarrassed to go home and ask her parents for money. They didn't want her moving south to begin with, and told her she was making a mistake. She needed to prove them wrong.

After that day, we started hanging out. She'd come to the dorm, help me with my homework, and I'd invite her to games. Our friendship turned romantic a few months later, and after a couple of years of dating, I asked her to marry me. I thought I had found my soulmate. It turns out I was just her meal ticket to stardom.

It's funny when you're in a life and death situation. You say a lot of things to the people around you. For me, I've always dreamed of playing professional football. I worked my ass off in college to achieve my dream. Elena's dream was to work in marketing or advertising. That was until we started dating seriously, and her social media skyrocketed. Then, her dream was to become an influencer and eventually a model. I supported each change in her career wholeheartedly because I wanted her to be happy, and I was in love with her. I *thought* she was in love with me. She told me we had to have a house in Orange County even though we lived in Portland, Oregon. At first, I didn't understand why but still gave her what she wanted. Everything became clear when some reality TV show about wives announced she was joining the cast. The show was a hit. Her fame grew. And suddenly, she wanted to be an actress. By now, through all of this, we have two children and are splitting our time between Portland, Huntington Beach, her parents in Delaware, and mine in Michigan. An endless cycle of traveling. I tried to talk to her about it. I tried telling her something had to give. At first, she was defensive, telling me I was trying to stifle her creativity. Then she said if I really loved her and the kids, I'd ask for a trade to one of the teams in California. When I told her no, she uttered the word I never thought I'd hear—divorce.

My world was rocked.

When all of this happened, Elena and my kids were my world, and I couldn't imagine my life without them. I spoke to my agent, asked what I could do to move to California, and thought about how I'd have to approach my career—that was until I found out she had an affair.

While I was busting my ass on the field, providing the lifestyle she wanted, she thought it would be smart to sleep with her co-star from her theatrical debut. She forgot about the prenup she signed, and now I'm the bad guy.

Now, here I sit, in the house we bought together, the place we planned to raise our children, at a standstill. I want the kids to live with me in Portland, and she wants them to live here with her. My argument is that our oldest, Reggie, is already in school. He has friends and plays Pee-Wee football. Roxy, our youngest, is only three. She doesn't grasp everything that's going on and knows Mommy and Daddy sometimes work away from the house. But most often, I'm gone for a couple of days when we have an away game.

"Julius, we need to make a decision," her voice is like

nails on a chalkboard. I used to love listening to her talk, but now, I never want to hear it.

"I've told you my stance, Elena. It doesn't make sense to pull Reggie out of school to move down here. Plus, this puts unnecessary travel on me when I want to see my kids."

"Well, I can say the same thing," she fires back. "I'd have to travel to Portland to see them."

"You've done one movie, E. One. With no other movies lined up. It doesn't make sense for you to be here if you don't have to be. You can stay in the apartment in Portland, and I'll go to a hotel. We can swap or whatever. Others have done it."

"And that doesn't make sense for me, Julius. My job is here, and this is where I live." She spreads her arms out, almost as if she purchased the house with her own money.

"Not for long, I'm going to put the house on the market."

"You can't."

I look at her and cock my eyebrow. "I can, and I will."

"I'll sue you for the house *and* alimony."

I let out a chuckle and decide to stand. I walk over to the window and look out over the expansive ocean. We have a view—that's it. If we want to go to the beach, we have to drive to it. "You signed a prenup, Elena. A very particular one that states I don't owe you anything if you partake in an extramarital affair."

"I never cheated. I only started seeing Sonny after we decided to divorce."

I turn to her and shake my head. "You must think I'm stupid. I have the photos. I have videos of him coming into the house and leaving in the morning."

"Those don't prove anything."

My hands go to my head, and I groan. "Just stop, Elena.

You're getting the divorce—that's what you wanted. The rest, I'm not budging on. There is no way in hell I'm paying you alimony, you know this, and your only fight is for the kids. Tell me, what are you going to do if you get a movie role that films out of state, huh? Leave them with a nanny for months?"

"They can go live with you."

"And interrupt their lives? No thanks."

I'm about to sit down when the front door opens, and a voice calls out, "You better be naked and ready for me because I'm . . ." his voice trails off when Sonny sees me standing in the room.

I look at Elena and shake my head. "Really? On a day we're supposed to be trying to work on the arrangement for our kids." I point at her boyfriend while keeping my eyes on her. "And what if they were here, huh? You just gonna keep them in their rooms so you can get fucked on our white leather couch?"

Elena says nothing. She won't even look at me, Sonny either. I think he's afraid of me, which is good. Although, I would never jeopardize my career for the likes of him. He's a pretty boy, the current Hollywood heartthrob.

"I'm so glad I wasted my day off to fly down here to talk to you. If I were you, I'd talk to ole Sonny boy about shacking up," I pause and scoff. "Oh, that's right, his wife kicked him out for having an affair. What a pair."

I brush past Sonny and head toward the door without saying another word. I'm beyond pissed and hope I send that message to them when I slam the front door. Thankfully, I have a rental car parked in the driveway, which should've been a clue to Sonny that someone was inside the house. Right now, I think they're both out of their minds. It's the lust fueling them. Once the newness wears off and reality sets in, they'll both realize how badly they fucked up.

I head toward the airport, weaving my way in and out of traffic. It's never wise to drive when you're this angry, but I need to get the hell out of here, even if it means I'll have to sit in the terminal lounge until I can get a flight. At this point, I don't care.

After dropping the rental off and catching a shuttle, I flag down a security guard and ask him to get me through security. Sometimes, I wait with the rest of the travelers, but I'm not in the right frame of mind to deal with fans. The last thing I need is some media report calling me an asshole because I wouldn't pose for a picture or some shit.

Once I'm through security, the guard drops me off at the terminal lounge. Inside, there's a concierge type person who can help me with my flight. Unfortunately, the next flight to Portland isn't for a few hours, and it's full, which means I'll be on standby until my scheduled flight at eleven tonight.

As soon as I sit down at the bar, the bartender asks what I want to drink. I order my usual "whatever you have on tap" choice and ask if I can get a burger and fries. Not ideal, but it's been a long day, and it's going to be a long night.

One stool away from me moves, and I glance to my right. She's blonde, in a suit, and screams sophistication. Our eyes meet, and she smiles. She's beautiful, and for a moment, I think about what it would be like to just say fuck it, throw all my morals out the window like Elena has, and ask this woman if she'd like to come with me to the bathroom. The bartender isn't going to care or even bat an eyelash. He's paid for his discretion.

"What's your name?" I ask her.

"Mariana," she tells me in a sweet voice. "Yours?"

"Julius. My friends call me Jules. Can I buy you a drink?"

"I'd like that." I motion to the bartender, and she tells him what she wants. She pulls out her phone and starts typing away. I wonder if I just got played. Does she know who I am or am I overthinking this entire situation? Either way, it's okay. As much as I'd love to get some aggression out in the form of a bathroom fuck, I'm not ready. Elena did a number on me, and it's going to take some time to recover. Most of my teammates tell me to start sowing my oats, but I've never been "the hit it and quit it" type. Again, I blame Elena. And if Mariana's telling her friends, good for her. Let her live in the moment.

At this point, everything is Elena's fault.

THREE

AUTUMN

I lost track of the hours it took to make my drive from Dickinson to Portland. I had a few days to do whatever and mapped my journey ahead of time, pinpointing stops, and booking a hotel. However, I did not plan for the long drive through Montana and ended up staying an extra night at some random hotel along the way. While the trek was beautiful through the state, it was exhausting. I think I danced a bit in my seat when I saw the Welcome to Idaho sign. I also regretted not staying in the small town of Coeur d'Alene because it looked so beautiful. I made a note to add it to my list of places to visit once I've settled in Portland.

When I gave my notice to my boss, he told me not to wait, to just go ahead and leave. I found it to be rather rude but figured I might as well use the vacation time I had and enjoy Portland before I have to jump into the fray of telling the fine folks of the Rose City about their weather.

The only issue I had with leaving right away was I didn't have a place to live. However, thanks to my new assistant, Lisette, she found me a cute apartment, close to the water and within walking distance of everything I will need. I ordered furniture online, hoping it would be comfortable, and had it delivered before I arrived. The drawback is I have to drive to work once I start my rotation because there is no way I'm walking in a city, by myself, at night. Still, I love the idea of walking around my new neighborhood and exploring all the cute, quaint cafes near me.

My apartment complex is bustling with activity when I step off the elevator. I'm on the fifth floor with a usable balcony overlooking the street. I smile and wish the door attendant a good day before I begin my walk toward the station. The sun is shining, I have a fresh cup of coffee in my hand, and my earbuds are playing an audiobook I started during the trip here. I thought I'd have some first-day jitters, but I seem relatively calm for starting a new job in a much larger market. I do remind myself that this is what I went to school for—to be a meteorologist—to be on network television. Portland is the place that could catapult me into stardom.

The walk to the station is thirteen blocks, which is doable except for having to walk under an overpass of a major interstate. Thankfully, Portland has a light rail system called Max, and there is a stop near me. I don't mind public transportation and became used to it when I lived in Chicago. My friends and I would often take the L train to the baseball games.

As luck would have it, the MCAX station is on a slight incline. I refrain from calling it a hill because I've seen some of the hills in Portland, and unless I'm looking to strengthen my calf muscles, I'm going to avoid walking up to them any time soon.

"Good morning," I say to the lady at the reception desk. "I'm Autumn LaRosa. Mr. Woolworth is expecting me."

She smiles and welcomes me before calling Sherry. We've spoken a few times since our original call, and I'm fond of her. Sherry has been accommodating with this transition. The side door opens, and a woman with a beaming smile comes out, followed by another.

"Autumn?"

"Yes, hi." We shake hands.

"I'm Sherry, and this is Lisette. I believe you've spoken."

"Oh my," I say as I pull her into my arms. It's forward, but I'm indebted to her. "You've saved my life with this move. How can I repay you?"

Lisette laughs. "It's my job to help. I'm very thankful everything went smoothly. Believe me, I've had challenges before."

"Come on," Sherry says as she motions toward the door. "We have a lot to do this morning." I follow behind her, with Lisette behind me. Sherry starts talking about the city, the station, and how we're a big family, which I didn't have in North Dakota. Every time we run into someone, we stop, and chat and they tell me how happy they are that I've joined the team. After we stop in human resources to get my ID badge, Sherry tells me I'll join Leon for lunch. Once she's gone, Lisette shows me to my dressing room.

"Whoa." It's all I can mutter when I step inside.

"Is something wrong?" she asks.

Slowly, I shake my head. "Absolutely not. At the other station, I had a closet, and I had to make my own vanity, which I brought with me, just in case."

Lisette laughs as she moves about the room. "Anything you need, you let me know, and I'll take care of it." She turns on the light to the bathroom. *My bathroom.* It's not huge by any means, and neither is my dressing room, but the bathroom has a stand-up shower and a toilet, of course.

My dressing room has a love seat, which pulls out to a bed, according to Lisette.

"The sheets are fresh, as are the towels in the bathroom. We have a laundry service that picks up on Friday if you want to use it or bring things from home. This afternoon, you'll meet with a rep from Meyers to go over your wardrobe."

"My wardrobe?"

She nods. "Meyers is a fashion company. They 'dress' people," she says, using finger quotes. "The station provides your clothes."

My throat tightens. "I'm sorry, what?"

Lisette looks at me like I have two, maybe three heads. Honestly, I feel like multiples are resting on my shoulders right now. Clearly, I misunderstood.

"Did Leon not go over the benefits? No, I'm sure he didn't. He never does," she answers her own question. "One of the benefits, aside from the standard sick time, vacation time, etc., is clothing. We want our team to look their very best, and in this day and age of social media, people are quick to point out when an outfit is worn more than once. Leon hates it when his crew is the butt of jokes. This is where Meyers comes in. They work with all the stores and designers to provide the news team with the latest fashion and trends. You wear it on air, we post where someone can buy the outfit, and the store or designer gets credit during the broadcast. It's a win-win for everyone."

"Wow, I'm. . . well at a loss for words."

She places her hand on my forearm and gives it a little squeeze. "I like you," she says. "You're going to fit in perfectly." Lisette takes me to a small conference room on the top floor of our office building, which apparently used to be apartments until the station bought it. People are milling around and eating lunch from the buffet set up against the wall. Leon hollers my name, and everyone turns to look at me. It's not awkward at all. I'm sure my cheeks are flaming red right now.

"Autumn, this is Selena Rich and Arthur Brentwood, the evening and late-night anchors." Lisette points to the people whose faces I've studied for the past two weeks. "Over there, the guy stuffing his face is Aiden Marchetti. He does sports. This here," she says as she pulls a guy toward her, "is Marvin Adams. He will be your main cameraman. If you ever feel lost up there, you look for him."

"Got it."

Leon finally comes over and welcomes me. He puts his arm around me, resting his hand on my shoulder. "Every-one," he says, getting their attention. "Meet Autumn LaRosa. She comes to us from Dickinson, North Dakota, after graduating from Northwestern with a degree in broad-cast journalism and meteorology."

"Great, she's coming for my job," Arthur says, much to everyone's delight. "Welcome," he adds.

"She's traded in the snow for the rain," another person says; someone I haven't met yet.

"Thank you," I tell the group. "I'm happy to be here, to learn about this great city, and become a part of the community."

"When's your first on-air date?" Selena asks.

"Tomorrow," Leon says, which is a shock to me. I thought I'd have a few days to acclimate and learn the ropes.

"Wow, Leon. Just throwing her to the wolves, huh?" Selena quips. I'm with her though, what the hell is he thinking?

"Well, I guess I better cancel my hair appointment for tomorrow," I say jokingly. Good thing I didn't have one booked. I suppose things could be worse. I could attempt to do the traffic in a city I know absolutely nothing about. At least, with the weather, it's pretty easy to tell people when it might rain. Being a meteorologist is literally the only job where you can be wrong and never get fired.

Leon leaves me to mingle, which I'm a little unsure of. I've never been shy, but there is something about being the new girl that makes me feel—skittish? I don't know. It's hard to pinpoint exactly what I'm feeling other than grateful...and maybe a little overwhelmed but in a good way. As I look around the room at my new co-workers, grateful is definitely how I feel. I've been given this opportunity, and I plan to make the best of it.

The buffet is calling my name, evident by the low rumble in my stomach. I place my hand over my midsection to stifle the noise and walk as quickly as I can to the table. Fresh fruits, sandwiches, salads, and cookies fill the space.

"I'm Aiden."

I look up from the plate I'm trying to fill and smile. "Nice to meet you. I'd shake your hand but . . ." I shrug and show him that both of my hands are full.

"No worries." He reaches across me to add a sandwich, a bag of chips, and a stack of cookies to his plate, and then he waits for me. When I'm done, he motions for me to sit down. "What do you think of Portland?"

"I like it so far. It's definitely a change from Dickinson, but right in line with Chicago."

"Is that where you're from?"

His question catches me mid-bite. I shake my head and then cover my face with my napkin. Eating in front of people can be so embarrassing. "No, I'm from Corpus Christi, Texas."

"Wow." His eyes go wide. "You're really expanding your horizons. How come you didn't go back to Texas after school?"

"I wanted something different, and I don't necessarily want to live in Texas for the rest of my life. Going back to visit my family is enough for right now. Where are you from?"

"Here," he says. "My wife and I have a house across the river in Vancouver. Both of us were born and raised in the area."

"Well, then I know who to come to when I need something to do."

Aiden laughs. "My wife would love that. She's a party planner. Does mostly weddings and fundraisers."

"That sounds like a fun job."

"She loves it. I'll have her stop by the station soon so you can meet." We're silent for a moment until he asks, "Do you know Peyton Westbury?"

I shake my head. "No, should I?"

"Leon said you went to Northwestern, right?" I nod. "She's from there as well. Sometimes Peyton fills in for me when I'm out. She works for the Portland Pioneers."

"Really?"

"Yeah, she's about your age. I guess I figured she recommended you to Leon."

"No, I don't think so, but I'm going to have to look her up."

"I'm sure you'll meet her eventually. She's here a lot."

"I look forward to it."

After lunch, the Meyers rep shows up, and I sit, well, mostly stand, through a three-hour fitting. I don't remember the last time—if there ever was a time—I tried on so many outfits and pairs of shoes. I swear, my body is moving in a constant up and down motion from all the high-heeled shoes. The rep seemed satisfied when she left, though, and told me I'd have an outfit hanging in my room when I came in tomorrow. Once she and Lisette finish chatting, Lisette and I walk to the newsroom to watch the evening news broadcast.

Seeing my co-workers deliver the news is exciting. I'm eager to stand up there and provide the weather, but when I hear Selena tell the viewers that I'm starting tomorrow, my heart beats faster. I'm excited and ready, and Selena, Arthur, and Aiden seem eager as well.

It's dark when I leave the station. Aiden offers to give me a ride home, which I graciously accept. He goes into what I call "Dad mode" and tells me I need to either take a rideshare home from work if I'm going to walk in or drive both ways at least until spring when it's light enough to walk after the five o'clock segment and then drive back. I appreciate someone looking out for me.

When I get back to my apartment, I pour myself a glass of wine before going through one of the boxes I haven't emptied yet, looking for my college yearbook. I thought it odd that my mother insisted on me buying them, but I did. I flip through the one from my senior year, searching for Peyton, and find nothing. Then my junior year, still nothing. It's not until my sophomore year that I come across a Peyton. Only her last name is Powell-James. Nothing close to what Aiden had said. Her bio says we were in the same sorority, but I don't remember her at all.

With my curiosity piqued, I pick up my phone and call Veronica, one of my sorority sisters. She's a year ahead of me, and we talk often. She never mentioned a sister living in Portland though when I told her I was moving out here.

"Hey, please tell me you made it to Portland."

I laugh and realize I forgot to text her when I arrived. "Yes, sorry, V. I'll send you pics when we hang up. My apartment's great. I met everyone at work today. I think I'm going to love it here. But hey, that's actually not why I called. I have a question. Do you remember a sister named Peyton?"

"Peyton," she says her name slowly. "Yes, she graduated with me. Don't you remember us doing that massive fundraiser for her? She was the one who left school because she was in a horrible accident."

"Oh yes, now that you mention it, I do remember something, but not specifically her."

"You might not have met. She lived off campus her senior year. Why?"

"Well, the sportscaster at work says she lives here, and I thought I'd reach out, one alumnus to another."

"Oh, you know, now that you say this, yes." Veronica fumbles with her phone and then apologizes. "I think Peyton is married to someone in the NFL. I don't remember off the top of my head."

"She works for the team, from what my co-worker says."

"Oh, maybe that's it. Do you have her email? You should send her a message."

"I don't. I'm sure I can find it in our alumni book."

"Here, I'll give it to you. Tell her I said hi though."

Veronica rattles off the email address. We stay on the phone for another ten minutes or so before she has to go. I keep good on my promise and send her pictures of my apartment before sending an email to Peyton. Chances are, she may never respond, but if she does, hopefully we can meet up for coffee. Having a friend that isn't a co-worker would be lovely.

FOUR

JULIUS

Behind me, Reggie talks about last night's football practice and how Miss Meghan kept yelling for him to tackle the other guy. "Only," Reggie says, "the other guy is on my team, and we're not supposed to tackle. I told Miss Meghan we could only tackle during games. Not practice."

I glance over my shoulder in time to see Reggie shake his head and sigh. It's comical. He's very dramatic, especially when it comes to football. He's told me many times that I'm his role model, but he's also told my best friend and teammate, Noah Westbury, that he's also his role model. Honestly, I'm not sure where I stand with my son in this sense.

"Daddy, I spill." The sweet voice of my daughter, Roxy, sings out. Instantly, I'm next to her and cleaning up the small dribble of milk that came off her spoon.

"It's okay, baby girl," I tell her as I run my hand down her hair. I've worked hard to keep my frustration with their mother hidden. They don't need to see the anguish she's putting me through, because they're going through their own pain. I come from a long line of married family members and have a hard time accepting that my marriage is over.

"I sorry," Roxy says, looking up at me and batting her big brown eyes.

"I know you are. We cleaned it up. Everything is good." Roxy is like this because her mother would yell at her, which I've deduced is because Elena felt guilt over what she was doing to our family. Maybe there's another excuse for flying off the handle and screaming at the kids over something as trivial as spilled milk, but I doubt it.

Roxy goes back to scooping her cereal into her tiny mouth without a care in the world. This is how her day should always be, carefree and without worry. Reggie watches me. Is he waiting for me to freak out, to start yelling? It's not going to happen, at least not in front of my kids. I'll let myself go when I'm at the practice facility where I can punch a bag or scream out on the field, and no one would know why. The thing is, they'd likely start screaming with me, thinking I'm trying to hype myself up or something.

"Eat up, Reg. It's almost time to leave for school."

"I go to practice?" Roxy asks. As much as I'd love to take her with me, today is not the day.

"Miss Meghan will be here soon. I think today is story time at the library, and then I believe she's taking you to the zoo."

Roxy nods as if she has her schedule with her nanny down.

"Is Miss Meghan taking me to my practice?" Reggie asks as he gets up from the table. He carries his bowl to the sink and then places it in the dishwasher. I have to say I'm rather impressed with him right now. We had a long talk after Elena went back to Los Angeles about stepping up with his sister, and he's taken it to heart. He knows that Miss Meghan is here to care for him and his sister, but not wait on them or clean up after them.

"Yes, but if that changes, I'll let you know."

Reggie finishes in the kitchen and then heads off to his room. It's just Roxy and me. I pull the chair out from under the table and sit down beside her. "I'm going to eat your breakfast."

She smiles brightly and giggles. "No, you not, Daddy."

"Uh-huh," I tell her. My hand starts moving toward her spoon, and she laughs louder. She squirms in her chair and then holds her arms out for me. "Are you all done?" I ask as I bring her toward me. Her dark hair is a mess of curls, going every which direction. I'm thankful Meghan is around to help me. Otherwise, I'd feel lost when it comes to my kids. I kiss Roxy on the nose. "I love you, bug."

"I lub you too, Daddy."

"Come on, let's clean up."

Roxy gets down from my lap and takes her bowl over to the sink. I hoist her up onto the counter and let her wash her bowl before setting it into the dishwasher. The front door opens, and she screeches out Meghan's name. I've barely put Roxy on the floor before she's off and running toward her nanny.

"Good morning, Mr. Cunningham." Roxy is in her arms before I can even mutter a good morning.

"Morning. Thank you for staying with the kids yesterday and last night. If you need a day off this week, let me know."

"It was my pleasure. We had a good time, right guys?"

Both kids nod.

"I'm going to take Reggie to school now," I say. "You're picking him up, right?"

"Yes, but you'll call me if anything changes?"

"I will." I kiss Roxy on the cheek and then holler for Reggie. He tells Meghan good morning before following me to the door.

We live on the top floor of a new apartment complex. Technically, we have a penthouse, but it's nothing over the top or extravagant. I'm not the guy who spends an ungodly amount on living expenses or frivolous things. I want to make sure my children have the best education possible and can go to college. I was lucky, I had football to pay my way, but Reggie's path may differ. Same with Roxy.

Our building is on the waterfront and within walking distance to most things—even Reggie's school. During the season, I drive Reggie to school. In the spring, we walk. Most days, even in the fall and winter, we walk around our neighborhood, do our shopping, or hang out in the park. I love it here in Portland, because no one cares that I play professional football. The gossip hounding media, on the other hand, is a whole other story.

"Is Mom coming home?" Reggie asks when we step into the elevator. He knows I went to see her yesterday, but I haven't sat him down to tell him we're going to divorce. I don't even know how to start a conversation like this with my son. Part of me thinks he's too young to hear about all this adult drama, but the other half of me doesn't want to lie to him. When he goes to L.A. to see his mother, something tells me she doesn't plan to hide her new boyfriend from the kids, and they should know about him ahead of time. Do I tell them, or does Elena? Is it possible we can be amicable enough to sit down and tell them together?

"She's busy, bud," I say but sigh heavily. It's not intended. I'm just thoroughly exhausted with all of this.

"Are you getting a divorce?"

I say nothing. I'm unprepared to answer his question.

"Mom has a boyfriend."

I look at my son, who is staring at the door. "Where did you hear this?"

He glances up with unshed tears in his eyes. At this moment, I want Elena to see what she's done to her children. "It was on TV last night."

Motherfucker. I swallow the knot in my throat. "I'm trying to protect you," I tell my son. "I don't want you to have to deal with all this adult stuff." He looks at me with sadness as my head shakes back and forth slowly. My heart hurts. It breaks for my children. "Mom is going to stay at the house in California for a bit, but you can go see her whenever you want."

"She doesn't love us anymore?" he asks, the dam of tears finally spilling over. I crouch down so we're eye level, and I wipe his damp cheeks.

"She loves you, Reggie. She wants you to go live with her, but I want you and Roxy to stay here with me. Maybe I'm being selfish and should ask what *you* want."

"Can I think about it?"

As much as it's killing me inside, I nod and stand back up. He doesn't need to see that his question is ripping me in two. When we reach the garage, I rush to my SUV and click the fob to unlock the doors. Reggie and I climb in and say nothing to each other until we're at the drop off in front of the school.

"I love you, Reg. Have a good day."

"Love you too. Tell Noah I said hi." He climbs out and doesn't look back as he runs toward his friends. I wonder if he'll talk to them about what's going on or if he'll keep it bottled up. The latter isn't good. I pull my phone out and send a text to my agent, asking him to find me a local family counselor. My kids need someone to talk to that isn't their mother or me.

By the time I pull into the practice facility, the tension in my body is rolling off me. It's a good thing we don't have a game for a few more days because I'm not sure I'd be able to focus. I'm heated, angry, and emotional. Not a great combination of feelings when I need to focus on running routes and catching torpedo passes from my quarterback. This year, we have a good team, especially with the draft picks the general manager and our coach made. In my opinion, which, let's be honest, probably doesn't amount to much, I think we have a shot at the playoffs.

The locker room is empty, which is odd but also a relief. Only Noah knows I went to L.A. yesterday to see Elena, and I don't really want to talk about what I did on my day off with anyone. Although, I guess if people saw the same shit my son caught on TV last night, the cat is out of the bag.

I find my teammates in the weight room. Loud music is playing, and some of the guys are walking around in spandex shorts or pants and no shirts, while others are wearing team workout gear. I bypass everyone and head for the treadmill. I want to get five miles in before I start to lift. Today is cardio, weight training, and skills practice. Tomorrow, we run through mock plays, on Thursday we'll hit, and Friday is another walk through with game time situations. Coach always has us down by seven when we run our simulations. He says it keeps us humble.

The five-mile run seems to go faster than I expected. I don't feel like I've exerted enough energy to be cordial to anyone. I look around the room and spot Noah. He's in the corner, chatting with our cornerback, Cameron Simmons. I head over, and the three of us shoot the shit for a bit until Cameron is called into the trainer's room.

"You look pissed," Noah says. He picks up a weight and sets it on the bar. I match him and realize this set is for me. Noah lifts, but never over a certain amount because he's afraid to fuck up his arm.

"I am." I lie down on the bench and place my hands on the bar. Inhale. Exhale. Pushing the bar up, I lock my arms until I feel the burn of the weight. Noah's behind me, his hands poised to grab the bar if needed.

"Ready?" he asks.

Up. Down. Inhale. Exhale. Grunt.

Repeat.

Repeat.

Repeat.

"I take it things didn't go well?"

"Met the boyfriend," I tell him through gritted teeth. "He came into my home saying something about how my wife better be naked and ready for him."

"That's messed up, man."

"She also wants to separate the kids since I want to keep them."

"I'm not a parent, but I think that sounds ludicrous."

"It is. I told her the kids should stay with me. They have a life here and a solid routine. Down there, they'd be with a nanny all the time. If she gets an acting gig, it could take her away from them for months, or they'd have to go and interrupt their lives to accommodate her. I also pointed out the only reason she wants the kids is because of child support."

"Prenup?"

"Solid as a rock. A nice little clause in there about extramarital affairs. The irony of it is she added it because she was afraid I'd fuck a fan or a cheerleader. Do you and Peyton have one?"

Noah laughs and shakes his head. "Nah, we both know we're not going anywhere. She knows I won't cheat on her, and if she ever cheated on me, I must've done something terrible to deserve it. I love that woman more than my own life. If she told me to quit football and wait on her hand and foot, I would."

"You don't ever worry about your age difference?"

"Nope. I've known most of my life I was going to marry her. I probably would've done it when she turned eighteen if it wasn't frowned upon by society. All through college, I wanted to be with her, but it wasn't legal, so I kept my distance."

"That must've been hard."

"You have no idea," he tells me. "Listen, I know you're hurting from the wife thing, but come over Friday night. Peyton and I are having some people over. My friend Quinn will be here, and possibly Peyton's sister, Elle. It'll be very lowkey."

"Elle's a bitch," I tell him.

Noah laughs. "Elle is engaged, and even if she wasn't, she's not the one for you. Come on, let's get this lift in so we can get the hell out of here sooner."

FIVE

AUTUMN

I thought starting a new job was nerve wracking, but nothing compares to meeting a sorority sister who seems to have hit the jackpot when it comes to life. After I sent the "hey, let's be friends" email to Peyton, I spent the next hour or so of my life on the couch with a glass of wine in my hand, looking her up. Why? Because I'm a glutton for punishment, apparently. I had it in my mind that there was no way in hell someone like her would email someone like me back. I am a Plain Jane, the *I don't belong in her circle* type of person. All over the internet, Peyton is living this luxurious life. Her father is a drummer in a very popular band. Her husband is the quarterback of an NFL team. Her sister is one of the most sought-after band managers, who it seems took their brother's band and skyrocketed them to stardom. Who am I? Someone she may have crossed paths with in the halls of our sorority house. And that's a big giant maybe. Honestly, I should've done all this research before sending her an email because now I feel like a complete fool for reaching out to her.

The café Peyton chose to meet at isn't far from my

house. I made sure to let Lisette know I was busy until about three, just in case. I'm not suspecting any earth-shattering weather patterns to arise, but you never know, and since I'm new, I want to make sure everyone at the station understands I'm dedicated to my job.

My eyes are constantly roving over every face that comes into view, even the men. There have been a few times since I've sat down that I've looked from a very handsome face to a left hand, just to check. Not that I'm interested in dating, at least I don't think I am. I remember when I took the job in North Dakota. I told myself I'd wait six months before I start looking for someone to spend time with. I tried dating, but the few men I went out with made it such a huge deal that I was on television. Honestly, it's a turn-off. I want someone to like me for me not because I'm the person in front of a green screen telling you how much snow you're going to get on Wednesday.

I'm in a daze, staring off into the abyss of moving bodies when I hear my name. The woman in front of me, dressed to kill in a pantsuit and heels and putting my flats to shame, is definitely Peyton Westbury. She looks exactly like the photos I found online, with long chestnut hair and a rock of a diamond on her hand that I found a dozen or so articles written about. She married a childhood friend, and there's an age gap between them that critics have questioned. "Are you Autumn?" she asks again.

"Yes, sorry." I hold my hand out to shake hers. Peyton pulls the chair out across from me and sits. The next thing I notice about her is she's beaming, making me feel as if this meeting is actually a good thing.

"I was so excited to get your email. It's not often I get invited out for coffee."

My mouth drops open at her admission. "I'm sorry, what?"

"What?" she asks, looking at me like I'm speaking another language.

"Okay, don't get me wrong, but you're Peyton Westbury. I looked you up on the web. You're famous without being famous. I honestly thought you wouldn't give me the time of day."

Peyton chuckles. "I'm not famous. My dad, uncle, brother, and husband are. Even my sister could be considered famous. I'm just me." She's humble, a rarity these days.

"Well, I appreciate you meeting me. Being new to town, I want to branch out from work friends and really get to know the area."

"And this is perfect because I want friends who aren't associated with football. I think it's a win-win. So, tell me, what have you done in the few days you've been here?"

Before I can answer, our waiter comes to take our order. We both ask for coffee and a blueberry muffin. "Let's see," I start as soon as the waiter moves onto another table. "I've walked along the harbor, this neighborhood, and the station. That's about it. It's been a week, but I'm eager to explore so much more. I think when we have a storm or something, I'll see about doing some remote work."

"Leon is a great guy to work with."

"Oh, that's right. I almost forgot that you fill in for Aiden on occasion. He's actually the one who told me you lived here. Do you mind me asking how you got into sports?"

The waiter is back with our coffee and breakfast. Peyton doesn't hesitate and picks up her fork. I find myself watching her, mesmerized for some odd reason. Here she is, with this ridiculously famous family, and she just wants friends. Suddenly, I don't feel so lonely.

"So good," she mumbles and covers her mouth. "Sorry, I love the muffins here. They're baked fresh and have that melt in your mouth feel to them. This café is by far my favorite. Well, except the one my mother-in-law owns."

"You're close with her?"

Peyton laughs. "My family story is odd, to say the least. For the longest time, growing up, everyone assumed Noah—that's my husband—and I were related. Our moms are best friends. Our dads are as well. Noah and I were always together. To our families, it wasn't a big surprise that we started dating or got married. The people in our hometown, on the other hand, were a little taken aback by the idea. But my mother-in-law, Josie, I grew up calling her my aunt, and then I married her son—do you get what I'm saying?"

"I think I need a family tree or something."

She laughs again. "You and me both. But, back to your original question before this delicious muffin entered our lives. My dad was really into football. It was our thing. When he died, I just hung onto it. With Noah playing his entire life, I was there, watching and learning. When I was five, my uncle Liam—that's Noah's dad—started teaching me how to play the game."

"Wait, I thought your dad was a drummer?"

"Wow, you really did look me up. He is. My biological dad died when I was five. It's a very long, drawn-out saga."

"You should write a book," I tell her.

She smiles and sighs. "Someday, although my life is anything but interesting."

I find this hard to believe.

"Anyway," she continues and finishes telling me her story. I'm completely sucked in and have so many questions, but I don't want to ask her something intrusive. By the time she's finished talking about her life, her husband, and Portland, two hours have passed, and panic sets in that I'll be late for work.

"Shit," I say when I look at my phone. "I don't want to be that person—the one who eats and runs—but I go on air at five and still need to do my hair and make-up."

"Oh gosh, I'm so sorry. I talked your ear off. I hate it when I do that."

"No, I loved listening to your stories, and besides, I asked, so please don't feel bad."

"Listen," she says. "Noah and I are having a couple of people over tonight. I know you do the eleven o'clock news as well, but maybe you can stop by. We live only a few blocks from here so you wouldn't have to go far. I'd love to introduce you to people and get to know you. I promise I won't talk too much." Peyton giggles and then shakes her head. "Sorry."

"You're fine, and honestly, I really enjoyed today. Count me in for later. I can come down between airings."

Peyton stands. "Perfect. I'll text you the address. It's super casual, nothing fancy."

"I'll be there." We hug, and then I'm on my way. I can't help but think I've just made a new friend. One that I'll be able to share my secrets with, meet for lunch and spa appointments, and go shopping with. Exactly what you'd expect from a sorority sister.

I STAND OUTSIDE THE BUILDING, which I believe is where Peyton lives. I look at my phone, the address on the door, and then the street sign, making sure I'm at the right place. I'm not confident I am, especially since the city is crazy with its streets—Southwest, Southeast Avenues, and Boulevards.

"The only way to find out is to go inside." I give myself a pep talk before opening the sizable ornate steel door. My footsteps echo against the marble floor as I make my way toward the reception desk. "Hi, by any chance, are there apartments here?"

"The onsite realtor has gone home for the day." The man behind the desk tells me. He slides a business card toward me. I take it out of respect.

"I'm actually looking for Peyton Westbury. I believe this is her address."

He turns stone-faced and says, "We protect our resident's privacy and do not divulge whether they live here or not."

"Of course, and I'm not asking you to. I'm new to town, a bit confused about where I am, and want to make sure I'm in the right location. Is this the address?" I turn my phone to him so he can see the text exchange with Peyton. He nods, and I turn my phone back around. "Phew," I say, hoping to lighten the tension. "Peyton gave me a code for the elevator."

This man is a statue. His face has no expression, and he's watching my every move. There are two sets of elevators, one on each side of him. Now, I can gamble and go to the right and be wrong, or I can plead with this guy to help me out. Something tells me he's not going to fall for an eyelash batting crazy woman, though.

Without taking his eyes off me, he picks up his phone and presses a couple of numbers. "Mr. Westbury, this is Bernard down at the front desk. Mrs. Westbury has a guest requesting access. Yes, of course." He hangs the phone up and then points to the left, saying nothing else. As far as first impressions go, I bombed this one.

The elevator is all glass, and as soon as it moves past the first three floors, I can see why. "Holy shit," I mutter as the city comes into view. "So, this is what money buys you these days?" I'm completely taken when the doors open and loud voices wash over me. I turn and find that I'm standing there, gawking. Peyton beckons me forward, and in good time because I barely miss the doors shutting on me.

"I'm so glad you made it. Come on, let me introduce you to some friends." She takes my hand and pulls me into the living room. When she said a few people, I thought she meant two or three, but there has to be at least twenty, if not more, standing around mingling.

"First, this is my husband, Noah."

He reaches out and shakes my hand. "Peyton talked non-stop about you today. It's very nice to meet you."

I'm dumbstruck, totally caught off guard by how good looking her husband is. The pictures I saw online did *not* do this man justice. "It's nice to meet you as well. I look forward to catching one of your games." I have no idea where this came from, but it seems like the right thing to say.

"Well, let Peyton know when you want to come, and we'll be sure to put tickets at Will Call for you." Noah walks off, leaving me to think he probably suspects I'm using his wife for tickets.

"Shit," I mutter.

"Is something wrong?" Peyton asks.

I shake my head quickly. "No, just stupid things come out of my mouth when I'm nervous."

Peyton sets her hand on my arm in a reassuring fashion. "Don't worry about it. Everyone here is super chill."

She takes me around, introducing me to other friends of theirs. Staff who work for the team, neighbors, and a couple of the players. When she gets to her brother, I know exactly who he is, thanks to the web.

"This is my brother Quinn and his fiancée, Nola. They're visiting from Cali this week."

We shake hands and exchange pleasantries. There's small talk about my move to Portland and questions asked about my job. Nola has a ton of questions about the weather, predictions, and the science behind it. She speaks with a southern accent, which I find enduring and cute, and makes me wish I hadn't worked so hard to get rid of my Texas twang.

We stand around together, talking about everything from clothes, Peyton's sister, who, from what I'm gathering, can be a pain in the rear at times, to babies. Peyton's mother is eager to be a grandma and isn't shy about telling her daughters every chance she gets.

Then, the most awkward and uncomfortable thing happens. Peyton is called away, and Nola excuses herself to use the bathroom, leaving me as the wallflower. I stand there for a moment until I move toward the sliding glass door. I step out onto the balcony, only to find a man sulking in the corner. By the look he gives me, it's clear he wants to be alone.

"Oh, sorry. I didn't know anyone was out here."

He sets his glass down onto the table. The ice inside rattles against what's left of the amber liquid. He stands and comes toward me. The muscles in his arms flex, and his jaw clenches as he strides toward me. He's three, maybe four inches taller than me, with black hair and the most gorgeous blue eyes. With each step he takes, the hair on my skin rises.

"I heard everyone talking about you in there," he says in a sultry, husky voice. "The new weather girl."

"Meteorologist," I squeak out.

"I find it odd that you haven't been here a week and already have your claws into Peyton."

"I'm sorry, what? We went to school together."

"Right, and you just so happen to need to climb the network ladder, knowing full well how popular she is in town. I hope for her sake, she sees through your bullshit before it's too late."

"Listen, buddy," I say, taking a step back. "I don't know you. You don't know me, so why don't we just walk away from this conversation?"

"Whatever you say, *Weather Girl*." He keeps his eyes on me before stepping into the house. He goes right to the bar and makes another drink. I tell myself this guy is drunk, nothing more, and didn't mean a single thing he said. Except, the doubt lingers in my mind. What if this is how Peyton feels about me?

SIX

JULIUS

The bourbon numbs everything except my thoughts. This room is full of people kissing ass and taking names to better themselves in their careers. The media management companies are trying to brand Noah and Peyton, then there's the rookie running back who makes sure to tell Peyton how pretty she is every day, and the new weather person for who knows what station. If I had to guess, it's probably some online-only type broadcast because the internet is the wave of the future. Honestly, they're right. I rarely watch the news because I can't filter what they show. At least, with the web, I can go right to the information I want. Probably not the best way to get my news, but whatever. ESPN is pretty much the only channel I watch because they're nice enough not to comment on my marriage, but they're sure to point out when I have a lackluster game. Fun times in the land of Julius Cunningham.

What bothers me the most is the new person in the crowd. *What did she call herself? Oh yes, a "meteorologist."* Even as I say this in my head, it sounds pretentious and snobbish. Did she have to go to some special school to tell people it's going to rain? Hell, I can do that just by looking at the clouds. And seriously, this is Portland—it's going to fucking rain, and then in the summer, it's going to get so fucking hot, people are going to wish for rain. It's an endless cycle.

I watch her, this weather girl, as she moves around the room. She's schmoozing, taking names and numbers, and working the room. She's using Peyton to advance her career because it's likely she wants to be the next Barbara Walters, and standing in front of the map talking about the rain accumulation is just her way of getting her foot in the door.

When this woman heads toward Quinn, I am certain she's just here to use Peyton, and I hate it. I overheard earlier that they went to school together, yet Peyton has never mentioned her until this evening. What bothers me is that Noah doesn't seem concerned. Normally, he's a hawk, protecting his wife from everyone. His sheltering comes from Peyton's accident. She almost died, and it still haunts him after all this time. I remember it all, clear as day. Noah almost quit, gave up his career to be by her bedside while she was in a coma. I was so angry with him, not because he wanted to leave the team. I was mad because he had a girl at the time, and to me, this was cheating. Dessie thought so as well but stuck by him. She tried to confide in me when all of this went down, but I turned her away. Elena didn't trust her, and as it turned out, with good reason. Still, I had beef with Noah until he told me why he put Peyton before anything. He was in love with her and had been most of his life. The minute he found out about her accident was when he knew he had to make changes in his life, or he would never be truly happy. This isn't to say Noah still didn't make a few mistakes where his life is concerned. Now though, as I watch him, he's always gravitating toward Peyton. He always knows where she is and always knows when to look at her at the right time.

I thought I had that with Elena. Boy, was I wrong! The more time I think about my life with Elena, the more I realize she used me. She came to Alabama for one thing—a ring—and she got it, but that's all she's getting out of me.

Noah nods in my direction, and I raise my glass to him. He comes toward me and pats me on the back. "I'm glad you decided to stop by."

"Nothing else to do," I tell him. "Are you coming to Reggie's game tomorrow?"

"Yeah, I'll be there. Eleven, right?"

I nod. "I'm hauling ass after our walk-through. I'm hoping to make it by kick-off." I'm thankful we have a home game this weekend because it gives me a chance to watch my boy play.

"Did Reggie's coach decide on a position for him yet?"

"Nah, man. The kid has a canon but can run like the wind."

"How's he doing with Elena being gone more?"

I take a sip of my bourbon and scan the room for another look around. My eyes immediately hone in on the weather girl. She's laughing, enjoying herself, and I'm finding that it bothers me. Did she not hear what I said to her outside?

"Reggie knows she has a boyfriend. He saw it on one of those entertainment shows the other night. I told him his mom wants him and Roxy to go live in L.A. with her, and he asked me if he could think about it."

"Probably not the question you expected."

"Not in the slightest. That's why I asked everyone to come to his game. I want him to see he has family here, even without his mom being here." I motion toward the weather girl. "Who is she?"

Noah clears his throat. "Autumn LaRosa. She's the new weather personality at MCAX."

"How does she know Peyton?"

"She doesn't or didn't. Aiden Marchetti asked Autumn if she knew Peyton since they both went to Northwestern. It turns out they were in the same sorority, only they never knew each other because of Peyton's accident and then moving off campus."

"Do you trust her?" I ask.

Noah laughs or coughs. I'm not sure which. "Yes, why? Do you know something I don't?"

I shrug and sip on my drink. "Just find it odd that she's here, new in town, and attaching herself to Peyton almost immediately."

"Huh," is all Noah says.

"Where's your bitchy sister-in-law?" I ask, hoping to lay my eyes on the knock-out. It's odd how Peyton and her sister are identical yet so far apart in personalities.

"Are you looking to have your balls busted or something?" Noah asks while laughing.

Again, I shrug. "She's nice to look at."

"She's engaged," he reminds me again.

"Eh, I said look, not fuck. Although . . ." I don't finish my sentence because I know Noah will punch me if I do. Ever since Elena left, I've fantasized about other women. It's natural, I think. Right after my separation, Elle came to town. A group of us hung out, we started drinking, and my thoughts started wandering right into the gutter where Elle is concerned. I didn't necessarily see her as the stepmom type, but more so the one I'd go to if I needed to feel pain. Elle comes off as the type of woman who will—as Noah put it—bust your balls, slap you with a whip or paddle, hogtie you, and leave you for dead, all while you're begging for more. I'm not into role-playing, but if I were, Elle would be in all leather and bossing me around.

Noah groans. "Are you seriously thinking about sleeping with her?"

My eyes widen, and I shake my head slowly. "There is absolutely no sleeping going on in my thoughts."

Noah rolls his eyes. "I'm glad she stayed home. The last thing I would want to hear from you is how she rejected you."

"Don't worry I'm not looking to hook-up with Elle, or anyone for that matter. I'm swearing off women. They're nothing but trouble, and that's something I don't need right now."

Noah pats me on the back. "Things will work out," he says to me. I appreciate his optimism, but my future looks bleak.

Peyton comes over to us with the weather girl in tow. I down my drink, preparing for the tongue lashing I'm going to get from Peyton on my mistreatment of her friend. "Julius, I'd like to introduce you to Autumn LaRosa. Autumn, this is Julius Cunningham, wide receiver for the Portland Pioneers."

In complete shock, Autumn extends her hand to shake mine. I do, and as soon as our skin touches, I recoil. My actions affect her. She's hurt but masks it quickly by dropping her hand and changing her stance.

"It's nice to meet you," she says. I don't know what game she's trying to play, but I don't like it, and I find it odd she's acting like we haven't already had a conversation.

"Didn't we meet on the terrace, Weather Girl?" I raise my eyebrow, sending my jab with emphasis.

She blanches and looks down briefly before saying, "I should really get back to the station."

"Later," I say without taking my eyes off her.

Peyton's not happy. I can tell by the expression on her face and the intense stare she has aimed at her husband. I don't dare look at him. I'm already in hot water with Peyton, that's enough.

"I'll ride down with you, Autumn. Noah, take care of this." She points at me, and I know I'm going to get shit for my attitude.

As soon as they're out of earshot, Noah says, "What the fuck?"

"She bothers me."

"Then let her bother you on your own time, man. Peyton is livid, and she's going to want some answers. Did you hook up with Autumn or something? Is she a one-night stand?"

I shake my head. "Nope, met her here tonight. I just have a bad feeling about her."

"Okay, well, tell Peyton in private, not in front of everyone. Jesus, Julius. You don't want to ruin this woman's career before it even starts here. That's the last thing either of you need."

As much as I don't want to admit it, Noah's right. But I'm not going to apologize. There's something about the weather girl that is off-putting. With everyone at this shindig, she just happens to be the one who needs a boost in her career, and she just happens to be a sorority sister of Peyton. Never mind Peyton's job, her connections, her husband, and her famous family. I don't buy it, and it smells like a heaping pile of shit.

"I'm out," I say to my very pissed off quarterback. Yep, I

can kiss my Sunday stats goodbye at this point. I'll grovel tomorrow when I'm sober and not so angry.

"Good thing you can walk home from here," Noah says.

"Yep, see ya in the morning."

"Set your alarm. You don't want to miss the walk-through."

He's right. I don't. Once I'm out in the hall, I pull my phone out and set my alarm for six a.m. Instead of heading home like I should, I walk a few blocks to the local bar when I get outside. It's empty, except for two guys in the back, playing pool. I take a seat on one of the stools and order another bourbon. I'm three glasses deep when the news airs. The bartender turns the volume up and hollers to the guys in the back that the news is on.

"Did I miss something?" I ask, wondering why it's so important.

"Ever since they hired the new reporter, I've been more interested in the news."

"Same here." A guy next to me slams his hand down on the bar. "Man, I can't wait to see her out and about. I'm going to shoot my shot for sure."

I'm confused until the anchor says Autumn's name. The camera pans to her. She's standing there, in a form-fitting blue dress, with her hair curled and her legs looking like sin. "Fuck," I mutter as my pants tighten around my crotch. Heels and long legs. The bane of my existence.

"What a babe," another guy says.

"MCAX is now my favorite station. I'm going to have to record the news twice a day just to see her," another adds.

"I wonder if some old boyfriend has nudes of her," says the guy standing next to me holding a cue stick.

"Shut the fuck up," I say to him. "Don't be such a pig."

The asshole doesn't say anything but mumbles to his

buddy. These guys are trouble, and I don't need it. I throw a couple of twenties down, and the bartender asks me where I'm going.

"Home."

"But we haven't even got the good part," one of the guys says.

"There's nothing good about Weather Girl," I mutter and walk out.

SEVEN

AUTUMN

I t's a rare fall day in Portland. The sun is shining like I said it would, and the temperature is hovering in the mid-seventies. The leaves are the perfect blend of red and gold and give the city a picturesque fall afternoon. I have to say I'm impressed with the foliage, although I will always feel as though Chicago has the best fall colors. With that said, I wouldn't know much about the foliage on the east coast, which I've been told rivals any other location.

I'm in full swing, so to speak, at the station. My time slots are solid, the team I work with is fantastic, and the staff here at MCAX really puts the station in North Dakota to shame. I get that I needed to work there to appreciate what I have now, but they could stand to learn a thing or two from MCAX, or really any other station for that matter.

The knock on the door signals it's time for me to make my way to the sound stage. Even though I feel like I've done my job a million times, I still get nervous. Talk to anyone on the street, and they'll tell you being a weather personality is easy. At least it looks easy to them. You stand there, you point, and you say whatever comes up on the teleprompter because that is what the viewers see. They see me on their screens, doing just that. They have no idea the research that goes into predicting the weather or how one colleague may say a storm will move north, but when you're looking at the calculations and the jet stream, you believe it's going to move south. No one also considers that whatever we tell you on air, we've written. This means, when I mess up, it's my onus. I hate being wrong.

I open the door to find Lisette standing outside of it. Well, not exactly. She's leaning against the wall, writing furiously on her clipboard and nodding. It took me a few days to remember Lisette is always wearing a headset and often talking to others when she's with me. We fall in line together, walking toward the sound stage. As soon as I enter the space, I'm mic'd up, and powder is brushed onto my face.

"Yeah, she'll be there."

I glance at her without turning away from the young woman making sure my face doesn't glow under the heavy lights. "Is that about me?" I ask, trying not to move.

"Yes," Lisette says. "You've been invited to do the coin toss at the Portland Pioneers game this Sunday."

"I have?" I turn this time to look at my assistant. "Wow."

She smiles and then lets out a hearty laugh. "In case you haven't noticed, you're pretty popular. Your Chatgram is growing by the thousands."

"I have Chatgram?"

Lisette nods and pulls her phone out. She clicks on an icon, and my face appears. "I started it when I realized you didn't have an account. It's the wave of the future. Everyone is using it. We can post images, videos and do live feeds. When you're on location, I'll be with you and will manage this for you. But you can post whenever you want or send pictures to me, and I'll do it for you."

"Can you go back to the popular part?"

As soon as I ask the question, Leon walks in. His smile is beaming, and he claps his hands together. "Popular is an understatement. I'm fielding calls left and right about having you on their radio programs, at their sporting events, and another station even asked if we'd loan you out."

"This is crazy. I just report the weather."

"Our male demographic for viewership has increased substantially since you went on air." Lisette flips through the papers on her clipboard and shows me a chart.

"I mean, that's good for the station, but—"

"Yeah." She nods. "Sex symbol status isn't what you're going for."

"No, it's not." I didn't have this problem in North Dakota. There, barely anyone paid attention to me. I never thought things would be different, in this sense, in another market.

Leon steps forward. "Lisette will be with you whenever you're out of the station on a promo event or special assignment. We'll also have security with you."

"Do I need security?" I ask.

My boss shrugs. "I'd rather be safe than sorry. The last thing I want is an overzealous fan trying to get to you. Your safety is our priority."

"This is crazy," I mutter.

"And definitely unexpected," Leon adds.

Marvin, my cameraman, signals that my segment is about to start. I make my way to the stage during a commercial break and chat with Aiden and Selena for a bit before the countdown to return to live TV starts. I get into position and wait for my cue.

"Welcome back," Selena says. "Now, here's a look at your evening weather with Autumn."

"Thanks, Selena," I say as I stand in front of the green screen. The preview monitor has my report on it, making it easy for me to point where I need to. "Your drive home is going to be gorgeous but don't forget your visor. The position of the sun could be a bit blinding. Tonight is a good night to fire up the grill because tomorrow could be a bit iffy. Rain is expected overnight but will dry up by the mid-morning rush. Tonight, we'll dip into the forties. Make sure your plants are covered because some regions may see frost. Now, here's a look at sports with Aiden."

The camera cuts away, and I sigh in relief. Not because my job is stressful but for complete relaxation. Once the news is done, I tape a couple of spots highlighting the weather that will air in between the national news, and then head off to my dressing room. I change quickly, putting on a pair of jeans, sandals, an oversized sweater, and then request a rideshare.

"Dinner plans?" Lisette asks.

"Yeah, with the Westburys and Marchettis. Nothing like being a fifth wheel with the power couples."

Lisette laughs. "I can always set you up with someone." I shake my head, and her eyes go wide. "We could totally do a 'Find Autumn a Date' segment!"

"No. No way. Not gonna happen."

"Why not? Leon would totally jump on board."

"Nope. Autumn is happy being single," I tell her. Although, I'm really not. I see the love between Noah and Peyton, and Aiden and Haley. I want that. I want a guy to look at me the way these men look at their wives. But I'm not willing to join a dating app or make my love life a public spectacle. At the end of the day, I want privacy like anyone else.

Aiden and I meet in the lobby and head toward the restaurant together. The rest of our dinner party is waiting out front when we arrive. Aiden rushes to his wife, they embrace, and a pang of jealousy washes over me. Maybe Lisette is right in the sense that I should find someone, but I also worry about my career. If what Lisette says is true, people will scrutinize my every move, and I need to be cautious.

After greeting Aiden's wife, Haley, and Peyton and Noah, Peyton links arms with me, and we follow Noah into the restaurant. He talks to the host and then comes to sit down next to us. "Is it going to rain on Sunday?" he asks.

"Nope," I say, shaking my head. "I'm going to be there."

Peyton's eyes go wide. "You're coming to the game?"

Her excitement is infectious. My head nods so fast my hair whips me in the face. "Lisette told me earlier that I'm doing the coin toss."

"Aiden, did you set this up?" Peyton asks him.

"No, it must've come from the team."

"I'll make sure you get an on the field media pass," Noah says. "Normally, they'll usher you off the field, and that's it. This way, you can hang with Aiden or Peyton."

"Yeah, Peyton can teach you all about football," Haley says.

Everyone laughs, and I somehow missed the inside joke among friends. "Okay, what am I missing?"

Haley waves her hand. "Peyton has tried to teach me, and still to this day, I know nothing. Noah throws the ball, someone—hopefully from the Pioneers—catches it. That's all I got."

The host calls our party, and we follow him to our

table among hushed whispers. Noah's name, as well as Aiden's and mine, are said as we pass by. We're seated in a corner, far from anyone but not far enough away from the stares.

"Does this get easier?" I ask.

"Nope," Noah says. "Peyton and I grew up with this because of our fathers. We learned early on to ignore it."

"Your dad is so hot," Haley says with a sigh. Aiden elbows her, and she shrugs. "It's the truth."

"I hated it when I was younger," Peyton adds. "I used to get so jealous if someone spoke to my dad or if a little kid came up to him. We used to go to Disneyworld a lot when we were younger, and there was always a crowd. Mostly women, throwing themselves at my dad or my uncles. It was annoying."

"How did your moms cope?" I ask Peyton and Noah.

"Well, my parents have a long . . ." Noah pauses and looks at Peyton before continuing. "Someday, I'll tell you about my parents. For right now, let's just say, my mom didn't handle it well in the beginning."

"Okay," I say, dragging the word out.

Peyton smiles. "These days, my mom doesn't care. But it wasn't always this way." It's apparent by the way she hangs her head that she doesn't want to talk about her family. I get it. I'm sure I'd be the same way if my family were uber-famous.

After dinner, Aiden and I head back to the studio for the eleven o'clock set. Lisette finds me in my dressing room changing into my work outfit. She shows me her phone. On it, a picture of the five of us at dinner.

"People are intrusive."

"Viewers are curious," she corrects me. "You're always on, even when you're not, which is why I tell you to keep your blinds closed at home unless you want someone and their high-powered telescope looking into your bedroom."

"I didn't have these problems in Dickinson," I point out. "No one cared."

"You're young and beautiful," she tells me. "You're going to attract all sorts. Just be careful."

"We should be able to use my growing popularity to our advantage, right? Like, fundraisers and such."

"We can."

"Let's do it. I'll work extra if it means we're raising money for the children's wing at the hospital, the science centers, and the museums. This would also allow me to be out, meeting the people of the Rose City."

"I like the way you think, Autumn. I'll talk to Leon."

LEON LOVED my idea to have Lisette book me for as many social events as possible, and while the coin toss for the Pioneers wasn't on our list of ideas, I'm happy to be at the stadium. The PR rep for the team sent over a welcome bag, complete with gear for me to wear for the game. I opted for a shirt to go with my jeans and flats and decided to braid my hair into a mermaid tail.

When I arrive at the stadium, the PR team greets me. They give me a tour of the stadium, show me where I can rest, get something to eat if I need some space away, and direct me to Peyton's office.

"Wow," I say when I walk in. She smiles and comes over to hug me. "What is it that you do here again?"

"Player analysis. I break down the game, point out the weaknesses, the abilities, and pinpoint where the players and coaching staff need to make adjustments."

"So, what you're saying is you're the boss around here?"

Peyton laughs. "Not even close. The players and coaches don't have to listen, but normally they do. I spend a lot of time watching game films and comparing our players against the team we're playing on Sunday. If I can expose a weakness on either side, we're better for it."

"And you enjoy this?"

She shrugs. "It's different, and I love football. I've always wanted to be around sports, and this way, I am."

"And you get to work with your husband," I point out.

Peyton nods. "There is that benefit." The use of the word benefit makes me wonder what kind of perks she's talking about. I've read enough romance novels to assume there's some hanky panky going on when no one is around. Not that I'd ask her.

She takes me down to the field and introduces me to a few more people and some of the players. A couple of them ask for my number, to which I tell them to call the station. They act surprised and maybe hurt but laugh it off. It's when I'm standing there, looking around at the crowd of people filing into their seats, that I spot Julius. He's at the wall that separates the spectators from the field, and he's holding a little girl in his arms. There's a woman in front of him, and she cups his face with her hand. I feel . . . angry when I see this happen in front of me. This guy was nothing but a complete jerk to me and yet, made me feel something I hadn't felt in a long time. Desire and longing, even though our exchange was anything but cordial.

Julius turns and sees me staring. His soft features turn hard, and he hands the young girl back to the woman. "Definitely his wife," I mutter to myself. My problem is I can't look away, even as he heads toward the field. I'm watching him and the woman. Back and forth, my head goes until I finally give up. My first encounter with Julius was anything but enjoyable and needs to be forgotten.

The teams leave the field but only for a few minutes, according to Aiden, who is standing next to me. He gives me a run-down of what will happen while the stadium crew sets up for the game. It's like the atmosphere changes on a dime when the music switches. The crowd goes crazy, and instantly, there are people around me. Both teams come running out onto the field, and the Pioneers are bouncing on their feet, working everyone up.

"Welcome to today's match-up where we've been promised to have nothing but clear skies for the day." Everyone cheers, and suddenly my cheeks are on fire. The announcer goes through the starting line-ups, the National Anthem is sung, and then it's my turn. "Let's welcome to Portland, the newest member of the MCAX team, Autumn LaRosa."

I step out onto the field, turn and wave, take a few more steps and continue to wave until I'm at the center of the field, where a referee and six hulking men greet me. The only one I focus on is Julius. He's glaring at me. If he were a bull, there would be steam coming out of his nostrils.

The referee puts the large gold coin in my hand after showing it to the men standing in the circle. Julius yells out tails. I toss the coin and wait for it to fall.

"Heads," the referee yells, much to the delight of the other team, who runs off toward the sideline.

Julius stands there, staring off. He finally looks at me and seethes. "If we lose this game, it's your fault."

JULIUS

When Elena touches my face, I want to bat her hand away, but I can't. The media reports on our marriage have been nothing but speculation at this point and I'm not interested in giving them anymore dirt. The segment Reggie saw on the entertainment show was denied by Elena's team, even though everything the clip said was true. She's having an affair or had one, and we're getting divorced, except neither of us have submitted the necessary paperwork or spoken to an attorney. I'm hoping everything can be agreed to without bringing lawyers in because then it just gets messy. I know what I want. I know what she wants. I also know what she can have or I'm willing to give her. Money is out of the question unless the kids are living with her full-time. I'll support my kids, but not her. Not after she's done me like this.

However, this pretend shit has to stop. I don't want to play nice for the cameras and it's only sending the wrong message to the kids. With Elena standing in front of me acting like she's the doting wife in front of our parents, I can only see Reggie's eyes. He doesn't hide things well and the straight up confused look on his face screams loudly. Everything happening right now doesn't jive with what we discussed a couple weeks back, and that's his mother's fault. She knows I'll play nice for the media because a confrontation right now would take away from the game, and make me look like a complete asshole.

"What are you doing?" I ask her. My voice is calm because I'm holding Roxy in my arms. Her tiny arms are clinging to my neck and her head is resting on my shoulder pads. Again, this is her mother's doing. The "let's show the world we're one big happy family" moment Elena strives for. Public perception is everything to her. It is to me as well, but faking it is becoming too hard and the effort is exhausting.

"She wanted to see her daddy," Elena says. Okay, I can give her that. I spent the night in the team hotel because it's policy and worked out perfectly for Elena to come see the kids. I knew the kids were coming to the game with my parents but didn't expect Elena to show up—or her parents for that matter.

I bounce Roxy on my hip and look at her. "Did you miss me?"

She nods and sticks her thumb in her mouth. Over the past few months, we've been working on not sucking her thumb, but I think all this shit with Elena not being around has made Roxy regress a little. I could be wrong. I'm certainly no expert on parenting a toddler.

"On Tuesday, we'll go to the zoo or something," I tell her. It's my day off and I fully plan to spend it with her.

"That'll be so fun." Elena reaches across the railing and runs her hand down Roxy's hair. "I'll check the weather and make sure we have the right clothes."

And this, right here, is what I have a problem with.

"Elena, when do you go back to California?" I ask in a harsh, biting tone meant to be direct and to the point. If the enunciation of my words doesn't send the message, then my facial features should definitely do the job.

"I thought I'd stay for a bit."

I nod. "Then we'll work out some living arrangements." I start to hand Roxy back, but the announcer's voice stops my movements. I hear the name that has grated my nerves since our first introduction. I look around, to my left and then right, to find the woman who hasn't been far from my thoughts, despite my desperate attempt to keep her out of my head. For some reason, I loathe her while, at the same time, feel like I should get to know her. Still, when I stare at her, I find her irritating and I can't place why. What I'm feeling has to be more than me assuming she's using Peyton to further her career, but then again, she's standing on the sideline, watching me, and proving my point. She used Peyton to get here today.

I give Roxy a kiss on her cheek and then hand her back to Elena. "Good luck today," she says as her hand caresses mine. I really want to tell her to take a hike, but the kids are near her and so are her parents, who I have a feeling know nothing about what's going on. Whereas my parents know everything. Reggie holds his hand up for a high-five and tells me to kick some booty. We fist bump and go through our handshake routine. I'm not superstitious, but I believe in rituals, and this is something Reggie and I do whenever we're at a game together. When we have an away game, we do it the night before I leave.

The team leaves the field to go into the locker room. It's more for a pep talk than anything else right now. Bud Walter stands in the center of the room. Each player takes a knee, almost like we're bowing to him. I suppose, in a sense, we are. Today, like any other day, he's our leader. The commander. We're going to do or at least try to do everything he's asked of us. To some, Bud is a coach. A guy who is paid millions of dollars to tell athletes what to do. To us, his Pioneers, he's our confidant and a father figure. Bud cares about us and not the scoreboard, which is a far cry from some coaches out there. The only problem with this is, if we don't start winning to the point where we are in the playoffs and a Superbowl contender—Bud could lose his job. Worse, trades will start to happen. We're on the cusp and I feel like this could be our year.

A team rep lets us know it's time to go back onto the field. Game day is all about the media and what they have worked out with the NFL. They set the schedule and we follow it. It's all about the show and when it comes right down to it, we're the entertainment. We run out to music, which honestly, we can't hear because the crowd is that loud. We are currently 3 – 0, and the city loves it. The fans do as well, and more are jumping on our undefeated bandwagon. Whatever, I'll take it.

As I run out, I salute Reggie and Roxy, letting them know I'm thinking of them. Along with me are Jesse McAvoy and Tank Arthur. We head to the center of the field and shake hands with our opponents. It's then that I see the weather girl walking toward us.

"What the fuck?" I mutter under my breath. How did I not hear that she was here to do the coin toss? If I had, I wouldn't be standing here right now. I can't stand her, yet I find myself focused on what she's wearing. Any other time we've had a woman out here, she's in heels. But not Autumn. She's in flats, with tight fitting jeans, and a Pioneers T-shirt. Her long dark hair is braided, but it's not one of those tight ones I've seen so many times. This one is messy, almost as if she didn't care she was going to stand in front of thousands of people and do something important. Well, it's important to me. To the teams playing today. It might not be to her.

The referee starts talking, repeating the same thing we hear week after week. Autumn stands in the center of us and asks if we're ready. Everyone nods or mumbles a response, except for me.

"Home team, what's your call?"

"Tails," I say as I meet Weather Girl's gaze. She tries to smile but her attempt fails. She takes a deep breath and then tosses the coin in the air. All eyes are on it as it spins through the air, somersaulting until it bounces on the turf and then finally settles on a side.

"Heads!" the referee yells out and instantly turns his attention to our opponent.

I'm fuming. I have never lost a coin toss at home before. Ever. And this chick shows up and we lose. I find myself stepping toward her. "If we lose the game, it's your fault." Her mouth drops open, but she says nothing. I don't give her a chance because I'm running toward the sideline. I'm not paying attention to where I'm going and almost run right into Noah.

"Well, this is different," he says. I know he's joking but I'm not in the mood. Not between my ex showing up and now the weather girl. Why can't I have a normal day where nothing bothers me?

"Why is she even here?"

Noah looks at me. "Who?"

I shake my head. I'm not sure who I'm referring to, Autumn or Elena. Both of them are in my head and that's not a good place for either of them to be. Especially right now. I don't know what it is about Autumn but I need to get her out of my thoughts. In the long run, she's inconsequential to me. She's nothing and her presence should not have any effect on me whatsoever. Elena on the other hand, I have to find a way to deal with her and set her straight on the reality course of life—we're getting a divorce. I'm not going to pretend that she didn't have an affair and brush it under the rug because she's had a change of heart.

WE WON THE GAME, and instead of celebrating with my teammates, I'm hiding out in the training room. I waited until everyone left before getting into an ice bath. I played like shit and needed to numb the stench of feeling like a loser away. Our trainer is chatting away, but I'm not listening. I'm fucking cold, my limbs hurt, and my muscles are tightening up. I need to get out but I'm stubborn and want to make sure the locker room is clear before I head in there.

During the game, Coach ripped my ass. I dropped too many passes, couldn't complete a route, and ran right into tackles. He asked me one too many times what the hell was wrong with me. I wanted to tell him, but I have a strict "keep home life at home" policy. No one on the team needs to know that I'm bothered by Elena being at the game or how phony she is for the cameras, and they really don't need to know that being in the same vicinity or hearing Autumn's name infuriates me to no end. The latter I can't explain and it's really bothersome.

The trainer tells me time is up. He's right, even though I don't want to admit it. I put my hands down on the top of the tub and push myself up, only to stumble back into the water.

"I knew you were gluttonous for punishment when you

got in," the trainer says as he puts his forearms under my pits and guides me to standing. "You good?"

I nod and step out. I'm shivering and my teeth are chattering. Fuck, am I stupid or what? He hands me a couple towels and tells me to warm up. I could go into the sauna or steam room, but I opt to head to the locker room. At some point, I need to face what's waiting for me at home. Elena can stay in the apartment with the kids while I get a hotel or something. I know they miss her and the last thing I want to do is take what little time they're getting with her lately away.

Thankfully, the room is clear of any team members when I walk in. I change quickly, run a comb through my hair and grab my things. On my way out, I pass a few staff members who greet me, but don't tell me I had a good game because they know I didn't and there is zero point in lying to me. I sucked ass and I should've been benched. Hell, if I were the coach, I would've sat my ass after my first fumble.

The parking lot is empty of cars except for a few. I think I'm in the clear until I hear my name. Elena and the kids are coming toward me. I drop by bag and crouch down, waiting for their tiny arms to wrap around me. They're my salvation, my reason for living.

"Tough game, Dad."

"I know, buddy. I'll do better next time," I tell Reggie.

"Guess we aren't going to watch the game film, huh?"

I shake my head. "Miss Peyton is going to have enough to say to me when I see her on Monday, I don't want to have to live through it more than once." Reggie nods. For being eight, he gets it.

"How come you guys are still here?" It's rare that they wait for me after the game. Since Elena left, my parents have taken on the responsibility of taking the kids home after the game.

"Mom said we should wait for you."

I glance at Elena, who waves. The gesture is off-putting. "Go wait in the car, okay. Reggie, make sure Roxy gets buckled up." My son reaches for his sister's hand and takes her toward the SUV. When they're inside and the door is shut, Elena comes toward me with her arms out as if she's going to hug me.

I hold my hands up, motioning for her to stop. "What the fuck, Elena?"

"What?" she asks, looking surprised.

"What do you mean 'what'? What are you doing here? More importantly, why are you still here?"

"Julius, stop."

"No, I won't stop. You chose another man over your husband, over your family. And you think it's okay to show up here, with your family in tow, to what, freeload off of me? How come you're here but couldn't make it to Reggie's game yesterday? Neither could your parents?" Just as I mention her parents, they appear from behind my SUV and walk toward us. "Fucking great," I mutter. "I don't have the patience to deal with your shit, Elena. Or this," I say as I point to her father.

"Julius," her mother says. "All this fighting isn't good for the children."

"No shit," I say. "But neither is showing up unexpect-edly at my game, pretending like we're all one big happy family. I played like shit today because of you." I point at Elena who gasps. Her father puts his hand on my arm and I swing my arm up to get him away from me.

He stumbles and goes down onto his knee. Elena and

her mother start yelling, and I can hear the kids crying from inside the car.

"I'm done. I'm so fucking done, Elena." I head to my car, needing to get to my kids. There's a voice in the back of my head telling me to look over my shoulder, and when I do, I find *Weather Girl* there, watching everything.

"Just fucking wonderful."

NINE

AUTUMN

Despite it being fall, the weather in Portland is gorgeous. The days are unseasonably warm—at least to me—and the colors of the leaves are so vibrant, I feel like I'm looking at a painting. Each morning, I start my day with a run along the harbor and stop at one of the many food trucks I come across for breakfast on my way back. Some days, I sit on one of the many benches and people watch. It's incredible what kind of stories you can come up with about someone you don't know just by focusing on what they're doing.

I've created a nice routine for myself. On Tuesdays, I meet Peyton for brunch. It's her one day off during the season, and we're taking advantage of it. Every day, I tell Aiden I'm thankful he mentioned her on my first day because she and I have bonded and become really great friends. I'm grateful for her and also for Noah, who is one of the nicest men I've met in a long time. That's not to say the teammates Noah's introduced me to aren't lovely. Most are, except *that* one.

That one, in particular, seems to hate me, and I can't

figure out why. Julius definitely has the wrong idea about me, and from what Peyton has told me, he's one of the nicest guys out there. I don't see it, especially after everything I witnessed on Sunday, which I plan to ask Peyton about when I see her.

After my shower, I put my hair in a loose braid, slip into a pair of leggings and throw on an oversized sweater. Having a wardrobe at work is a godsend. I absolutely love the lack of stress that comes with this perk.

The café Peyton and I are meeting at is halfway between our respective places. While I'm on the water, she and Noah live about six blocks away from it. Of course, their view of the harbor is something I'd take in a heartbeat over the proximity. Don't get me wrong, I love my apartment and the location, but the idea of sipping my coffee from my balcony while looking over the city is appealing as well.

Peyton is already at the table when I arrive. She waves and tells me she already ordered us mimosas as I sit down. "How was your run?" I've begged her a couple of times to come with me, but she declines. I wonder if it's because she genuinely doesn't like to run or if this has something to do with her accident. I did look it up online, and it was horrific. The article I read said she wasn't expected to survive, and the interview her dad gave was heartbreaking. The way Noah hovers over her, it's like he's waiting for something to come out of the sky and take her away from him. It's endearing and completely makes sense to me now that I know about the trauma she's been through.

"My run was great. The weather is perfect today."

Peyton laughs. "Almost as if you predicted it yourself."

I follow suit and shake my head. "Puns for days," I say to her. "I keep seeing this older couple. I don't know, I'd guess they're in their eighties or something, but each time I see them, they're holding hands and seem so in love. My grandmother is always talking about how my granddad is driving her crazy and says they've been married way too long."

"My mom's parents are still alive, as is my father's dad and my dad's mom."

I hold up my hand. "Okay, explain the dad/father thing to me."

Peyton smiles and readjusts herself in her seat. "My *dad* is Harrison. He adopted my sister and me, and my mom adopted his son, Quinn. They're my parents. They have been together since Elle and I were about six. My *father* is Mason, and he died when I was five."

"You sometimes talk about your father like he's still part of your life."

"That's because he is, sort of. Football was his thing. He played in high school with my Uncle Liam and played in college. Then he started coaching back at his high school. My sister gravitated toward my mom, and I was my father's football buddy. My dad has always encouraged us to talk about our father. There are even pictures of him up at my parents' house."

"Got it, I think." Our waitress arrives at our table with our mimosas and takes our order. Once she's gone, I continue. "And Noah has always been there?"

"Every memory I have, he's in."

"That's so crazy. You'd think you'd be tired of each other. My parents are like that, high school sweethearts. How long have your parents been married?"

Peyton's eyes widen, and she lets out a chuckle. "They're not. My mom wasn't ready to get married, and my dad said a piece of paper isn't going to change how he feels.

They've been together for over twenty years, but you'd think they're still in the early days of dating. My sister, brother, and I have walked in on them way too many times."

I want a love like that, something that spans years and decades but never fizzles. Something tells me that Peyton and Noah have that one of a kind of love, where absolutely nothing else matters in their world.

"Okay, I have to ask, what is the deal with Julius Cunningham?"

"What do you mean?"

I lean forward to talk quieter. You never know who is eavesdropping. "At the game, daggers. This man loathes me, and I don't understand why. I know he thinks I'm using you, but his anger toward me has to be something else. Then, I see him after the game. He's in the parking lot with his wife, and things are not going well. I can tell they're heated, so Lisette and I are trying to keep to the shadows. Some older man comes up to Julius, and he sort of shoves him away. I can hear kids crying. His wife and an older lady are screaming. It was all a mess. Worst part—Julius saw me there."

Peyton clears her throat. "I don't want to speak for Julius."

"I know, but why does he hate me so much?"

She shakes her head slowly. "I don't know. It's so unlike him."

Our server brings our breakfast, and we focus on our food for a bit. Peyton sets her fork down and asks what I'm doing over the weekend.

"Nothing, why?"

"There's a fundraiser for the Children's Museum on Saturday. The team is going because Alex Moore's girl-friend conned them all into volunteering. There's a silent auction, some raffles, dinner, drinks, and dancing. Noah and

I will be there. Aiden will likely be there. You should come, hang out, and meet a ton more people."

"Don't you guys have a game on Sunday?"

She shakes her head. "It's a bye week, which works out because our GM is big on social events. Anything to put the team in a good light."

"Sounds like fun. I'll be there."

WHEN THE DRIVER of my rideshare pulls up in front of the Benson Hotel, my stomach flip flops. I press my hand over it to quell the unease I feel. "What did I agree to?" I mutter in the backseat. There are photographers, bright lights, and a freaking red carpet.

"Ma'am," the driver says to get my attention.

"Thanks for the ride."

This is the last place I want to be right now. Peyton never said anything about a dress code, but the people walking in— the ones who are having their pictures taken—are dressed like they're at a Hollywood Premiere while I'm dressed like I'm going on a date. "Oh, why did I agree to this?"

"Autumn!"

I turn at the sound of my name and see Leon coming toward me. "It's nice to see you here tonight."

"You're a sight for sore eyes," I tell him. "I wasn't expecting this."

"Yes, well, we are among celebrities tonight."

What the hell is he talking about?

"Wait, I thought this was a team event?"

Leon chuckles. "It is, but mostly a fundraiser, and from what I hear, her father and his band are coming."

Just then, a roar deafens my eardrums. A long, black limo stops in the middle of the road. Security guards, who have appeared out of nowhere, work to hold the crowd back. Within seconds, chants start. Names shouted. Squeals emitted. And I stand there, dumbfounded.

The door to the limo opens, and a woman steps out first. She looks identical to Peyton, and I'm going to assume it's her sister, followed by three men in tuxedos. More names shouted, screamed actually, and the camera flashes are going wild.

"Holy shit, that's Liam Page," I mutter. Leon laughs.

"I take it you're a fan?"

"I'm actually not a fan. My mother is die-hard though. She's going to be so mad I didn't invite her."

"Come on, let's go in."

Thankfully, Leon guides me to the door where we run into Peyton. She smiles when she sees me, and we hug. "You didn't tell me you invited your dad and his band."

"I'm a great keeper of secrets," she whispers. Before I can respond, she calls out for her dad. I stand there, in awe of watching a celebrity interact with his daughter. It amazes me the pedestal we put people on when they're just as ordinary as the rest of us.

"Daddy, I want you to meet my friend, Autumn." Her father sticks his hand out to shake mine.

"It's nice to meet you," he says. "I'm Harrison, this is Liam, and that's JD. Peyton has told me a lot about you."

"Same," I say stupidly. "I feel like I already know everyone."

He laughs and steps aside. Did he seriously laugh? Was it a good laugh or an I-think-she's-bat-shit-crazy-laugh? *Aw crap.* There isn't a doubt in my mind I'm going to embarrass myself tonight. In fact, I'm willing to bet I do so in a colossal way.

Bring it on.

The elegantly decorated ballroom is booming with people when I finally walk in. If I had any hope of hanging out with Peyton tonight, that notion is long gone. I stick to Leon until I find Aiden and his wife, and then I attach myself to them. We mingle, introductions are made, and careers talked about. Every so often, I zero in on one of the guys from the band, curious to see how they handle their fans, and each time I see them, they're walking around, talking to whoever stops and talks to them. Like I said, ordinary.

As the night goes on, I have minor run-ins with Julius. This game he's playing, the "let's-make-sure-Autumn-knows-I-don't-like-her" game, is getting on my nerves. I don't understand it. Besides Peyton, we have nothing in common, and he's just butthurt that she's my friend. It's almost like he wanted her to get his permission or something. None of it makes sense. Yet, wherever I go, he's there, watching me like a hawk.

When it's time to sit for dinner, I'm surprised to find I'm at Peyton's table and sitting next to her. She introduces me to her sister, who asks me tons of questions about the weather. Their father asks a few as well, but it's JD and his British accent that has me in stitches. I could spend hours talking to him about nothing, as long as he's the one talking. According to Peyton, JD is laying it on thick tonight because I'm infatuated. I don't care, either way, as long as his words continue to flow in my direction.

When dinner is over, Noah whisks Peyton off to the dance floor. Harrison follows with Elle, leaving me sitting with two of the hottest older men I've ever been around. I've always been a date near my age type of woman, but damn it, this older gentleman vibe is definitely something I might want to try.

If I was expecting either of them to talk to me, I was sorely mistaken. Within minutes of everyone getting up, they did as well. I knew any fantasy I conjured in my mind would have to stay there for a lifetime. I do, however, follow their lead and decide to head toward the auction room. I see Julius's name down on a bid form—something about a handyman, jack of all trade sort of thing—and put down a bid. I'm sure I'll never win, but it's for the kids. If I do win, I think he could wash my windows, or maybe I'll tie him to a chair and keep him there until he tells me why he hates me so much. The latter is very unlike me, so windows it is.

I bid on a few other things before making my way back to the table. A crowd has formed, and the conversation seems lighthearted. I hear "weather girl" and groan. I've never hated a nickname more in my life than I do that one. I ignore Julius because flipping him off in public could be a bad career move.

"Gentlemen, if you are up for auction, please come to the stage."

"I hate this shit," Julius mumbles as he sets his drink down. He hates it, yet volunteers? I don't get him at all. I do, however, keep my eyes focused on him as he walks to the stage. His black pants are form fitting, hugging his tight muscles and firm . . . I clear my thoughts. There is no need for my mind to go into the gutter where this man is concerned.

Each player has their name called, and each winner comes forward. When Julius steps up to the front of the stage, I smirk and take a sip of my gin and tonic. Some unlucky person is going to have to spend the day with him, and I'm thankful—

"Congratulations, Autumn LaRosa."

I spit my drink out, sputtering, and some kind person pats me on the back. I bend at the waist, trying to regain some semblance of composure. "Shit," I mutter and stand upright, only to come face to face with Julius.

"Tell me how much so I can write you a check."

"Excuse me?"

"You heard me, Weather Girl. How much did you bid? There is no way in hell I'm spending the day with you."

At this moment, I realize my only mission in life is to make Julius Cunningham miserable. "I hope you like windows," I say before turning and walking away. I may look confident on the outside, but my nerves are frayed. By the time I make it to the bathroom, I'm ready to hurl.

TEN

JULIUS

My weekend sucked. I somehow convinced Reggie and Roxy that we needed to stay in on Sunday. I kept the blinds closed, helped them build a blanket and pillow fort in the living room, turned my phone off, and laid under the tent with the kids watching movies. I may have taken a nap or two as well. Mostly, I laid there and allowed Roxy to climb all over me while I battled the demons in my mind. It's funny how what I call demons are images of two women: my ex and the Weather Girl.

Weather Girl pulled a fast one on me the other night when she won the auction. I'm confused why she would even bid on me. It's not like I want to spend time with her. Hell, I can't even stand to be in the same room as her, and I don't get it. I don't know what it is about Autumn and why I'm so hung up on her. I just am, and I hate it. I hate that she's on my mind. She shouldn't be. Yet, each time I close my eyes, she's there, smiling and doing a hair flip, even though I've never seen her do such a thing. Every time I see her, she's poised and unaffected by my brutish behavior. Clearly, whatever subtle message I'm trying to send isn't working, and I'm going to have to use the powers that be to let her know *this,* whatever the hell you call it, isn't happening.

By the time I get to the practice facility, I'm in a mood. I'm not sure I ever came out of my funk, but nonetheless, I'm angry. At the world. My life. Everything around me. Usually, on a bye weekend, I use it to my advantage by taking the kids someplace fun. I should've bailed on the fundraiser and taken the kids to Disney or something, but then I'd have to see Elena. After her last trip here, I think it's best we stay away from each other. Elena gave me some song and dance on how her father is considering pressing charges against me for shoving him. It's so rewarding seeing your family members evolve over time. I go from being the best thing to ever happen to their daughter, to the worst. Good times.

As soon as I walk into the gym, the guys start catcalling me. *Assholes.* "I don't know what you guys are doing, but stop," I tell them as I step onto the treadmill.

"Where are you going on your fancy date?" one of the rookies asks.

"What date?" I start with a slow jog.

Chase Montgomery chimes in with, "The one with the hot reporter." *Weather Girl.*

I ignore my teammates and push the button to increase my speed. Someone hops onto the machine next to me.

"She's a knockout." I glance quickly at the voice next to me and groan. Brandon Garrison, our running back and resident loudmouth starts jogging next to me. "You'll have to take her somewhere cheap so the rest of us can shoot our shot with her. Why she thinks you're worth it, I'll never understand."

"Feel free to take my date," I tell him. "I'm not interested."

His eyes widen, and his mouth drops. "Give her my number."

I sort of shake him off and continue my run. Giving her his number isn't an option because I don't plan to spend any time with her at all. Brandon starts running, making me think I'm in the clear, but it's nothing but a guise.

"Honestly," he says while jogging next to me. "What's going on with the two of you?"

"Nothing. I don't even know her."

"She bid on you and not the rest of us. Do you expect us to believe you're not hitting that?"

I push the stop button and set my feet to the side until the belt stops moving. "I don't know her, aside from an introduction at Noah's. If you want to take her out, call her. I'm sure Noah can give you an introduction."

"Julius," the soft voice of Peyton rings out. I look toward her, and my insides drop. I expected Peyton to talk to me last week, but she never got me from practice or requested a meeting. Yet here she is. I swear, she's like a principal or something. Anytime she shows up, we know we're in trouble. The catcalls from earlier turn into heckling as I make my way toward her.

Peyton smiles when I'm near her. "Film time," she says. To the outside world, Peyton is this tiny woman who doesn't say boo, but to us, she's this powerful female who knows more about football than the players. She never tells us we are wrong or makes us feel stupid. Her game film sessions are different. By the time she brings one of us into her office, which is a large room with a massive viewing screen, she's broken our plays down and asks us to go over them with her. Her favorite question is, "What could've been done differently here?" Peyton never blames one person but the entire team.

I follow her to her office. The entire walk there, she keeps her head down, almost like she's shy. I mean, I know she is, but she's worked here for a few years now, and I've known her a bit longer. I remember when she would come to see Noah play. She would always spend time with us afterward, something that angered his girlfriend at the time, but Noah never cared. When Peyton walked into a room, Noah's world changed. Before I really knew Noah, I had asked him how long he and Peyton had been hooking up. He was mad and confided that he had only been with her once but never got that night out of his mind. He was in love with her but was afraid of what people might think of him if he pursued a relationship with a teenager.

Peyton sits down at the conference table in her office and presses a few keys on her laptop. On her wall, the film from our previous week appears. A few more clicks and the screen changes to multiple boxes of plays, each one is showing me. I groan.

"Can I preface this by saying I know I had a bad game?"

She looks up from her computer. "You can, but it's not going to change the outcome of the meeting."

Ouch, nothing like getting slammed in the gut, but she's right. I allowed my personal issues to interfere with my job, which should have never happened. I know better. I could easily blame Elena—I mean, it *is* her fault for showing up— but at the end of the day, the onus lies with me. I have a job to do, one which pays me very well to do it , and I need to get it done.

Play after play, Peyton breaks down what I could've changed, where I ran the route wrong, and where I took my eyes off the ball. Losing sight of the ball is the biggest issue.

Peyton points out that I'm a second or two late in turning my head toward the pass.

"Something to work on in practice," I say.

"Yes, I already gave my report to Bud," Peyton shuts the screen off. I'm thankful I don't have to stare at my errors anymore. "I do have a list of things you did well during the game if you'd like to go over them?"

I shake my head. "We both know the list is short. I had a bad game. I own it."

"You did some good things," she says. I think she only tells me this because she spent the past hour or so pointing out all my mistakes. "I understand the personal part of your life getting in your head though. It happens."

"But it can't continue to happen."

She shakes her head. "Anything I can help with?"

"Maybe," I say and then pause, wondering if I should really go where I'm about to go. Peyton stares at me with her eyebrows raised. "What's the deal with Autumn LaRosa?"

She smiles. "Why? Do you want to be set up?"

I jump back in my chair. "Hell no. I want to know where the hell she came from. I'm not trying to stir up any trouble, but I find it odd that she appears out of nowhere and is suddenly everywhere."

"Oh," Peyton says. "Autumn was a sorority sister. We were in the same media program."

"Yeah, Noah mentioned some of this. I don't know. There's something about her that rubs me the wrong way."

Peyton eyes me warily. "I think you watch too many documentaries on crime or something, Julius. Autumn is probably the most genuine person I know."

"Don't you feel she's attaching herself to you because of who you are? I mean, you're married to an NFL quarter-back, your dad is a famous drummer, and your brother is the lead singer of one of the most popular bands out there right now."

Peyton sits back in her chair and crosses her arms over her chest. By the look on her face, I know I've said something wrong. I'd take it all back, but the truth is, I'm bothered by Autumn, and I can't figure out why.

"First off, if I thought people were hanging around me because of who I am, who I'm married to, or because of who my family is, I'd be holed up in a dark corner of a room somewhere, afraid to come out. I learned a long time ago to give people a chance to show they're genuine.

"Second, the only reason Autumn reached out to me is because Aiden suggested it *after* he told her we were at the same school. She had no idea until another sister of ours told her. I had moved out of the sorority house by the time Autumn moved in. Her being in Portland is pure happenstance and a testament to what she brings to the news.

"Third, I see the way you look at her, Julius. And while I know you're going through some things with Elena and the separation, maybe you can use the date Autumn won as a new stepping stone into a friendship with her."

My eyes widen at the mention of the date I have to go on with Autumn. "Speaking of, how do I get out of the date? I tried to pay her off, but she won't take my money."

"Pay her off, why?" Peyton asks.

"Because I don't want to go with her. I literally loathe her."

Peyton laughs. "Oh, Julius." She shakes her head. "You have a crush."

Before I can respond, Peyton stands and goes to her door. She opens it and stands there, waiting for me to leave. When I'm near, I open my mouth, but words fail me. Peyton smiles and tells me to have a great day.

WHEN I OPEN the door to my apartment, everything is quiet and dark. There's a faint glow coming from the living room, and as I step into the room, I find Miss Meghan and Roxy snuggled on the couch, asleep. I leave them there and use the time to check on Reggie. I knock on his door, and he tells me to come in. My heart seizes for a second when I find him curled up on his bed. Immediately, I'm by his side with my hand on his forehead.

"Are you sick?"

He shakes his head and sniffles.

"What's going on, bud?"

"I'm mad at Mommy."

I sigh and lay down next to him. I don't know if I'm doing this right, the whole parenting thing when it comes to divorce, but I'm trying. "I get that you want to be mad at her." Hell, I am too.

"She doesn't love us anymore."

"No, that's not true, Reg. She loves you very much."

"Then why is she with that man?"

"What man?" I ask.

Reggie pulls his phone out from under his pillow. At eight, I believe he is too young to have a phone, but his mother insisted and went behind my back. I have taken the thing and put so many parental controls on it, and still, the wrong shit finds its way onto it. He taps the screen and then flips it around so I can see. There is his mother, in an embrace with her boyfriend.

"Where did you get this?"

"There's more," he says as he takes the phone away and swipes through a series of photos. My blood boils. I'm angry at Elena for being so public with this new romance, especially after pretending we were one big happy family last week.

"Reggie, where did you find these pictures?"

"Owen sent them to me. He called my mom a whore."

I groan angrily. I don't know who Owen's parents are, but I'm going to find out. I delete all the photos and then go to the deleted folder and remove them again. I hand Reggie his phone back and then use my finger to prop his chin up so he can look me in the eyes.

"Your mom is not a whore. I don't ever want to hear you say that word again. Not about your mother or any other woman. Your mom and I are getting a divorce. This means she's allowed to date other men, and I'm allowed to date other women. This does not mean we love you or Roxy any less. The two of you are our worlds. We'd do anything for you."

"But Mommy loves someone else."

I nod. "I know, bud. And I know that hurts you. It hurts me too. We can be sad about it, and we can always talk about what's going on, and you can also talk to your mom. Tell her how you feel when you see those things."

"Okay."

I pull my son into my arms and rest my chin on top of his head. I imagine Elena lying next to us, creating a Reggie sandwich, which we've done so often. Except, when I close my eyes, it's not Elena's face I see . . .

. . . it's Autumn's.

ELEVEN

AUTUMN

I'm thankful for the mild fall weather. When I lived in North Dakota, venturing outside at a time like this never boded well for my running habits. I never enjoyed jogging until I started my job. At first, I couldn't run for five minutes without having to stop. Five turned into ten, and that ten finally turned into a mile. Now, I'm up to at least five miles before I need a break or lose total interest in what I'm doing. One of the perks of being in Portland, in the downtown area, is the waterfront. There is a nicely paved pathway that affords all sorts of recreational activity. Every morning, I encounter bicyclists, rollerbladers, and a slew of other joggers. One of the perks is looking out over the water to see the boats. From what I hear, fleet week happens in May and June, and it's a sight to behold. Not gonna lie, I'm looking forward to summer.

After last night though, I'm considering taking up boxing. Peyton called in between my broadcasts and told me that Julius Cunningham, the jerk I won in the auction and who has made me feel completely unwelcome, asked about me. Color me stumped. When Peyton said this, my mouth dropped open, and at first, I thought, "Wow, this guy is coming around." Nope, nada. He despises me, and for what—I have no idea. Peyton thinks it's because he likes me, but there's no way. We aren't in the first grade anymore. There is no "be mean to the new girl because you have a crush on her" game of tag happening on the playground.

We're adults, but Julius doesn't act like one. He's a giant man child with a chip on his shoulder the size of the Grand Canyon, all because he thinks I'm using Peyton. I find him sad, honestly. Peyton says he's going through a few things with his wife but won't elaborate, which I'm okay with. The last thing I want is to know more about him. And to be honest, I don't want to spend the day with him. I have a feeling it's going to be a nightmare of a time, and I'll likely end up crying through most of it. Maybe I should've taken him up on his offer and accepted the check he wanted to give me. Nope, I paid for him, and I plan to use him to my fullest pleasure. He's going to rue the day he decided to talk shit about me.

When I come around the bend, my apartment complex is within sight. Usually, I go home but the morning is so lovely I decide to spend some time at the park. There was a time in my life when I thought I wanted to be a nanny. I love children and want my own someday, but loved the thought of taking care of babies. I was also sixteen at the time and thought I'd be an au pair in France or find a wealthy family in California that would take me on their vacations to Bali with them. I head toward the playground and sit down on the first empty bench I can find. I'm surrounded by strollers, moms, dads, and nannies talking to each other or chasing a toddler around. The sight brings a smile to my face. I hate that my clock is ticking and I have no one.

For the longest time, I thought Camden and I would get married and start a family, but he's out living his best life, chasing storms, and doing what he loves. I love my job too, but I'd give it up to be a full-time mother in a heartbeat. For this to happen, I have to start dating or go to a sperm bank. Neither idea seems ideal. Dating scares me. I see the tweets I get from random men and the stares when I'm out alone. The double-takes are what get me. Believe me, I'm not looking at men on the street wondering if they're the next man in my life. And the idea of going to a clinic to comb through a million profiles to find the right combination of eye, hair, height, and intelligence is such a turn-off. It's like dating, but without any commitment from the other party.

After watching the action in front of me for a few minutes, I decide to close my eyes and tilt my head back to enjoy the sun. It's in the mid-fifties. Not too warm, but not cold enough where you have to wear a parka either. I know many will disagree with me, but I find this weather perfect.

I listen to the chatter around me. Someone is talking about going out to dinner and mentions a place I haven't heard of. As tempted as I am to open my eyes and pull my phone out to put the name of the restaurant in my notes for reference later, I don't. If I forget, there are hundreds of other places I can try. Another voice piques my interest. It's a male, and if I had to guess, he's on the phone. I hear bits and pieces of his conversation and quickly deduce that someone in his life has had an affair. I tune him out, not wanting to feel like I'm a creeper and eavesdropping, even though he's talking about personal things in a park where anyone can hear him.

I settle deeper onto the bench and relax, knowing that I could easily fall asleep right now, except something is touching my leg. I open my eyes and sit up, startling the little girl next to me. "Hi," I say to her.

"Yous the lady from TV."

"I am. My name is Autumn." I hold my hand out for her, but she jumps at what I suspect is her name being frantically yelled. I glance around the play area, looking for her parent, only to find Julius storming toward us.

"Roxanne Cunningham, you know better than to run off."

"Is that you?"

She nods but doesn't seem fearful of her father. I would be, but he probably likes her.

"Daddy, wook." She points to me while staring at her looming father.

Julius and I make eye contact. I give him a soft smile and wave. "She yours?" It's a stupid question, but I have nothing else to say to the man. Much to my surprise, his daughter climbs onto the bench and sits next to me. Her little legs are bouncing up and down with excitement.

"Roxy, you shouldn't bother people," Julius says. "Come on, let's go."

She shakes her head and hides her hands under her legs. "I stay."

"She's not bothering me," I tell him, meaning every bit of it. I glance down at her and match her toothy grin with one of my own. "Hi, Roxy, it's nice to meet you."

"I see you on the TV."

"Well, I'm happy that you watch my weather reports. Now tell me, Roxy, do you like the rain or the sun?"

"The sun," she says.

"Roxy, we should go."

I turn my attention toward Julius and shake my head a

bit. "Honestly, she's not bothering me, Julius. I don't mind talking to her."

He nods but says nothing. He stays nearby, undoubtedly watching us like a hawk.

"How old are you?" I ask Roxy.

"Dis many." She holds up three fingers. "How old is you?"

Wow, I didn't expect her to come back with this question. I hold up both hands and say, "I am many more than this."

"Yous old." She laughs. If she weren't so cute, I'd be insulted.

"Sorry," Julius says. "She doesn't have a filter, so she says whatever comes to mind."

I wasn't aware he was close enough to listen to us, but it makes sense. He probably doesn't want me asking his daughter anything he would deem inappropriate. Not that I would.

Another child comes up to us. He looks to be around Roxy's age. I'm about to ask if she knows him when she yells out his name.

"Henry, she is on TV."

"You famous like her dad?" the little boy asks.

"No, I just tell you what the weather is going to be like."

"I don't like the weather," he tells me. "It's stupid. Sometimes it rains and then I can't go to the park. This one time, it snowed, and I got to stay home with my mom, but she was mad."

"I'm sorry."

"Do you make the weather like my mom makes my lunch?" he asks. "Because you should make it rain cats and dogs." Henry starts laughing and slaps his hand down on his leg.

"You're a funny guy, Henry."

"I know."

So humble.

Henry decides to call the entire playground over by telling everyone that I can make it snow or rain. The kids find it fascinating, while the parents use the free time to their advantage and check their phones. Honestly, I don't mind talking to them, but I hate disappointing them when they think I can change the weather.

The alarm on my phone goes off. I'm one of those people who sets reminders to do things, like eat lunch. I give myself an hour and a half to figure out what I'm going to do. Lately, I've made this my big meal during the day because the break between the evening news and night news is often too busy. I tell the kids that I have to go. Some scatter, but a few linger. Glancing around the park, I scan the space looking for Julius. He's over by the fence that keeps people from going into the river. I look down at Roxy and hold my hand out to her.

"Come on, I'll take you to your dad." She takes my hand without reservation and follows me toward her dad.

"Do you want to skip wif me?"

Hell yes, I do. "Let's do it."

Roxy and I start skipping until we reach Julius. He smiles, and my heart stops. Deep down, I know it's because his daughter is with me, but I swear he looked right at me when he did.

"I have to go," I say when we reach him. "I didn't want to leave her on the bench by herself."

"I appreciate that." He takes Roxy's hand. "She likes to wander off sometimes, as you can see." He looks down at this daughter, who is beaming up at her father.

"She's sweet, Julius. I enjoyed my time with her."

"What do you say to Miss Autumn?"

"Fank you for bisiting wif me."

I crouch down, so we're level. "You're welcome, Roxy. I hope we can hang out again real soon."

"Me too." She wraps her arms around her dad's leg, suddenly shy.

"Have a great day, Julius. It was nice to see you." It wasn't, but I'm a firm believer in killing people with kindness. I leave them there and head back toward my apartment. I'm tempted to look over my shoulder to see if he's watching, but I don't want to give him the satisfaction of knowing I care whether he's paying attention to me or not.

Once I'm back in my apartment, I head to the sliding glass door and step out onto the balcony. I find myself surveying the area for Julius, wondering if he's still out there or if he's left. I'm curious where he lives and why he would be in this neighborhood. According to Peyton, most of the guys live in the suburbs, at least the ones with children, while a few of the guys live in the same building as her and Noah. When I don't see him, I step back inside and head for the shower.

One thing is for sure—the Julius Cunningham I've met and encountered since moving here is *not* the same man I spoke with today. When his daughter is around, he's soft and vulnerable. The bad attitude, the snark, and disparaging comments don't exist, and that is something I could definitely get used to.

TWELVE

JULIUS

After practice, Noah and I head to the golf course. The sun is shining, and we want to get as many rounds of golf in as we can before the course closes for the winter. Granted, we still have time, considering it's only mid-September, but with our schedules, it's hard to say when we can come out again.

I tee off from the fifth and watch my ball sail through the air until it lands approximately one-hundred and fifty yards from me.

"Not bad," Noah says as he pushes his tee into the ground and sets his ball on top of it. He takes a few practice swings and then finally centers his driver behind the dimpled ball and swings, hitting the stupid white orb about twenty yards farther than mine. I'm starting to think there isn't anything Noah Westbury isn't good at. I've seen him play baseball when he volunteered for the Pioneers for a charity game. The dude can not only pitch lights out but is a beast with the bat. And he can even sing, but it's a rare day he belts out a tune.

"Did you get good grades in school?" I ask as we head back to the cart.

"What do my grades have to do with golf?"

I slide into the driver's seat and wait for Noah to sit down on the passenger side before taking off toward my ball. "It doesn't. I'm trying to find something you're not good at."

Noah laughs, which sort of makes things worse because he's leading me to believe he's some genius who probably could've gone to MIT or something. "My grades were decent, and I'm not good at everything."

I scoff.

"I'm not," he adds. "You have to remember I chose football over baseball and didn't have a scholarship when I went to Notre Dame. I was a walk-on."

"Yeah, why did you do that?"

I look over at him as he shrugs. "Lots of reasons, really. I knew I could play baseball anywhere I wanted, but football was my passion and something I had done all my life. Growing up, I expected I'd have offers from every college out there, but only a few came in, and they weren't schools I wanted to play for. I took a chance at Notre Dame because their program was something I believed in. However, being a walk-on affords you nothing. I was a practice player until I got my shot, and once I did, I didn't let the coach down. So, no, I'm not good at everything and have often thought about giving up on football and going back to baseball."

Noah's confession causes me to hit the brake on the cart. We lurch forward, and I mutter a weak apology. I don't know what I'd do without Noah and know that we won't be on the same team forever. Trades happen, or contracts don't get renewed, whether we like them or not.

"Are you planning on leaving the Pioneers?"

He looks at me quickly and then back at the green. "I think about leaving all the time. I'm not sure if I'm good enough for the Pioneers or able to get them to the next level. Every draft, I'm on pins and needles, waiting to see what management will do with their picks. If they take a QB, I feel like that's my sign to go."

I put the cart in park and wait a moment before exiting. Noah follows me to the back, where we each take an iron out of our bags. Noah walks with me to my ball and waits for me to set up my shot. You never realize that most of the time it takes to golf is because you have to look down the fairway, test each angle, practice your shot and imagine the ball landing somewhere near the pin. If you're really good at the game, you're checking the wind speed and direction and mentally calculating the trajectory.

My second hit barely escapes the sand trap and rolls to the edge of the green. "Better, but that'll be a long putt."

Noah laughs and walks toward his ball. I head back to the cart and don't bother to put my iron away so I can catch up with him. Noah walks through almost the same motions as I had and finally sends his ball through the air, landing not far from mine.

"I'm about to say something, but it has to stay between us. This means no going home to tell Peyton."

Noah looks at me warily. "I don't like to keep secrets from my wife."

"I know, but this one is important, and I don't want her to know anything, at least not yet."

"Okay..." he says hesitantly.

I motion for us to get back in the cart, and as soon as we do, I inhale deeply and ready myself for what I'm about to say. "I think I may have misjudged Autumn."

Noah lets out a strangled laugh and then coughs. He

apologizes, but I know he's done it on purpose. "Why's that?"

"Well, I saw her a little over a week ago at the park by my house. Roxy ran right up to her, like she's known her for years, and had a conversation. Autumn didn't care that a toddler took up any of her time, and then more kids came over, and she just sat there, entertaining all of them. Ever since, Roxy insists on watching the weather every evening, and naturally, I watch with her because I'm her dad."

"Is that what you tell yourself?" he asks. "Or is there another reason?"

"Another reason entirely," I tell him. "Why didn't you slap me in the head when I first met her? She's so freaking beautiful."

Noah sighs and then chuckles. "You were drunk when you met her, and I think deep down you remember being angry when all of this happened, so you manifested this issue between the two of you into something that it isn't. I know you're worried about Peyton and thinking Autumn is using her, but she's not. You gotta remember, Peyton is an excellent judge of character, and if she felt Autumn had ulterior motives, she'd keep her at bay."

"Yeah, Peyton said something similar to me when we had our last session."

"At what point do you admit you like Autumn?"

I don't normally blush, but there is definitely a temperature influx happening on my face. "I . . . uh . . ." Noah shows his phone to me. On it is my Twitter feed. Instantly, the heating of the cheeks I thought I might have felt moments ago is back with a vengeance.

"I," I pause because I don't have a decent excuse as to why I started sending tweets to Autumn. When I glance at Noah, it's clear he's waiting for me to start talking. I sigh heavily and say, "This all started a few nights after I saw her in the park. I'm lying in bed one night, and I hear her voice on the television, so I sort of watch her segment, while I'm scrolling through my Twitter feed, and I happen upon a tweet she reshared from Marchetti. I clicked on her profile and accidentally hit follow."

"And you can't unfollow after that?" Noah interjects.

I shake my head slowly. "Nope. I do what any guy who has nothing to lose would do: I start tweeting her about her segment, and man, I'm a fool because I have no idea what I'm saying, but she reshares each one and sends laughing or smiling emojis back."

"Sounds like you've made a connection."

This time I eye him. "I'm pretty sure she hates me and is just saving face on social media."

"Why do you think this?"

It takes me a moment to respond. I'm not proud of what I'm about to say, but if he's asking, maybe that means Autumn hasn't complained to him or Peyton. "Because when I first met her, I called her weather girl. I know she's insulted by it, but I haven't stopped because I'm an idiot."

"Yeah, you are." Noah sighs and then starts laughing. "If you weren't going through everything you are, I'd suggest you talk to Autumn. You might find that you like her."

"I do like her," I tell him. "That's the problem. I've made such an ass out of myself over the past few weeks, I'll be lucky if she gives me the time of day. If I were her, I'd hate me."

"Autumn doesn't strike me as the type of person to hate anyone." Noah pauses for a moment and then says, "What about Elena?"

I grimace at the mention of her name. "We haven't spoken much since my trip to L.A. and when she randomly showed up at the game, but it's clear she's moved on. I have it on my to-do list to call the lawyer and get the paperwork finalized. We'll end up fighting over the kids and alimony, which she's not entitled to, so it'll come down to child support. We both want full custody, but I feel like her real motivation is to get more money. The whole thing is very uncomfortable."

"I can imagine."

I chuckle at his statement. "No, you can't. You and Peyton are perfect. You're like the spec model for marriages."

Noah doesn't say anything in return but does crack a smile as he steps up to his ball. He swings through, and that stupid white plastic thing lands right on the green and rolls toward the pin.

"I give up." I hang my head and walk toward the cart, all while my best friend is laughing behind me.

Noah and I finish our round of golf and head back to our training facility where I make the mistake of going inside to grab a few things from my locker.

"Julius, I'm so happy I've caught you. I was about to email you," Maggie, the general manager's secretary, says.

"What's up?" Maggie is one of those people you either love to run into or dread. Sometimes, she's the bearer of bad news, and you never know what she's going to say.

"Autumn LaRosa emailed. Your date has been set."

Part of me is excited by the word date, but the other half of me is dreading what's coming my way. "And when is it?"

"Tomorrow."

"Tomorrow?"

Maggie nods. "There was a little back and forth about your schedule, but tomorrow seems to work."

"And what if I have plans?" I ask.

"Change them. I'll forward Ms. LaRosa's contact information but expect to meet her outside her apartment in the morning."

"I don't even know where she lives," I state.

"It'll be in the email," she says as she walks off.

I stand there, speechless and groaning on the inside. I'm equal parts pissed because I don't have a say and excited because I like a woman who takes charge of a situation. However, I'm leery because Autumn could make me do anything she wants and there isn't shit I can say or do about it. I'm at her mercy. The only thing I'm sure of is I won't have to mow someone's lawn or pick up anyone's leaves—unless she has decided to farm my services out.

On my drive home, I think about what I'm going to say to Autumn when I see her. I should apologize for being a complete d-bag when we first met, and I should definitely tell her I'm sorry for calling her weather girl. Although, I do think the nickname is cute.

Every thought I have right now is about Autumn as I head toward the elevator with a smile on my face. I'm curious what she's going to have me do on our date, and I've concluded that I don't care as long as she's with me. Of course, the likelihood is I'll have to do some menial tasks while she sits back and laughs at me. It's okay. I deserve it.

I'm lost in thought when the elevator door opens back up and someone steps in. The only reason I look up is that there's a very audible gasp. I glance at the person in front of me, and my smile fades because the first thing that comes to mind is that Autumn is stalking me.

"What are you doing here?" I ask her.

"I could ask you the same thing."

I let out a small chuckle, mostly to curb my impending ire. "I live here, so what's your excuse?"

Autumn's mouth drops open and then closes quickly. "I live here as well. The fifth floor."

Unbelievable.

"Penthouse."

"I guess this makes us neighbors?" Before I can respond, the chime dings, and the number five illuminates. "Guess I'll see you tomorrow," Autumn says as she starts to step out. She pauses and looks over her shoulder.

"I'll see you downstairs in the morning, Weather Girl," I say with a wink.

THIRTEEN

AUTUMN

I'm trying not to focus on what my head is screaming while I get ready for my date with Julius. It took me a bit to come up with something I felt would be appropriate for him while getting some humor out of it. I thought about having him stand on the street corner, directing traffic with one of those signs for insurance, or having him dress up as a chicken and dance around Pioneer Square. Neither seemed clever enough for Mr. Cunningham. One thing I knew when I started planning was I wanted him to see me in a different light. He has such a preconceived notion about me that I'm hoping to change his mind.

Of course, there is the slight issue of him winking at me yesterday when I stepped off the elevator. I have no idea what possessed me to turn and look at him, but I did, and wow! Just freaking wow. There is no mistaking the fact that Julius Cunningham is a fine-looking man. No, he's better than fine. Some would say he's handsome or good-looking, while others—me being in the "others" group—would say he's smoking hot with a side of gorgeous. As much as I hate to admit this, I find the man incredibly attractive. More so since I met his daughter. The way he was with her, I never expected the man I met weeks ago could be so gentle. It was like he was a completely different person with her. But then again, he called me weather girl, so his use of this nickname negates any personality change.

I stand in front of the mirror, turning from side to side. I opted for the casual look today, with jeans, a T-shirt, and a sweater. I never gave the Pioneers office any instructions on what Julius should wear, just that he needs to meet me in front of my . . . *our* apartment complex. I step closer to the mirror and shake my head. What are the chances that the man who had been a thorn in my side since I moved to Portland would live above me? Granted, he's *way* above me, but that's to be expected. With one last look in the mirror, I grab my things and head toward the elevator. As soon as I step out into the hallway, I find myself looking in both directions, half expecting Julius to be coming toward me or even lurking around the corner. Would he do something like this? It's unlikely, although he does seem a bit childish at times.

My nerves are on edge by the time I step out of the elevator. I scan the lobby and even peek inside the restaurant for any sign of Julius. I requested he meet me outside, but again, I find myself second-guessing whether he will follow the rules or not. And even though he said he'd see me today doesn't mean he will show up. He was pretty adamant about paying me back for the money I spent on winning him.

When I step outside, I use my hand to shield the sun. Across from the entrance to my building, a man stands. He's dressed in khaki pants, a white dress shirt, and has a dark-colored jacket or sweater in his hand. I swallow hard at the hulking form coming toward me. It doesn't take long for me to recognize Julius, and with each step he takes, I start to see him in a different light.

"Good morning," he says when he stops in front of me.

"Morning," I somehow choke out even though my tongue feels four inches thick. There's a slight breeze, and I get a good whiff of his cologne. My knees go weak. It's woodsy with hints of spice. Very masculine and very sexy.

"I didn't know what you meant by casual," he says as he looks himself over. "If this isn't okay, I can run up and change."

"No, it's fine, you're perfect. I mean—" I cover my face with my hand and shake my head. I inhale deeply to center my thoughts. "What you're wearing is fine for what I have planned. Are you ready?"

Julius holds his arm out and tells me to lead the way. I point back to the door. "We need to go get my car."

"Do you want me to drive?" he asks, and I shake my head. I don't bother to check and see if he's following me. I can sense him . . . or rather *smell* him. He's close, right on my heels. Instead of going to the elevator, I head for the stairs. I don't want to be trapped in a small box with him right now because my mind is in the gutter, counting the ways I could climb him like a tree.

When we get to the garage floor, Julius steps in front of me and opens the door. "Thank you." I know chivalry isn't a lost art, but it's becoming harder and harder to find someone who still wants to open doors for women. "My car is over there," I say, pointing to my black Tucson.

"Do you like this car?" he asks.

"I do. It gets great gas mileage." I hit the fob and unlock the doors. I'm sort of expecting Julius to open the driver's side to let me in, but he doesn't. What he does do, is wait until I'm inside before getting in. "How's Roxy?" I ask as I start my car and back out of my space.

"Roxy's great. She's a handful but worth it."

"She's a cutie. I enjoyed meeting her." I exit the garage and head toward work. It's a short drive, which works out well since neither of us is talking. When I pull into the station's garage, Julius asks what we're doing.

"Well," I start by saying, "Since I live in an apartment, I'm sort of limited on what I can have you do. I don't have a yard to maintain, and washing the windows is probably against the ordinance. Not to mention dangerous. The Pioneers made me sign a form saying I wouldn't do any bodily harm to you, so putting you on a street corner in a chicken suit is out as well."

"You were going to make me wear a chicken suit?" he asks in a voice that borders on panic.

We get out of the car, and I glance over at him. He seems genuinely concerned. To put his mind at ease, I tell him, "It was an idea. Believe me, what I came up with is much, much better." I give him a soft smile and motion for him to follow me. He's next to me in a flash and stepping ahead of me to get to the door.

"I've never been here."

"I'll give you the tour."

I like that Julius is nervous and doesn't know what to expect. His punishment, for lack of a better word, will be much more appreciated this way. Once again, I opt for the stairs. The drive over was torture with him sitting so close. Until now, I never spent longer than a few minutes with him, and the conversation centered around him telling me what he thought of me. And those thoughts haven't been very nice. Plus, I don't trust myself not to drool in front of him. Julius is hot, sexy, desirable, and completely off limits.

When we reach my floor, I open the door this time. I'm confident he would've done it had he known where we were going, but I'm also okay with it. There is nothing written in arbitrary rules saying I can't hold the door for him.

Julius follows behind me. We walk down the hall, passing a couple of the offices. I hear a few chairs scrape against the floor after we go by and a sure sign of someone rushing to the door. I have no doubt tomorrow it'll be the Spanish Inquisition when I come to work. We walk by the reception desk, where I give the new girl a little wave. Her mouth drops open, and it makes me wonder if she knows who Julius is or if she's just a fan of how good-looking he is right now.

"Everyone is staring," he mumbles into my ear. For him to be this close, he has to press against my back, which means I can feel his hard chest against me. I'm angry at myself for wearing my sweater and wish I had half the sense Julius did and just carried it.

"You're famous," I remind him. "Aren't you used to this?"

"Yes, but most people just approach me, ask for an autograph and a picture and then go on their way. These people are staring."

"Huh," I say as I open the door to the stage.

"Whoa." Julius walks past me and takes in the set. "This looks nothing like what we see on TV."

"I know, it's crazy."

"Where do you stand?" he asks. His question gives me pause. Up until now, he's never asked a single thing about my work. He's only berated me and called me weather girl. I point to where I stand, and he looks confused.

"Wait, where's your map?"

"In here." I tap my temple and smile. I don't explain

anymore and ask him to follow me again. We leave the set and head back toward the office. I take him to meet my assistant Lisette, who does ask for his autograph, and they pose for many pictures. She even makes him pick her up. Julius does everything she asks and does it all with a smile.

"Do you have an office?" he asks.

"Not exactly. I have a dressing room, and when I need to use the computer or something, I go to the media room. It's where most of us work when we're not on air."

"How come you're not working today?"

"How do you know when I work?"

He shrugs and blushes slightly. "I may have looked you up the other night when I was tweeting you."

"You were tweeting me?" This question displeases him. His smile disappears, and he looks confused.

"Well, I thought it was you. I guess I have the wrong handle." Julius takes his phone out and shows his social media.

"No, that's definitely mine, but sometimes Lisette will retweet things during my broadcast. She really manages most of my social media stuff."

"Ah, so I was flirting with your assistant and not you?"

Now I'm the one blushing. "I'll be sure to add the app to my phone."

There's an awkward pause between us—the "should I say something, or should he?" moment when neither of us knows what to do or how to act. I finally give in and look away from him before acting like I've come up with the most fantastic idea ever.

"Do you want to see my dressing room?"

Julius nods, and we head a few doors down from Lisette. Thankfully, we have a cleaning crew, so last night's dinner isn't stinking up my room. "It's not much, but it's ten times what I had when I lived in North Dakota." He walks around, touches the clothes on the rack, and then sits down on my sofa.

"Damn, this is comfortable. I'd probably fall asleep on this if we had couches in the locker room."

"You do. I've seen them."

Julius shakes his head and gives me a disgusting look. "Heed my words, never ever sit on anything in the locker room, ever. Footballers are gross. We walk around naked, take quick showers, and believe in superstitions."

"Okay, well, I feel sick now."

He pats the cushion next to him, and as much as I'd love to sit next there and get lost in his baby blue eyes, I can't. I won't put myself through unneeded agony. I opt for the chair at my vanity. It's far enough away, and I won't want to strangle him when his mood shifts.

"So, you have me at the station and gave me a tour. What is it that you want me to do for you?"

"This is a date, right? With no time limit?"

He nods.

"Well, first things first," I say as I stand. "You need to sit here so I can put some make-up on you."

"Haha, very funny."

Except I'm not laughing.

I see nothing but fear written all over his face. "For what?" he asks.

"You're going on air, Julius. You're going to do the weather, *weather boy*."

His mouth drops open, and I know I've beaten him at his little game.

FOURTEEN

JULIUS

"I . . . uh . . . there's . . ." I don't even know what I'm trying to say, but every word possible fails me. There has to be some mistake, right? I must've misheard Autumn because there is no way the station will allow someone who has no idea what they're doing to go on air and report something as scientific as the weather. Then, it hits me. This is a joke because I made fun of Autumn's job, and she's trying to prove a point. I start to chuckle and nod. "I get it. I'm sorry for making fun of your job. What you do is very important."

"Well, I'm certainly glad you have recognized that my job does require some skill, but you're still going on air."

"Wh-what? Why?" I stammer.

"Because it's going to be a humbling experience for you," she says. "And I think the viewers will love to see Julius Cunningham in a different light."

"So, this is about PR?"

"No, it's about showing you there is more to the world than football. Now, come sit." Autumn pats the black chair and swivels it around so the seat is facing me. I look from it to her and see she's serious about me doing this. *Fuck.* Autumn pats the chair again, and I groan. Each step I take is staggered. I'm dragging my feet like a three-year-old who has been told to come to the dinner table and eat broccoli. I really want to ask her if I *have* to do this, but I'm afraid of the answer. She bought me for the day and technically can tell me to do whatever she wants me to do. And I guess this is better than standing on the street corner dressed as a chicken. Although, no one would really know it was me. Nope, I have a feeling Autumn would alert the news or something. In hindsight, this will be the lesser of any other evil she could come up with.

I finally sit, and my body sags. Autumn spins me toward the mirror, and I lean forward. "Are those bags under my eyes?" The large light bulbs surrounding her mirror illuminate my face. I look horrendous like I haven't slept in years. I don't remember looking this bad when I left the house, but hell, maybe I did.

"Yes," she says. "Not getting much sleep, huh?" Autumn is at her counter, going through her bags and drawers of what I'm guessing is make-up.

"Understatement. Have you ever had a toddler's feet in your face while trying to sleep?"

Autumn laughs and comes toward me with a brush and some brown stuff. "Can't say that I have. I'm sure that makes for a crowded bed at night."

"It shouldn't since Roxy is so tiny."

Autumn continues to brush cream or something all over my face. I can't really say if I like this or not. It's definitely different, and I'm happy I don't have to do this for any of my interviews after the game. What a nightmare.

"What does your wife do for work?" she asks.

I sigh and close my eyes when her fingers are nearby.

"My soon-to-be ex-wife is trying to make it as an actress in Los Angeles."

"I'm sorry."

"For what? The fact that she's my ex or an actress?"

Autumn pauses and then goes back to her counter. "I didn't mean to pry."

"You're not. It's somewhat public knowledge, especially if you watch the gossip shows. She has a boyfriend. She wants a different life."

"For that, I'm truly sorry."

"Me too. I have a question."

"Shoot."

"Do you like your job?"

"I love my job," she says without hesitation. "There's a joke that goes around about how being a meteorologist is the only job where you can be wrong and not get fired."

My eyebrows raise. "That's a good point."

Autumn laughs lightly, and I find that it's a sound I'd like to hear again. "Do you like your job?" she counters.

I shrug, and she steps back. "Don't get me wrong, I love what I do. Otherwise, I wouldn't put my body through it, but sometimes I wish I had that nine-to-five."

"What does Roxy think about her dad?"

"Roxy goes to the games for the hotdogs and cotton candy. My son, Reggie, he plays as well, but he's just in Pee Wee."

"You have a son?"

I nod and close my eyes again while her brush moves gently over my skin. When the sensation stops, I open them and find Autumn staring at me. "He's eight," I tell her. "Is that a problem?"

"Why would it be a problem?"

"Dunno, didn't know how you felt about going on a date with a single dad?"

Autumn chuckles and returns to her counter. "I don't date men who tend to hate me."

"I don't hate you."

She scoffs. "You've treated me poorly since the day I met you."

"True, but I have excuses. Would you like to hear them?"

Autumn turns and points to the couch. "Your face is camera-ready, but we have a bit before you have to be out there. We can sit over there." She moves to the sofa, stops at the small refrigerator, pulls out two bottles of water, and hands one to me. We both sit, but Autumn angles toward me, waiting for me to give her every excuse I've come up with as to why I've been such a jerk.

"Okay, so the first night I met you, I had just come back from L.A. where I had gone to see my ex. The meeting didn't go well, coupled with some hard liquor and the fact that you're unbelievably gorgeous, I didn't know how to react. I heard you talking to Peyton and some other media people and just got it into my head that you were using her to get ahead in your career. There was another time, where I ended up at the bar, and the guys in there were catcalling you. I was pissed, and I didn't know why.

"Then you were at the game. Funny story, I had never lost a coin toss at home. You show up, boom, I lose. So, naturally, I'm angry. And after the game, you see the bullshit with my ex and her father, plus my kids are in the car screaming. It was like the universe put you in my path at the most inopportune times. If something bad happened, you were right there to witness it."

"You think I'm gorgeous?" Her voice is quiet, and her brown eyes are piercing.

My head shakes slowly. Not because I disagree with her, but because she even has to question it. "The night of the gala," I pause and put my thoughts in order. "Everyone stared at you, and it bothered me. I kept thinking, damn, whoever she pays attention to is the luckiest person on the planet because I want five minutes to apologize. I was so pissed off when the emcee announced you had won me, but deep down I was happy, even though I've had a hard time accepting the fact I like you and didn't want you to know. Or even admit it to myself."

"Could've fooled me by the nickname you gave me."

I chuckle and take a long pull from the bottle of water. "Yeah, I thought I was clever, but I'm just an ass. You have to admit, it's cute though, Weather Girl." I reach for her hand and play with her fingers for a bit before letting them go.

"It's grown on me. I don't hate it as much, but I'm not okay with anyone else saying it either."

"So, what you're saying is, it's our thing?"

Autumn shrugs, and I take this as a good sign. "You're a lot different than I thought you'd be today," she tells me. "I figured I'd want to get rid of you five minutes after our time started."

"I don't blame you for thinking that. I haven't been very nice to you."

"You were the other day in the park."

I nod, remembering the morning very clearly. "The way you were with Roxy." I pause and look at Autumn. "I left her sitting with you and walked away. The whole time I watched your every move. You treated Roxy as if she was someone important to you. After those other kids showed up, every few seconds, you'd put your hand on her leg or turn to her. To Roxy, you're the famous one because she can see you on television, and for you to make her a priority that morning, it meant the world to us."

"I know this is going to sound odd, but I felt like I had known her for years. She's an incredibly special little girl."

"Don't I know it." I reach over and touch Autumn's hand again. "So, would you date a single dad?"

Autumn shrugs, and my heart falls. She smiles, but it still doesn't do anything to lift my spirits. "It's really going to depend on the dad," she says with a wink. I laugh and groan, knowing I've been played.

AUTUMN TAKES me back to the stage. I expect everything to be different with cameras everywhere, and people running around, barking orders. But it's still the same, with the only exception being Selena Rich and Arthur Brentwood are delivering the news. To say I'm confused would be an understatement. Where are all the cameras?

"You okay?" Autumn asks.

"Confused." I'm sure the look on my face expresses this as well. "Who the hell are they talking to?"

Autumn pulls me a bit farther into the room, turns me around, and then points up. "Our producers and cameras are up there. The only one down on the floor with us is the teleprompter. All our communication is through our earpieces. Come on, I gotta get you mic'd up."

"Wait, I thought the entire set was one large microphone."

"Nope, here slip this wire under your shirt, preferably in the front, and clip the mic right here." Autumn touches my chest, and I shiver. Our eyes meet, and normally, this would be the right time to lean forward and kiss her. It's wrong for me to even think about kissing her because of the way I treated her, but I'm not sure if there is a better way to show her I'm not the guy she first met, that the one standing in front of her is the type of person I am.

"Got it," I hear her say.

"Huh?"

"I'm talking to Marvin. It's almost time. Come on, let me show you how to do this."

I follow Autumn. She shows me the teleprompter and introduces me to the guy who makes sure it's facing the right direction. Then, she takes me to this green screen, and that is when I freeze.

"I can't do this," I tell her, but she's not listening. "I suck at geography."

Her eyebrows raise as she smiles. "You're going to stand here and face the prompter."

"Where's the map?"

"There isn't one. Just read what the prompter says and point where you think you need to point."

Autumn helps . . . more like forces me to stand in a specific spot. She steps away and gives me a thumbs up. This isn't going to go well at all. There's a voice in my earpiece, giving me a countdown. My heart starts beating rapidly, and my palms sweat. I'm beyond nervous. I'm anxious and feel like I'm going to crumble to the ground in a heaping pile of embarrassment.

"Shit," I mutter.

"No swearing, please, Julius," the voice in the earpiece says. Of course, I cuss again, and then there's laughter. Great, they're all mocking me. I'm told I'm on the air and instantly start reading from the screen.

"Hey Rose City, it's me Julius Cunningham, wide receiver of your Portland Pioneers, and after the break, I'll have today's forecast and how the week is going to shape up for you." Something sparks within as soon as I mention the Pioneers. I can do this. I may not be good at it, and I may not even get any of this right, but I'm going to make this fun and memorable and make sure Autumn knows I'm taking my new job seriously.

Now that I'm on stage, I can hear everything. You really have to pay attention or at least know what your cues are. Selena Rich welcomes everyone back from the commercial break, and then a countdown begins in my ear. I'm poised, ready, and my eyes are focused on the monitor.

"Hey, Pioneer fans. I know you're excited about this week's game, and let me tell you, I am as well. Right now, we have a small cold front moving in, which will bring us a couple of days of rain, but by Friday, it'll be gone. You can expect clear skies on Sunday, but you'll want to mow your lawn today because the rain will be back Sunday evening." All while I'm standing, my arms are flailing about. I have no idea what the viewers see behind me, and I don't care because over in the corner, Autumn stands there, laughing. And to see her laugh, to see her enjoy what I'm doing right now, is the best feeling I've felt in a long time.

FIFTEEN

AUTUMN

I thought Julius would embarrass himself. At least, that's what I hoped would happen. I should've known his charismatic personality would shine through in a moment like this. I see the error of my ways. I shouldn't have tried to humiliate him at all. I'm not that sort of person, and I feel terrible.

One of the producers tells Julius he can leave the set; he comes toward me. He's beaming, and I can't help but match his grin with one of my own. Julius reaches for me and pulls me into his arms. His very strong, warm, and comforting arms.

"This was the most amazing thing ever. Thank you so much," he says quietly. Julius's mouth is so close to my ear I swear I feel his lips press against my skin. I know I probably imagine this, but the fact that he still has me wrapped in his arms and hasn't let go yet is sending my thoughts in a direction they should not head.

When he steps back, he keeps his hands on my arms, cupping my elbows. His response has caught me off guard. I expected him to tell me he hated being up there, that the lights made him sweat, or the teleprompter moved too fast for him. Or worse, that I made him look like a fool in front of his fans. The thing is, I'm excited he had so much fun. I want him to see my job as something that is serious but also entertaining. Many people think being on the news is stressful, but once the cameras stop rolling, it's a laugh a minute around here. Most of the time, we have dance-offs during commercial breaks, or Aiden is standing off to the side making faces at Selena or Arthur because Aiden thinks it's fun to try and make our composure crack.

"You were great up there. A natural. I think you've found your calling after retirement."

Julius nods. "I take back everything I said about you being a weather girl." He cringes at the sound of my nickname as he says it. "I was so wrong in making any assumptions about you or your job, and I'm sorry."

"You're forgiven."

"Are you sure?" he asks.

"I am." I motion for Julius to follow me. We are about to leave the sound stage when the crew comes up to us.

Marvin, my main cameraman, juts his hand out to shake Julius's. "It was a pleasure filming you today," he says.

"I'm hoping you captured my good angles." Julius turns and poses, and everyone around us laughs. Including me. "Seriously though, I had a blast. Anytime Autumn is out, don't hesitate to call me. I'll gladly fill in."

I lightly jab Julius in the arm. "Hey."

"What?" he pulls me toward him and wraps his arm around my shoulder. My co-workers give me a few looks, making me wonder what is going on in their minds. More so, what is going on in Julius's right now? He looks at me and winks. I like this. The feeling of his arm around me and the way he stares at me. He's not much taller than me, but it's enough to make me feel secure. Julius is a friend if I can be so bold as to even call him that. Up until now, I thought he hated me.

His deep-set, crystal blue eyes bore into mine. I swallow hard and try to disengage, but I can't turn away. Julius is attractive. He knows this, and I have felt this way about him since I saw him on Peyton and Noah's balcony. His attitude that day and the days following should've steered me down the path of avoidance, but each time I've seen him, I've greeted him with a wide grin only to be rebuffed by him. I should be afraid. Leery even. Except, I'm not. I'm interested and curious. Is this truly the *Julius* Peyton told me about?

"Autumn?" he says my name so quietly, I almost don't hear him. I snap out of my trance and realize people are staring at us. My eyes blink rapidly, and I look off into the distance to regain my composure. Julius's arm is still around my back, and his hand cups my shoulder. It's an intimate gesture. One that I like.

I finally clear my throat and face my co-workers. "You can't take my job," I say firmly as my eyebrow raises. I'm challenging Julius to say otherwise.

He doesn't.

Instead, he smiles so brightly and laughs. "Our girl has spoken," he says as his gaze leaves mine and his attention is back on the people around us. I feel like I should feel relieved, but the truth is, I'm on edge. My nerves are dancing at the edge of my skin, keeping me rattled. I can't tell if my speeding heart is because of the situation I'm in now or because of Julius and how I'm starting to feel about him.

My co-workers ask for Julius's autograph, and he agrees, which means he must let go of me. As soon as he moves his arm, I find myself stepping closer to him so I can continue to feel his presence. Julius tilts his head slightly and smirks. It's sexy and heart racing. I step back and give him the space he needs to be Julius Cunningham, Wide Receiver for the Portland Pioneers.

After Julius finishes and my work family is satisfied, we walk back to my dressing room. I think I feel his hand on the small of my back every few steps we take, but I most likely imagine his hand is there. It's one thing to show people you're grateful for an opportunity, but it's a whole other thing to openly flirt. I tell myself; Julius is not flirting. He's being nice.

"Okay, what's next?" he asks when we get to my dressing room. I honestly hadn't thought about what we'd do next and figured he would be so angry with me he wouldn't want to talk to me again.

"Well . . ." I pause and think about what we could do with the rest of the day. I had planned on taking a nap and trying to find a last-minute opening for a massage. "Shopping," I blurt out. "Yeah, we're going shopping. You get to see how I normally spend my day."

"What do you mean?" he asks and then shakes his head. "Shopping, really? You want to take me to the mall?"

I shrug because I don't know what I want to do, except I don't want our date to end. This *new* Julius is fun to be around. "You know I am usually on the evening and night-time news with Aiden, Selena, and Arthur, right?" he nods. "I made special arrangements today for all of this to happen. When I told them my idea, they wanted to be part of your broadcast, so we all swapped with our afternoon team."

"I still don't get where shopping comes into all of this?"

"It's part of my routine. Once a week, I go into Meyers and work with a personal shopper on the new items they've received. They fit me for my wardrobe, find things they think I'll look good in, and then I usually meet Peyton for lunch before I go to the station to work."

Julius reaches for my hand. He squeezes it and doesn't let go. "If I promise to go shopping with you later, can we do something else?"

I don't know what else to do. "Um . . ."

Julius takes my hand in his and squeezes it. "Do you trust me?"

No, the hell I don't.

"Okay, wrong choice of words." He laughs. "Tell me this. Have you done much sight-seeing?"

"No," I say, shaking my head. "I stay mostly by our complex."

He sighs. "I figured. Let me take you to my favorite place in the city."

At this point, I have nothing to lose. It's not like something is going to happen to me. Everyone knows I'm with him today. "Okay, show me." My statement is open-ended, and by the surprised look in Julius's eyes, he didn't miss the subtle innuendo.

We walk to the parking garage, and thankfully, no one stops on our way out. I'm excited to see where we are going. When we arrive at my car, Julius holds his hand out. "What?"

"I should drive."

"Why, because you're a man?"

He chuckles. "Believe me, no. I am all for equal rights. I know where we're going, and it's easier for me to drive than give you directions. The one-way streets can really mess someone up."

Ugh, I hate that he's right. I dig in my purse and hand him my keys. My hand lingers in his palm for longer than necessary, but I don't care. He's watching me, and I, him. There's an energy between us, one I felt when I first met him but also ignored. I'm not sure I want to ignore it anymore.

Julius walks me to the passenger side of my car and presses the fob to unlock the door like he's done it a million times. I know it's a fob, and most are standard, but I like that he's so confident in what he's doing. He waits until I'm settled and then closes the door and again goes around the front of the car so I can follow him. The sight of Julius in khaki pants is genuinely something to behold.

He gets behind the driver's seat and asks me how to adjust it. "There's a thingy on the side."

"A thingy?"

I shrug. "I don't know what else to call it."

"Thingy, it is," he says as he reaches down by the door. The seat slides back and he adjusts the seat one more time before pressing the push start button.

Julius pulls out of the parking lot and turns away from the downtown area. I don't know why, but for some reason, I thought we'd head toward the stadium or the waterfront. He continues to drive on the side street. Multi-colored leaves hang from trees, creating shadows with the sun. It's a beautiful day out. If I had paid attention to the forecast I delivered last night, I would've planned a picnic or something. Julius was right, shopping can wait.

We make idle chit chat during the thirty-minute drive. He asks me what I like best about my job, and I tell him that I'm fascinated with the weather. I pose the same question to him, and he tells me his career is fun, for the most part, but that he loves his teammates and the atmosphere around game day.

"Did you always want to be in the NFL?"

"Yeah, for sure," he says as he maneuvers a turn. "My dad, brother, and I would watch football all the time, and my brother and I would always toss the ball back and forth. In high school, I was a standout player, in basketball too, but football got me to college for free, and then to the NFL."

"Do you ever wonder what you'd be if you didn't have sports?"

Julius thinks for a moment and then shakes his head. "Not really. It's always been my life. What about you?"

"Oh, well, let's see. I wanted to be a princess, of course. Thought about being a lawyer because I used to love being on the debate team."

"How did you end up being a meteorologist?"

"My junior year of high school, I took a media class. We had our own television station, mostly for announcements and other important school things like the sports scores, weather, birthdays, and such. I worked the lunch gig and figured out I loved being in front of the camera."

Our conversation ends when we pull into a parking lot. Julius puts my car into park and pushes the ignition button to turn the vehicle off.

"Where are we?"

"This is an observatory." He gets out and rushes over to my side, opening the door for me. Julius extends his hand, waiting for me to take hold. I do. The gravel parking lot crunches under us until we reach a paved path. "This is my favorite place in the city."

"I expected you to take us to the stadium."

He looks at me oddly and then shakes his head. "I come here when I need to think."

When we get to the ticket booth, Julius leans down and has a hushed conversation with the clerk. I step back and let Julius conduct his business. Every few seconds, Julius looks over his shoulder and smiles at me. As I stand there, waiting for him, it dawns on me that this is precisely where I want to be right now.

SIXTEEN

JULIUS

I'm a fool for ever thinking such asinine things about Autumn. Not once today has she been the person I tried to make her out to be. I feel as though I need to apologize repeatedly for everything I said and did to her, especially making her feel like less of a person. I only hope she can forget the guy she met and like the real me because I like her a lot, even though I shouldn't.

I love that Autumn isn't from Portland. It gives me an excuse to see her again because I'm officially dubbing myself her tour guide. I'm going to show her everything I can when our schedules allow for it. I can't wait to take her to the beach. First, we'll go to Seaside, and then we'll drive south to Lincoln City or north to Astoria. I hope she's a fan of *Goonies* so I can show her the house where they filmed the movie. It's a bold assumption to think she even likes the beach. The mountains might be more her thing, although if I remember correctly from one of my numerous eavesdropping conversations, she's not a huge fan of the cold. Either way, I am looking forward to getting to know her more and am thankful she bid on me. Even though I know she did it out of spite. Whatever she would've had me do today, I would've taken the punishment like a champ because I deserve it after the way I treated her.

Throughout the drive to the observatory, I watch her as she takes in the scenery. She loves the old houses and how they're strategically built on a hill, and how the landscaping is mainly made up of roses and other perennials that have held onto their petals into the fall. Every so often, I have the urge to reach over and take her hand. I've done it a couple of times today and love the way her hand feels in mine. Except, I shouldn't feel this way. My heart should be cold and dead inside after the things Elena has done. It should also feel a pang of longing for my wife, and it doesn't. My heart jumps with excitement when I think about Autumn. It has since the night I met her on the balcony, and the rapid beating I feel when I'm with her—I can't ignore. I don't even want to, but a part of me is leery of pursuing anything. What if Autumn has an issue with the fact that I haven't filed for divorce yet? I might if I was in her shoes. Maybe this is the push I need to get the paperwork filed, and the process started. My future could be sitting next to me, and if I don't act accordingly, I could lose her. Something deep down tells me I don't want to lose Autumn.

As soon as I pull into the observatory parking lot, it hits me that she might have been here. I know I asked if she's done any sightseeing, but I never considered the weather station not far from here. She's probably been up here a million times already. I don't give her time to tell me she has. I'd rather not know and continue with my plan. After I park and shut off her car, I get out and go to her side to open her door. This is another excuse for me to hold her hand, which she doesn't seem to mind.

When I get to the ticket booth, Autumn lets go and

walks to the edge of the pavement. I wish it were spring right now because the colorful roses are a sight to behold. "Good afternoon," I say when the clerk sits down. "I'd like to rent the upstairs of the observatory for an hour, please."

"We only allow this with a reservation and a monetary donation."

I nod, knowing this policy as I've done this more often than I care to admit. I pull out my wallet and slide my credit card through the slot. "How much on very short notice."

The clerk looks at me, probably wondering if I'm serious. He has no idea how serious I am. He tells me he has to ask his manager and leaves me standing there. I use this time to spy on Autumn, to see what she's doing. I peer around the bend, catching a glimpse of her standing there, facing the city. I wonder what is going through her mind right now. Is she in awe of what she sees or completely bored?

"My boss said the minimum on such a short notice is two thousand."

"You have my card," I remind him. The clerk's eyes go wide. Again, I want the time alone with Autumn and am willing to pay for it. He processes my credit card and tells me his manager has gone up to close the observatory for us and says we can go up now if we'd like. "Thank you," I say as I take my card and receipt from him and head toward Autumn.

She's standing not far from me, resting against one of the columns. The way the sun beams down onto her hair makes her dark waves look red. I don't know how long I stand there, watching her, but when she turns around and sees me, I swear her eyes light up with excitement. I'm not going to tell myself otherwise because I don't want self-doubt to dampen my mood right now. I'll save those moments for later when I'm in bed, staring at my ceiling and asking myself what the hell I am doing right now. Pursuing the woman in front of me, that's what.

We both take steps toward each other, and both pause at the same time. Autumn throws her head back in laughter, and instantly another image comes to mind, of her on top of me and my hands cupping . . . I shake my head to clear my thoughts. This is not the time to let my imagination run wild. Autumn steps forward again, and this time I stay where I am.

"How do you like the view?" I ask her.

"It's amazing. I have so much exploring to do. I want to see every part of the city."

I like this idea, more so because I want to be the one to show her everything, all of the Pacific Northwest if she'd allow me to.

"Come." I motion toward the building. "There's something I want to show you." I hold my hand out, and thankfully she takes it. At the entrance, I hand over our tickets and give Autumn her stub. "I don't know about you, but I save all of mine."

"Me too," she says. Her smile is bright and infectious. "What is this place?" she asks as soon as we step into the elevator. Because we are already high above the city, we only go up three floors. I stall on my answer until the doors open, and we're in a glass room. Her audible gasp brings an insurmountable satisfaction to me.

"Oh my . . ." Autumn walks to the farthest wall. I hang back, taking in her pure enjoyment. "This is incredible." She rests her hands on the railings and looks out over the city. I stand behind her, softly pressing my front to her back and breathing in her perfume. God, she smells fucking amazing. Like sunshine, happiness, and the beach.

"This is my favorite place. Lately, I've come here a lot to think. It's peaceful and quiet, but you can see every aspect of the city from here, and I love it." I angle her in a slightly different direction and point. "There's the stadium, and if you look over here." I move her again. "You can see the antenna from the station."

"How do you know where everything is? I feel so lost, yet oddly at peace."

I chuckle. "Lots of practice."

She eyes me warily, calling my bluff.

I give in rather quickly and pull my phone out and tap the screen a few times. I hand it to her. "Hold it up to the glass and tap a section on the screen." She does as I say, and the map changes. It now shows her exactly where the landmarks and businesses are.

"I'm surprised Leon hasn't brought you up here yet."

"Why would he?" she asks as she moves around the room, tapping on my phone. Every so often, she finds a place and tells me about it. I don't have the heart to tell her I have the cityscape memorized, so I play along, although something tells me she knows.

"Because there's a weather station not far from here. I figured you would spend a lot of time there."

She drops her hands, and her eyes squint with confusion. "There's a weather tower?"

Had Leon seriously not told her about this? I nod and reach for my phone but end up taking her hand instead and walking her to the window. "Point in that direction, and you'll see it."

Autumn does as I say and mutters, "What the fuck," when she sees it.

"I can take you there if you'd like."

"No, it's fine. I'll ask Leon about it. Maybe he forgot."

Let's hope he did. I may not know anything about reporting the weather, but I think a weather tower might be necessary for a meteorologist.

Autumn and I continue to walk around. I stay close to her, using every opportunity I can to touch or brush up against her. When she asks where a particular place is, I stand behind her to show her and do everything I can to hide the fact that I'm giddy as fuck when she leans into me.

When she has looked over every inch of the city, I expect her to tell me she's ready to go, but she doesn't. She rests her head on my shoulder and sighs. "You're right. I feel at peace up here. It's like the view washes away your worries."

"During the summer, it's crazy, though. Lots of tourists and summer camps. The zoo and science center aren't far from here either."

"I want to go to the zoo. I hear it has one of the best elephant exhibits."

"It does. Roxy loves the elephants. They have a program where you can spend the night in the zoo, like a giant slumber party. I did it with Reggie a year ago and stayed awake all night long. I don't care that the animals are locked up. I feared for our lives that night."

"But you'd do it all over again for Roxy?"

"Without a doubt. Being their dad is the best part of my life."

"I feel like I should ask you about your ex, but then I feel like it's none of my business. I'm torn."

I shift slightly, so I'm in front of Autumn, and she's leaning against the railing. "There's time," I say. "Or at least I'm hoping there's time. I'm having an amazing time with you, Autumn. I want to see you again."

"I'd like that as well, Julius."

I haven't kissed another woman since college, and right now, I want nothing more than to press my lips against Autumn's. I lick my lips while I psyche myself up for what I'm about to do. My body leans closer, and my eyes never leave hers.

"Autumn," I say her name softly. A wave of excitement, longing, and desire passes over me. The tension between us is thick. Her tongue darts out, wetting her lips, and her chest heaves as she inhales. "I'm sorry for being a complete ass when we first met. Do you think you'll ever forgive me?"

"Uh-huh," she says as she nods slowly.

My mouth twitches in anticipation. I'm about to kiss the woman who has muddled my thoughts since the moment I met her. She's haunted my dreams, kept me awake at night and showed me what it feels like to lust after someone after the heartache I've felt.

My hand gently cups her cheek. Autumn closes her eyes and tilts her head into my palm, and pushes her lips against my skin. Electricity zings through my body, and the hairs on my arms and the back of my neck stand at attention.

"I can't wait," she says, launching herself into my arms and pressing her lips to mine. I stumble back a step or two and wrap my arms around her waist. Autumn knows what she wants, and when she opens her mouth, I give her any and everything I can in this moment. I walk us to the railing, needing it for support. One hand moves to her hair while the other pulls her tighter against me. Her lips and mouth are demanding, greedy, and I return her passion with reckless abandon. Why did I wait so long to talk to her? To apologize to her?

I blaze a trail of languishing kisses across her jaw and down her neck. She pulls at my shirt, yanking it from my pants. My mouth drops open when her hands caress my heated flesh, and her fingers dig into my skin. I step back and reach for the back of my collar, the intent of taking my shirt off when I realize where we are.

"We have to stop," I tell her reluctantly. "But please don't think I don't want to do any of this with you because I do." I glance down at my pants to prove my point.

"I got carried away."

"Sweetie, you can get carried away anytime you want." I cup her cheek again and run my thumb over her cheekbone. "Believe me, I want . . ." I let my words linger in the air before I kiss her again. This time, it's soft yet filled with passion. She tastes like heaven. When we part, I kiss her nose and then take her hand in mine.

"Where are we going?"

"Dinner."

"It's not time."

I laugh. "It will be by the time we get back into town and fight traffic."

SEVENTEEN

AUTUMN

Weeks ago, if someone asked me what I thought of Julius Cunningham, I would've told them he is nothing but a bully with a bad attitude and a chip on his shoulder. If someone asked me last week after I saw him with his daughter, my answer would be something like he's softening up or he's not so rough around the edges like I had thought. Ask me now, and I'd fumble for words because I'm drunk. Drunk off his lips and the way he cupped my cheek before he kissed me. Smitten by his kindness and how he knew I needed to see the city from this vantage point, and that he made sure we had the privacy to do it alone. I look over at him now, driving my car, and find it hard to believe he hasn't been in that seat for longer than a few hours. He fits perfectly. It's like we're on a date for the millionth time and not some paid-for excursion. Everything feels natural and not forced like I expected it to be.

I glance over my shoulder and imagine his children in the back and wonder if his son will like me or if his parents' divorce is proving to be too much for him. I've never dated a man with children before and am unsure how children become incorporated into a relationship. I suppose I'm ahead of myself, thinking there will be a relationship between Julius and me, or even the children and me, but the thoughts are there, and I can't stop them. Nor do I want to. He's a single father who I know puts his family first, which I respect and admire wholeheartedly.

A warm hand squeezes my thigh, bringing my attention back to the man sitting next to me. He drives with one hand on the wheel and the other now intertwined with mine. How did we go from barely speaking a cordial word to each other to this?

"What are you thinking?" he asks, almost as if he can read my mind.

I lean into the headrest and give him a soft smile. "Just wondering how we got here."

Julius chuckles lightly, winks, and turns his attention to the road. "I've been asking myself for weeks why I was such a dick to you."

"Did you ever come up with a good answer?"

He laughs again. "Nope, other than we met at a bad time. I think if it had been any other day, things would have been different. I've been attracted to you from the beginning, and I think I let all those thoughts I had play with what was really going on."

"Which was?"

Julius kisses the back of my hand. "I have spent my entire adult life with Elena, and unlike her, I never looked at another person. Then you walk out onto the balcony, and bam, it's like a ton of bricks are dropped on my head because there's this gorgeous woman standing a few feet from me, who is smiling at me—and I think 'wow, I'm an epic shit because I'm married.'" Julius pulls up to a red light and looks over at me.

"Except, I'm not. My wife, or soon-to-be-ex, has moved on and done so very publicly, and nothing is stopping me from doing the same. Once I realized this, you were all I thought about, but I still had a hard time reconciling this attraction. Once I started my 'I hate Autumn campaign,' it was hard to stop because deep down, I didn't want to like you."

"And now?" I think I already know the answer, but still want a little reassurance.

"And now I'd like to take you on a date or two or ten," he says with a shrug. "I guess what I'm trying to say is, I'd like to explore where this could lead."

"I'd like too as well."

My answer pleases Julius because he leans over and kisses me, much to the disgruntled driver behind us pressing down on the horn longer than necessary.

"I have a few choice words for whoever is behind us." Julius drives forward while shaking his head and muttering a few profanities. After a bit of silence, he says, "Have you ever dated someone with kids?"

I shake my head. "I haven't, but I also haven't dated a whole heck of a lot. Besides, I think there's a slight age gap between us."

Julius's mouth drops open, and he looks at me wide-eyed before busting into a fit of laughter. "Are you calling me old?"

"Not at all, but I wonder if you know how old I am."

He winks and chuckles. "I'm going to come clean here. I've spent some time looking you up online, so yes, I know how old you are, plus you went to school with Peyton, so that makes you a year or so younger than her. I guess the true question is, do you know how old I am?"

"I do." Honestly, I've never considered age to be a determining factor when it comes to dating. I've always been the type of person to encourage my friends to date whomever, as long as they're happy.

"And that doesn't scare you?"

"Not at all," I tell him.

Julius smiles, and it's heart-stopping. He's devilishly handsome with his blue eyes, dark hair, and a wicked smile. I'm definitely having a pinch-me moment with him right now. He pulls up to another car and then reverses into a parking spot. "That's it. I'm keeping you," I say after he puts the car into park and shuts the engine off.

"Why's that?"

"You can parallel park. That's keeper material."

Julius leans over the console and cups my cheek, which is turning into my favorite affection. I'm starting to love that he wants to look into my eyes and doesn't give me a chance to shy away from him.

"You're beautiful," he says. "Right now, I feel fortunate to be with you, especially after I treated you like complete shit. I really don't deserve any attention from you, but I'm thankful you're willing to look past my epic assholeness." He leans in and kisses me before I can say anything in response. "Come on, let's go eat."

Julius is out of the car and at my door within seconds. He holds my hand while we jaywalk across the street, dodging oncoming traffic and maneuvering our way toward a restaurant.

"You're taking me to a pizza parlor?" The question comes out of my mouth ruder than how it sounded in my head. "I'm sorry," I say as I tug his hand to get him to stop before we go inside. "That came out wrong."

"It's fine," he tells me. "This is my favorite place, especially when I have the kids, which is normally all the time. I just thought . . ." Julius pauses, his face scrunches up in thought, and then says, "We can go someplace else. You're right. This shouldn't be our first dinner date."

He starts to walk away, but I hold my ground. "No, this is perfect, and it's the place you wanted to bring me. I was caught off guard, is all. Do they have a salad bar?"

He nods. "One of the best around. They also have a fire truck."

"I'm sorry, what?" I ask, trying to hold back my laughter.

Julius shrugs and opens the door for me. He follows behind me until we get to the host stand and tells the young man we need a table near the fire truck.

"Is this a real—" my words are cut off by the sight of a full-sized fire truck parked in the middle of the room. "Wow, can't say I've seen one up close before."

"You can climb on it, if you want."

Oddly, I do want to. "Fascinating."

The host shows us to our seat, which is two tables away from the truck. It's nice, but not as intimate as I hoped. But then again, it's pizza. As soon as I look at the menu, a waiter sets two glasses of water down and asks what we'd like to drink. I'm taken back by Julius when he stays with water. I do the same. Our waiter tells us to help ourselves to the salad bar, which I happily do.

I'm digging into my leafy concoction when Julius asks if I like arcade games. With my hand over my mouth, I nod and try to swallow quickly so that I can talk to him.

"I'm a beast at air hockey."

"I'm the champ," he says as he flexes.

"Is that a challenge, Mr. Cunningham?"

"It is, Weather Girl." Normally, this irritates me, but the nickname has grown on me. But only if it's Julius saying it.

"I'll take this challenge, but after we eat because I'm

starving," I say as the waiter sets our pizza down. I reach for the serving utensil, pull a slice of pizza up, and put it onto one of the plates. I hand this to Julius, who looks at me in surprise. "What? Do you want another slice?"

"No." He shakes his head slowly. "I didn't expect you to plate my food for me."

"Why not?"

Julius shrugs and says nothing, making me assume his ex didn't do things like this. My mother always plates our food. It's her thing. I suppose I learned it from her.

We eat mostly in silence, and every now again, I find myself staring off into space or losing my thoughts while watching kids climb on and off the fire truck. Julius keeps his head down, and I wonder if it's because he's afraid someone will recognize him or if he's deep in thought. Under the table, we play footsie, and every so often, we hold hands across the table.

When we've finished off the pie, more so, when Julius has finished it, he asks me to follow him. Once again, he takes my hand, and I fall in line behind him. He walks us toward another room, one filled with young adults and kids. There are very few people our age here.

"Oh good, the table is free."

With a slight roll of my eyes, I let go of his hand and head to the end of the table. I have to inspect my mallet and make sure there aren't any obstructions on the bottom. The table comes to life, and the puck starts moving slowly.

"You should start," he says.

"Nah, I think I'll be okay." I'm confident in my game and push the red puck toward Julius. He eyes me, maybe with caution or trying to figure out if I'm bluffing.

We start, and the clanking of the puck grows incessantly. Neither of us has scored, but it isn't for lack of trying.

Every angle I hit, he blocks, and when he tries to speed the game up, I slow him down. Then he tries to do the same, and I reverse things on him and return my shots as hard as I can and as rapidly as possible. When the puck finally slips between his mallet and the goal, my hands go up.

"You owe me a beer." It's been my automatic response since college.

"You're on, but I was hoping we could play for something else." Julius winks, and my insides turn to mush.

"Keep it PG, Mr. Cunningham. There are children here."

He laughs and shakes his head. I drop the puck and send it toward him. He blocks me, and just as I send it back, someone yells his name, causing him to turn away.

"Score!" the machine says, and the mock cheering starts.

"That doesn't count."

"It does. Besides, you can't take a goal away."

"But—"

"No buts," I say. "You must focus on the game." I point to the table, and he groans.

"You sound like Peyton. She's always telling me to focus on this or that. I haven't played very well lately."

"Maybe you need a good luck charm."

Julius scoffs. "Maybe you should come to the game this weekend."

I return his guffaw. "I distinctly remember someone telling me I was bad luck."

Julius picks up the puck and comes toward me. "I had to blame you for something. The entire game, I watched men come up to you and flirt. I hated it. It wasn't your fault I lost the coin toss that day." Julius leans in to kiss me, and I shy away. "What's wrong?"

"Nothing." I shake my head slightly. "I just . . ." I just what? I don't even know what I want to say. Camden never believed in PDA. Everything had to be closed door. At first, I hated it and thought he was embarrassed to be seen with me, but after a while, I became accustomed. Julius is confused and rightly so, which isn't my intent. I lean in and press my lips to his, but he's not entirely receptive.

"Don't want people to know you're on a date?"

"It's not that. My last boyfriend wasn't affectionate in public."

"Well, we'll have to change that."

I can only bring myself to say, "Okay."

Julius hands the flat puck to me and tells me I'm about to go down, to which I snort.

I'm up four to zero when he finally scores. "I haven't had to work this hard before."

"You hate losing. Don't you?"

"Is it that obvious?"

"A little." I hold my thumb and index finger close together. "But I get it. It's your nature. You want to be successful at everything you do. I just happen to be the air hockey champion of Northwestern."

Julius sends the puck flying, and I block his attempt at scoring. He throws his hands up, and I laugh. I think he thought he'd catch me off guard, but I'm onto his wily ways.

When the score reaches seven and the machine shuts off, I do a little dance to celebrate. Julius pulls me into his arms and kisses me. I let him, enjoying every minute.

"Rematch?" he asks.

"Anytime."

"Excuse me, but are you, Julius Cunningham?" a little boy standing near us asks. I look at Julius and raise my eyebrow.

"I am," he says as he crouches down to this little guy's height. "What's your name?"

"Robert, but my friends call me Bobby."

Julius's large hand dwarfs this little guy's hand as they shake. "It's nice to meet you."

"Can I have your autograph?" Bobby holds out a napkin and pen for Julius.

"Of course. Are your mom and dad here?"

Bobby nods, turns, and points. A young couple wave, and the father starts walking toward us.

"Sorry about this," he says when he reaches us.

"It's not a problem at all. Do you have a phone?" Julius asks the dad. He fishes it out of his pocket while Julius and Bobby pose for a series of photos. My favorite being when Julius sets Bobby on his shoulder.

"That was amazing," I tell him after Bobby and his dad have left us. "You were so good with him."

"The little kids, I don't mind. Even the teens are good. But you get those older people, who act as if I owe them something because they bought my jersey or came to a game —they bother me. Oftentimes, they're rude and demanding or think they can cut in front of a little guy like Bobby. Give me hundreds of kids like him, and I'll sign and take pictures all damn day."

Julius and I are about to leave when another child comes up to us. From there, a line starts. I stand by, taking pictures when asked and even posing for a few when someone recognizes me.

What catches me off-guard is when a young lady asks Julius if I'm his girlfriend. I didn't say anything because I've never commented on my personal life before, but he had plenty to say. "Let's just say, I want her to be my person."

EIGHTEEN

JULIUS

When something you've said without thinking of the consequences spreads like rapid-fire, the only thing you can do is run with it. I wasn't joking when I said I wanted Autumn to be my person. I do. I love spending time with her, I'm attracted to her, and I can't stop thinking about her. Should I have said it on our first date?

No.

Should I have said it to her in private? Yes.

Should I have waited, I don't know another hour? Day? Week? Month?

Yes. Yes. Yes.

Do I regret it?

No.

I blurted the statement out without thinking. Call it the heat of the moment or fitting for the situation. I do want Autumn to be my person, but I shouldn't have said what I did to the people I did because within seconds, my words, in my voice, were all over social media. Unbeknownst to Autumn and me, someone recorded the impromptu autograph session at the pizza parlor and caught the entire exchange. I knew as soon as we got back into her car and my phone lit up, I had made a mistake.

Autumn and I live our lives in the media. More so her than me, it seems, because people really only see me on Sunday or if they happen to catch me out and about. No one is looking for me when they walk down the street or are buying groceries. But Autumn—she's new in town and like a shiny new toy to people. Her personality is infectious, and everyone seems to love her. Honestly, I was surprised we weren't stopped more during dinner. I saw people staring and pointing, and it wasn't at me. Viewers like her. In fact, the station's ratings are up for her time slot. Leon knew what he was doing when he hired a young, drop-dead gorgeous woman to do the weather. He brought in someone girls could look up to and gave men at home someone to gawk at. I'm just happy she's interested in me because, like I said, I want her to be my person.

What sucks is our schedules. When she is free, I'm at the practice facility. When she's working, I'm home. And since I don't have a live-in nanny, it's not like I can take the elevator down to Autumn's floor when she gets home from work or have her come to my place. As much as I'd love to spend some time with her in my apartment, I'm not sure the kids are ready for that. Well, Roxy is. She's infatuated with Autumn.

On the other hand, Reggie's had a hard time dealing with his mother having a boyfriend. I don't want to throw Autumn into the mix and really screw him up. I must tread lightly when it comes to my son, and I'm okay with that.

I rap my knuckles on his door and step in.

He looks up from his phone and quickly slides it under his pillow. My heart drops. There is something on there that he doesn't want me to see. I hate the fact that he has a phone. He's eight. He should be reading adventure stories or watching cartoons, not surfing the damn internet. It seems that no matter how many parental apps I put on his phone, he's found a way to get past them. I blame his mother, and the ever-growing tech world.

I put my hand out in a silent demand for his phone. Slowly, he places it in my hand, and I motion for him to scoot over so I can sit next to him. I type in his passcode, which is my number and the year he was born.

The screen lights up with pictures of Autumn and me, exactly what I didn't want to see but should've realized Reggie would find them sooner or later.

"Is she your girlfriend? Everyone says she is."

Is she? I don't even know if a label is needed these days.

"She's a friend and someone I like."

"What about mom?"

Weeks ago, I asked my agent to find me a family counselor, someone for the kids and me to speak with. He gave me a few names, but I didn't do anything with the information.

"Bud—"

Reggie moves away from me and says, "I know, she's not coming back." He gets off his bed and goes to the window. "I hate her."

"Reggie, come on, you shouldn't say that."

"Don't you hate her, Dad? We were a happy family, and she had to ruin it. She has a boyfriend, and now you have a girlfriend. I hate her!"

I'm off the bed in a flash and holding him to my chest. He's hurting, and I'm adding to the pain because of my big mouth. He has a point, but the last thing I want is for him to bad-mouth his mother or develop negative feelings toward

Autumn. Of all the people involved in my messy life, Autumn and the children are the innocent ones. They didn't ask for any of this.

I'm able to coax Reggie back to his bed, where we sit in silence for a few minutes. There isn't much I can say about his mom and her life because I don't know what's going on in her head. I can only speak for myself.

"I don't know what it's like to have your parents get divorced. You know grandma and grandpa are still married—"

"Grandpa drives grandma nuts," he says, interrupting me. Again, he's right. My mom is always whacking my dad with her handbag, the newspaper, or anything else she has close by, but they love each other.

"Yeah, he does," I say, laughing. "What I'm saying, though, is I don't know how to help you and your sister through this. I think we should see someone who can give us advice on how to cope with our feelings. I'm sure it's hard to see your mom with someone else, and it's going to be hard to see me with someone who isn't your mom, but it's going to happen, and I want to make sure you feel okay with it."

"What if I don't? Will you stop?"

His question catches me off guard. Will I? I find my heart seizing as I look at him. From side-to-side, my head moves slowly before I can get the words from my brain to my mouth. "If whoever I dated hurt you or your sister, I'd stop seeing them. I'm going to date Autumn and see how it goes, but I want you to know that you can always talk to me about anything."

"What if Mom comes back?"

What a loaded question. How do I tell my son that even if his mother returned, it wouldn't be to me? I don't want her anymore. The damage she's done to our marriage is unforgivable. I press my lips to his forehead and then pull him into my arms.

"I love you more than life, Reggie. I hope you know this."

"I do. I just hate my life right now."

"I know, Bud. What can I do to help?" I know I'm giving him the chance to tell me to stop seeing Autumn, but I don't think he'd say this.

"I don't know. I'll think of something."

Oh yes, the little con artist is back. I roll my eyes and tickle him, soaking in his laughs. "You gotta get to bed. You have a game at nine in the morning."

He gets up and goes to the bathroom. While he's gone, I go through his phone again, snooping like a nosy parent. I'm pleasantly surprised to find he doesn't have anything downloaded that I don't know about. Everything he found about Autumn and me is from Chatgram, which I've allowed him to have because he likes posting photos of him playing football, and I don't want to take that away from him.

When he comes back into his room, I hand him his phone. "I went through it," I tell him, wanting him to know.

"I'm not on anything I shouldn't be."

"I know, and I appreciate it."

Reggie hops into bed, and I cover him up. "So, early wake-up. I'll make breakfast, and then we'll head to the field."

"Is your girlfriend going to be there?"

"No, it's your game. I'll be there. And she's really not my girlfriend. We just really like each other."

"Oh," he says, confusing me. Minutes ago, he seemed angry about Autumn. I lean down and kiss him. "Goodnight, Bud. I love you."

"I love you too," he says. I'm halfway out of his room

when he adds. "She can come if you want her to." I let the words linger in the air for a moment before turning back toward him.

"Do you want to meet Autumn? Your sister met her at the park a couple of weeks ago."

"I dunno. Roxy likes her because she's on TV."

"Yes, but Roxy also likes everyone, so I'm not sure we can trust your sister's judgment."

Reggie laughs. "Roxy doesn't like the lady downstairs who serves the ice cream because she never gives Roxy enough."

"Point taken." I lean against the door jamb, wondering if I should test the waters with Reggie and Autumn. It might be too soon for my son, whereas my daughter is ready to jump in with both feet because she thinks Autumn is pretty.

"Goodnight, Bud," I say again.

"Dad," he calls out. "If you want, you can ask her." The mind of an eight-year-old gives me whiplash.

"Okay, I'll think about it. See you in the morning." I shut his door quietly and then cross the hall to peek in on Roxy. She's at the foot of her bed, lying horizontally. I'm tempted to reposition her, but if she wakes up, I'll never get her back to sleep.

I spend the next few hours picking up Roxy's toys, doing the dishes, and listening to a podcast about being a better father, husband, partner, and person. By the time I'm done, I have enough time to shower and get ready for bed, where I plan to watch the news. Until meeting Autumn, I didn't care what the weather would be like tomorrow and in the days to come, but now it's all I can think about.

When I get out of the shower, I find Roxy sprawled out on my bed. "Lovely," I mutter. Since her mother left, she's had nightmares—me too, but of a different kind. I slip into a pair of boxers, which I hate sleeping in and crawl into bed. As soon as I've situated my pillows, her tiny voice echoes through my room.

"Hi, Daddy."

"Hey, baby girl." I reach over and pull my comforter over her, but she has a better idea and decides to squirm her way over to me. I turn on the TV and turn the volume down until Autumn is on air. I love listening to her speak and don't even care if it's about jet streams and fronts.

Autumn stands in front of her five-day forecast screen wearing Pioneer colors. Every part of me wishes she did this because of me, but I know someone else picks out her clothes for her. Still, I feel like this is a message. Yes, I want her to be my girlfriend and a part of my children's lives, but is that what she wants?

When my phone vibrates at eleven-forty-five, a big smile spreads across my face. "I have to say, I loved your color scheme tonight."

She laughs, and the sound goes right to my groin. The most we've done is kiss, and I have a massive hard-on for her. If this is any indication of how I feel about her, the moment we get to be together, to make love to each other, it will be explosive.

"Thanks. I told Meyers we could add some more color to my wardrobe."

"Nicely done, Weather Girl."

"What are you doing right now?"

I groan. "I feel like this is a segue into phone s-e-x."

Autumn laughs again. "Roxy in bed with you?"

"Yep."

"It wasn't," she says, "But now I'm thinking about it."

"Stop," I warn. "Nothing good will come from it other than frustration."

"Okay, I'll be good."

"No, don't do that either. Gah, I'm confusing myself."

Again, with more laughter. "Okay, I'll behave even if I'm a bit jealous of your daughter right now."

"Oh yeah, do you want to be in my bed?" As soon as the words come out, I want to take them back. Yet, I don't.

"Can I be honest with you?"

"Please do."

Autumn clears her throat. "One hundred percent," she says.

"Mhm . . . we'll have to figure something out." I'm not sure what, unless Elena comes to town and I'm staying in a hotel, or my parents take the kids for a night.

"I can be patient, Julius."

I can't.

"I'm not sure I can, Autumn." I groan again and scrub my hand over my face. "I need to change the subject." I clear my throat and readjust in bed. "Reggie is sort of between two minds right now with hating his mother, not wanting me to date, and being a kid. But he asked if you're coming to his game in the morning. I hadn't mentioned it before because I don't know if you're interested in meeting the kids this way or even going to a Pee Wee football game first thing in the morning. If you're not, no biggie. If you are, you can ride with us if you want."

There's a long pause.

"I'm sorry," I add. "I know I rambled a mile a minute there."

"It's fine. What do you think, Julius? Do you want me there?"

"Yes, I do, but it's up to you. I know we just started

seeing each other, and while Roxy loves you, Reggie is older and struggling with his parents getting a divorce."

"Okay." Autumn inhales. "I'll go, but I'll drive myself. I don't want your son to feel awkward in the car. That should be his safe space."

For some odd reason, I feel insurmountable relief. "God, I can't wait to see you tomorrow."

"Same here. Maybe we should keep the PDA to a minimum, though? I don't want to upset Reggie."

"I agree. Besides, once Roxy sees you, she's not going to let me anywhere near you."

"Text me the address, and I'll be there, Julius. Goodnight."

"Goodnight, Weather Girl. I'll see you in the morning."

We hang up, and I quickly send her the address of the field and the kick-off time. I set my phone on my nightstand, turn the television off, and relax into my pillows. The only glow is from the city lights since I've left my curtains open. I should get up and close them, but I don't. The ambiance is excellent, and it gives Roxy a nightlight in case she needs to get up in the middle of the night.

As soon as I close my eyes, my wiggle worm of a daughter crawls onto my chest and relaxes. She started this after her mother left, and I don't know how to break the habit, but I need to if I ever plan to have Autumn spend the night.

NINETEEN

AUTUMN

I'm awake before my alarm goes off and tired. I didn't sleep well last night. Aside from tossing and turning, my mind raced with everything Julius said on the phone, and I still can't believe I hinted at sex with him. What the hell is wrong with me? We've been on one date—if you can even call it that—and I'm talking about taking the guy to bed. He really must think I'm some type of . . . I don't even know what the right word is. Whatever it may be, I am feeling it through and through. I should've never opened my mouth and said those things.

And now I get to face him all while meeting his son, who may or may not like me after today.

"No pressure," I say aloud to my ceiling. I want to meet his son. I know his children aren't going anywhere, and I would never ask him to choose between me and them, but I think this is worse than meeting parents. Kids can be tough. Harsh, even. What if Reggie hates me and Julius stops talking to me?

Too many what-ifs, and none of them are going to get resolved if I dwell on them.

I throw the covers back and get out of bed. Leaving my hair in the messy bun I put it up in last night, I step into the shower and let the hot water run down my back. I tell myself everything will be okay, and it will be if I manifest nothing but happy thoughts.

My nerves are on edge by the time I reach the parking garage. All morning, or at least the couple of hours I've been awake, I thought about texting Julius to cancel or check-in and make sure I'm still wanted at the game. I figured if his son had changed his mind, Julius would've told me.

With the address plugged into the GPS, I head toward the field where the game is. It's in a part of town I haven't been to, which isn't shocking since I haven't done much exploring since moving here, but on the way, I spot a donut and coffee shop and think I should bring some breakfast.

Except, while I'm standing in line, I realize donuts are not the most nutritious thing to give to children, and Julius may not appreciate the sugar rush. I think about heading back to my car, but I really need coffee and want to bring one to Julius. When it's my turn in line, I order a half dozen assorted muffins, thinking these are a safer choice than sugary donuts, and two large coffees, along with two bottles of chocolate milk.

When I get to the field, there's no mistaking there's a game going on or about to start. There are three small sets of bleachers on one side of the field, and numerous chairs are set-up, some with umbrellas. Most parents seem to have banners or some type of sign for their son, and I wonder what Julius brought with him.

I walk toward the stands with my arms full, hoping and praying Julius is already here and things won't be awkward. I'm thankful I decided to wear a ballcap and still have my sunglasses on. While I'm becoming more recognizable, I don't want to be today. I'm sure Julius draws enough attention by being at the game. I'd rather stay incognito. I don't wish to take any attention away from Reggie and his team. Unfortunately, Roxy has other ideas, spotting me and immediately yelling out my newest nick-name—TV lady. I don't understand what it is with these Cunninghams but their nicknames leave a lot to be desired.

Roxy is the first to approach me, and she does so in a fashion I'm unaccustomed to. Her little arms wrap around my legs, causing me to stagger a bit, and when she lets go, she jumps up and down, like she wants me to pick her up.

"Roxy, stop," Julius says, and she does. Julius reaches for the box of muffins, which has the drink carrier full of our drinks on top of it and takes it from me. I'm tempted to lean in and kiss him but remember how I've suggested the PDA be kept at a minimum, at least for now. We're friends until we reach a point of defining ourselves as more.

"Daddy says you was coming."

Julius chokes at his daughter's choice of words, and I feel my cheeks flush. Leave it to the three-year-old to say the most innocent thing, and her father and I turn it into a sexual innuendo.

"We're sitting over here," Julius says, motioning toward the bleachers. Roxy takes my hand and pulls me to follow behind her father. Julius looks over his shoulder and smiles instantly. My heart leaps with admiration for this little girl. I don't want to think how Roxy or I will feel if things don't work out for her father and me. I pick her up when we get to the riser and step up after her, apologizing to the few people I have to pass in front of.

"What's in the box?" Julius asks as I sit down.

"I brought us some muffins. One of the coffees is for

you," I tell him before looking at Roxy. "And for you, I brought chocolate milk. I hope you like it."

Her face scrunches for a second, and then her head nods in quickly. "I lub it."

Julius takes the cap off and then removes the seal from over the lid. He hands the bottle to Roxy and tells her to be careful and to take small sips.

"Can I has a muppin?" she asks.

"You already had pancakes," he tells her. I don't know why, but it feels like I've made a mistake in bringing them food. I should've known better. I grimace and look toward the field, feeling like a major idiot right now.

A warm hand rests on my back, and his fingers gently push into my skin. I glance over and see him leaning toward me. I do the same. Julius places his hand near my ear and whispers, "Thank you for thinking about the kids and bringing them something to eat. If I give Roxy the muffin now, she will ask for another one when Reggie gets his. As for coming . . ." Julius doesn't finish his sentence but nips at my earlobe. When he pulls away, he's flush, and the color of his cheeks likely matches mine.

I glance over my shoulder to see if anyone caught what just happened, and no one is staring, so I think we're in the clear.

"You are trouble," I say to him quietly.

Roxy hands her dad the bottle of milk and decides it's time to sit on my lap. She's a wiggle worm until she finds what's comfortable and tells me I should move closer to her father, so she doesn't have to stretch for her drink.

"Is she always this blunt?"

"Most of the time, it's worse," Julius says. He opens the box of muffins and lets out a swear.

"What's wrong?"

"They're warm."

"And that's a bad thing?"

He shakes his head. "Nope, it's an irresistible thing."

"I'll tell you what. Because I'm hungry, I'll share my muffin with Miss Roxy here, and you can eat yours, and then when the game is over, Roxy and Reggie can have theirs. Does that work?" I look at Roxy when I ask. She nods, and Julius finally relents. He hands me one of the blueberry ones, and Roxy takes it upon herself to spin herself around on my lap until she's facing me. I pick off a piece of my muffin, and before I can hand it to her, she takes her own piece.

"Dis good," she says, nodding and taking another piece.

"I'm glad you like it." She's right. The muffin is good.

With Julius sitting closer, I can feel his every move. His hand brushes along my arm, and his leg presses against mine. He bumps me to get my attention and nods toward the field where the game begins.

"What number is Reggie?"

"Eleven."

"Same as you," I state.

Julius looks at me and smiles. "You know my number?"

I shrug. "I may have done some online searching myself since we had our day together." This time I wink. Julius blushes and tries to hide his smile. I turn my attention to the field. I don't know much about football, but I'm a damn good cheerleader and have no qualms about making some noise when it's warranted.

During the game, I watch Reggie and the other kids on the field. They seem so small out there, playing this adult sport. I know kids start young and play through high school and college, but I have a different perspective after being on the Pioneers sideline.

Julius stands just as I notice that Reggie has broken away from his defender. He's running toward the end zone, and I don't know who I should watch, him or his father. I stand and place Roxy on my hip. She starts cheering right off even though I'm not sure she knows what she's doing. Julius is yelling, telling his son to run, and my arm is pumping in the air. The bleachers shake. They rattle and vibrate from the commotion, not only from us but the other parents. On the other side of us, the opposing team's parents are screaming for their kids to "get him," which I don't care much for, but I get it.

Reggie crosses the line, and even I know it's a good thing. He stands there for a second and sets the ball down— no celebration or anything, much like what his father does on the field. Granted, I haven't seen Julius score a touch-down yet, but I did find some videos of him online. Reggie then runs to the sideline and salutes. Julius does the same.

"Did you see that?" I ask Roxy. "Your brother scored a touchdown!" She's bouncing up and down in my arms. She's heavy, but I find that I like having her there.

Julius holds his hand up high, and I slap it. "Thank you for inviting me," I say to him because I'm happy to be here with him and excited to experience this side of his life.

"It was all Reggie."

"Well, I'll be sure to thank him after the game."

Julius unexpectedly kisses me right in front of Roxy and everyone around us. I don't know what to think, but Roxy does.

"Ew, Daddy." She pushes him away, and he laughs. So much for keeping the PDA to a minimum.

Roxy glares at her dad and wraps her arms around my neck. "She mine."

"You can share," he tells her.

"No, you hab Mommy."

Ouch, that stings, but I get it. Roxy is too little to understand that her mother has moved on.

Julius says nothing, which I do appreciate. What's he going to do, air his dirty laundry in front of all these parents? I'm sure they already have some idea of what's going on. One search on the web shows Julius's ex with another man, and there isn't anything in the pictures to suggest they are just friends. I'm sure seeing those pictures hurts Julius, and he deserves some happiness. If I'm it, why shouldn't he show it? I am, however, concerned with how Roxy and Reggie will respond if Julius and I become serious.

When the game is over, I help Julius pack up and wait with Roxy while Julius goes out onto the field. During the game, I asked if he would ever coach, and he said maybe in retirement, but by then Reggie will be in high school.

Julius and Reggie walk toward us. Julius has his hand on his son's shoulder and is carrying his pads for him. They stop in front of me, and I wait with bated breath for someone to say something. Finally, Julius clears his throat, and I feel like I'm meeting his parents or something. Honestly, this is probably worse.

"Autumn, I'd like to introduce you to my best friend and son, Reggie."

He sticks his hand out to shake mine. I'm not surprised he has impeccable manners because Julius does, too, once he's over his hatred for you.

"It's nice to meet you, Miss Autumn."

I crouch down so I can look this boy in his eyes. "It's lovely to meet you, Reggie. Thank you for inviting me to your game."

"Did you have fun?"

"I sure did! Here, I have something for you." I hand him the muffin and bottle of chocolate milk and realize this probably isn't the best gift. His eyes go wide, and he looks at his dad.

"Did you tell her chocolate milk was my favorite?"

Julius shakes his head. "Nope."

Reggie looks back at me. "Wow, thank you so much, Miss Autumn."

"You're welcome."

"Are you coming to lunch with us?"

I glance at Julius, and he shrugs. "Same place we had dinner the other night. I wasn't sure how you felt about eating there twice in one week."

I pretend to think for a minute. This is a no-brainer because I want to spend time with Julius, but I also want to see him in his natural state—with his children. They're part of who he is and will be part of our time together if we continue.

"I'd love to go," I say, much to Roxy's delight.

TWENTY

JULIUS

"Is she still there?" Roxy asks. I glance in the rearview mirror to make sure Autumn is still behind me.

"Yes, she is." Roxy wanted to ride with Autumn, but it would've been more of a hassle than necessary with her car seat. Honestly, I'm glad I had the whole seat thing as an excuse because I didn't want to put Autumn in an awkward situation. Not many people want a chatty toddler in the back of their car. Plus, my daughter can ask some really inappropriate things, and I didn't want Autumn to feel uncomfortable. Although, I'm relatively confident Autumn can handle herself when it comes to Roxy.

My phone rings, and Elena's name shows on the console. Internally, I groan and say "It's your mom," before I press the green button to answer.

"Hi, Mommy!" Reggie screams excitedly. Roxy follows him but is much louder because she squeals.

"Hi, my loves," Elena says. "How was your game, Reggie?"

"It was awesome. I scored a touchdown."

"That's fabulous. Did your team win?"

"Yes, by a ton."

"Two touchdowns," I mutter and give him a sideways glance. I'm trying to teach my son to be humble, that playing isn't always about winning. Is it nice? Of course, it is, just as losing is the worst feeling ever. But in the end, someone has lost, and they're sad. We have to respect that, especially when they're youngsters.

"I'm so sorry I missed it," Elena says. My eyes roll hard. I'm of the notion she doesn't care because if she did, she'd be here.

"When are you coming home?" Reggie asks. I can hear the longing in his voice, and it breaks my heart. My son wants his mother around, and as much as I can't stand to look at her right now, I want her to be around for him and Roxy. Kids need both parents.

"I don't know, Reggie. I got another part in a movie, and it'll start filming soon."

Wrong answer. "Are you filming now?" he asks.

There's a long pause. The level of anger I'm feeling starts to rise. I desperately want to hit the button and just stop this, but I can't.

I signal to pull into the parking lot next to the pizza parlor, remembering how Autumn doesn't prefer parallel parking. Again, I find myself tempted to shut the car off, ending the conversation, but I don't.

Elena clears her throat. "Sorry, someone was talking to me," she says, which I feel is a lie. She doesn't want to answer her son's question.

"What are you doing today?" she asks.

"Going to lunch with Miss Autumn," Reggie says.

"I like Miss Au-um. She's pretty," Roxy adds.

"Who is Miss Autumn?"

Before I can say anything, my daughter blurts out,

"Daddy's girlfriend." I glance at Roxy. Her legs are bouncing, she has a smile on her face, and she's looking out the window without a care in the world. She doesn't know the magnitude of what she just said. Roxy starts to unbuckle, ready to get out of the car and get some pizza.

"We're at the pizza place," I say. "The kids will call you later."

My finger is poised to press the ignition button and open my door, ending this call, but Elena blurts out, "Wait."

I pause.

"Take me off speaker, Julius."

I roll my eyes and look at Reggie. He has unshed tears in his eyes. I motion for him to get out of the car, and I reach for my cell phone, transferring the call. I don't say anything for a bit. Instead, I focus on getting Roxy out of the car. Autumn walks toward me, and I point to the phone and then to the kids and finally the door. She nods and takes Roxy's hand. As they walk away, I notice Autumn put her arm around Reggie and watch as he leans into her. Is she intuitive or just being nice to my son?

"What?" I bark into the phone.

"How long have you been seeing this new woman?"

My personal life shouldn't be any of her business, but we share children, and regardless of what she's done to our marriage, she has a right to know who is around her kids. My fear, which is sitting heavily in my stomach, is that she's going to ask that Autumn not be around the kids. I've done this with her boyfriend. In my defense, though, Elena broke our family up for this man.

"Things are new. We've known each other for a little bit and just started dating."

"And you're already bringing her around the kids?"

"That wasn't my intention," I tell her. "Someone posted

a photo of us, and Reggie saw it on social media," I say this, hoping that Elena understands the message I'm sending her. That each time she's out canoodling with her boyfriend, her son sees it thanks to the internet.

"And because he saw it, you decided to bring her home?"

"No," I say, trying not to lose my temper. "Autumn—that's her name—she's on the news, and Roxy recognized her at the park. They hit it off. After your most recent outing with what's his face, Reggie asked if Autumn could come to his game."

"Why would he do that?" she asks.

"I don't know, Elena, maybe because his mother won't." My words have a little bite to them. I regret them, but I don't apologize. "Because he sees you flaunting your relationship in the tabloids but can't be bothered to come to visit."

"That's not fair."

"Of course, it isn't."

"I think you should keep your girlfriend away from the kids until I've had a chance to meet her. I'm their mother."

"Then act like one. You're not filming anything that has you on set every single day. You can be up here, taking them to school, helping them with their homework, and spending time with them. But you're not. You're living the responsibility-free life while the rest of us watch it play out on the gossip shows."

"My manager says—"

"I don't care what your manager says." I cut her off. "Listen, I'm meeting with my lawyer this week. Because of the prenup, things will be easy. You just have to sign and send them back. Hire a lawyer if you want. I've said you can keep the house in Los Angeles, and I'll keep the apartment here. The kids will stay here until we can figure out a viable custody agreement, but as far as our marriage goes. It's over. I've accepted it, and it's time to end it."

"I agree," she says. "But I still want custody."

My thumb and index finger push into my closed eyes, and I groan. "And I will fight you on this. I don't care what it costs. The kids are better off with me. I gotta go." I hang up, not giving her a chance to disagree with me. She wants money, and the prenup is very clear. The only way Elena gets a dime out of me is if she has full custody of the children, and I can't let that happen. Not because I don't want to support my children, but because the money is the only reason she wants them with her. I don't want them living with a nanny while Elena is off doing whatever the hell she's going to end up doing with her life.

I make my way into the pizza parlor and tell the hostess my family is already inside. I have no idea where they're sitting, but I don't care. I'll wander around the entire place if I have to. I head toward the fire truck, knowing Roxy likes to sit by it and stop dead in my tracks when I spot Autumn and the kids.

They're sitting in the booth. There are drinks on the table, and the menu is gone, making me think Autumn has already ordered our food. But this isn't what has me standing still in the middle of the room. Roxy is on Autumn's lap, and Reggie has pressed himself right up tight to Autumn's side. The three of them are coloring and seem to be in a deep conversation about where each color should go. I don't know what part of the scene in front of me is making my heart twist in knots the most. Is it the sight of my daughter being attached to Autumn, Autumn caring for my children, or the look of happiness on my son's face? Ten minutes ago, when he was on the phone with his mother, he was sad. I thought lunch was going to be an emotional time for him, that he'd be despondent. But from the looks of things, Autumn isn't allowing any of that to happen.

I clear my throat as I approach the table. Three sets of eyes look up at the same time. "Hey, guys."

"Hey, Dad," Reggie says and then goes back to coloring.

"We ordered already, and I got you a soda." Autumn motions to the lone drink on the other side of the table. "Everything okay?"

I nod as I slide into the booth, feeling lonely because everyone I want to be with is across from me. "We can chat about it later."

"Only if you want," she tells me. I like that she's giving me an option and not demanding she be in the know. Honestly, I like that Autumn hasn't pestered me with questions about Elena or about opening up regarding my failed marriage.

"Dad," Reggie says, grabbing my attention. "Miss Autumn drew this, and then we started coloring it." He slides the placemat over toward me, and I lean in to take a better look. There's a house with windows and a chimney, a field with flowers and grass with two children standing in it.

"You drew this?"

She nods and adjusts Roxy on her lap. "My mom is an artist, so I know a few tricks."

"This is pretty awesome."

"Thanks, but the kids did all the work. I just gave them the outline. Reggie decided on what colors the house should be while Roxy worked on the flowers."

"I love it." I give it back to Reggie and place my hand on his, giving it a firm squeeze.

When our pizzas arrive, I suggest Roxy or Reggie come over and sit on my side. Neither of my children budges. I'm not sure if I should feel bad because they don't want to sit with me or happy because they like the woman I like. I feel like I'm losing no matter what, though. I *like* Autumn and want to spend time with her, without my kids, but something tells me unless I'm sneaking around or Reggie is in school and Roxy is with Miss Meghan, I'm not going to get much alone time with Autumn.

Autumn doesn't encourage either of them to move. She simply adjusts the way she's sitting so Roxy can stay on her lap while they both eat. Autumn even beats me to cutting Roxy's pizza and offers to do the same for Reggie.

"What, no way," he says. "I can eat it with my fingers." To prove his point, he picks up his cheese pizza, tries to fold the thick crust in half, and takes a bite. The only problem is, the pizza's hot and very cheesy, which means he's making some horrible noises with his mouth while cheese and sauce ooze everywhere.

"Reg." I reach for the pizza just as Autumn places a napkin under his chin. Roxy isn't helping matters by giggling. "Come on, dude." I take the slice out of his hand and manage to get the cheese pulled apart. "Manners," I remind him as Autumn is rolling the sauce and cheese-soaked napkin into a ball.

"Let's either wait until the pizza cools down, or I can cut you a smaller slice," Autumn says. While her voice is kind, I fully expect Reggie to start sulking. But he surprises me and says a smaller slice would be fine. Autumn places another piece onto a clean plate, slices it down the middle, and gives it to my son, only for him to repeat the same thing he did before. This time, successfully.

Once everyone is settled and the pizza mishap has been taken care of, we start eating, and I realize quickly, I'm watching a relationship develop between the woman I like and my children. Seeing this unfold in front of my eyes is heartwarming.

"You eat your pizza like you've been to New York City," she says to Reggie.

"I went a couple of times with my Dad, but I don't remember if I had pizza there. Have you had pizza there?"

Autumn nods. "But I like thick pizza like this." She holds hers up. "And New York has thin pizza."

Roxy chimes in with, "That's funny."

"Where did you live before you came here?" Reggie asks Autumn.

"Well, I was born in Texas, went to college in Chicago, and then I lived in North Dakota for a little bit until I moved here."

"Do you like being on TV?" he asks.

"Miss Au-um is boofiful on TV," Roxy says. Autumn gives Roxy a happy squeeze, and then Roxy does the unthinkable. She places both her greasy hands onto Autumn's face and brushes her nose back and forth over Autumn's. If Autumn cares, she doesn't show it and doesn't make a big deal about having greasy toddler hand residue on her cheeks. When Roxy pulls away from Autumn, they stare at each other, making me wonder what they're both thinking and making me wish I was on that side of the table too.

"I do like it. It's fun. And I love the weather."

"It's a bit ironic that you do the weather, and your name is Autumn," I blurt out, only to realize my statement is very random.

The three of them laugh.

Great, they're already teaming up against me.

"Complete happenstance," Autumn says. "My father wanted me to be a lawyer, and my mom wanted me to go to art school. I didn't decide I wanted to do the weather until after I got to college.

"Daddy, it be funny if yous name is football." Roxy giggles.

I reach across the table to tickle her. My hand brushes against Autumn and is instantly ablaze with heat and electricity. Our eyes meet, and I can only hope she's thinking the same thing I am. We need some alone time to explore what is building between us.

TWENTY-ONE

AUTUMN

As soon as I get back to my apartment, I go right to the bathroom and start filling my tub. I need a bath—a nice long soak to ease my muscles. I never knew holding a toddler on my lap for a couple of hours would put so much strain on my back. I didn't mind holding Roxy though, or sitting next to Reggie. This afternoon had to be one of my best afternoons in a while. Julius's children are a delight, and I've grown especially fond of Roxy.

As soon as there's enough water, I strip out of my clothes and climb in—feet only. The water is hot, and I need time to adjust. I move the faucet dial a bit to bring in some cold, swishing it around with my foot until the temperature is tolerable. I finally sit down and sigh. I wish I could stretch out, but my tub is a standard size, and my legs are a little too long to really allow for any comfort. After I pull my knees up a smidge, I'm able to relax more. Water sloshes at the nape of my neck. If I'm not careful, I'll spill over the edge. With my foot, I push the dial into the off position and then close my eyes.

Today replays in my mind. Images of Roxy and Reggie

laughing and having a good time brings a smile to my face. And then there's their dad—Julius. I'm smitten, and I like him, but I feel like he's holding back. I knew he was on the phone with his ex because Reggie told me that Roxy called me dad's girlfriend to his mom, and she sounded mad. I get it to an extent, but if I'm not mistaken, she cheated on Julius. He's the one who's entitled to be mad. When he came into the restaurant, I wanted to ask him if everything was okay. There wasn't any time. The kids never left our sides, and when they did, we followed them everywhere. Even when Julius and I had a rematch at air hockey, the kids were right next to the table.

The alarm on my phone goes off, and I groan. Mostly because my phone is on the other side of the bathroom, and I have to get out regardless. Plus, I don't remember setting my alarm to remind me I have something planned for later. My body is stiff and only slightly relaxed. I need to book a massage and maybe start using the hot tub we have in the building. I have yet to venture to the gym here, opting to run outside while the weather is still somewhat decent. With my towel wrapped around me, I make my way to the phone and silence it before going back to the tub to pull the plug. While the water drains, I check my calendar—*dinner with Peyton.*

"Huh, I can't believe I forgot." When Peyton invited me to dinner a few nights ago, I couldn't say yes fast enough, and yet, it somehow slipped my mind. I glance at myself in the mirror and lean forward to get a better look. I tug at the skin under my eyes and wonder if the night cream I use is doing its job in preventing wrinkles. "I need to book a facial," I mutter to my reflection. "And a haircut."

Standing there and staring at myself isn't doing anything for my self-confidence. Work keeps me busy, and the free time I've had recently I've spent with Julius. Today would've been a perfect time to go to the spa and eliminate some of the stress I'm feeling but spending time with him and his children is important. Finding a healthy balance is a must.

In my room, I slip into a pair of sweatpants and an over-sized sweatshirt. I have a couple of hours before my dinner date with Peyton and the book I started many moons ago sits on my nightstand, mocking me. I pick it up and head into the living room, stopping to pull a throw blanket out of the basket I use to store them in. Curling up on the sofa, I open the book to the last page I'd marked and start reading. None of this makes sense. I'm in the middle of the chapter, reading about two characters that I don't remember. Determined to keep going, I flip back to the front and start over. I've read half of the book, so I must've found it interesting and figure I can skim if I begin to remember the content.

Halfway through my reread, there's a knock at my door. Ignoring the knock seems like the best thing for me to do since it's likely someone from my floor selling their steak knives or boxes of popcorn. This is a drawback to living in such a large building—everyone is a door-to-door salesperson. It's the little kids that I can't say no to though, and they know it.

The knock sounds again. I set my book down, get up and tiptoe to my door to look through the peephole. It's Julius, standing there with his hand on the wall and looking down at the floor.

"What is he doing here?" I whisper, thinking I might answer myself.

"Autumn," he says as if he can sense I'm standing on the other side of the door. "It's me. Are you home?"

"Shit." I step back and straighten out my ratty clothes

and smooth my hair back. I really need to put a mirror up by my door for occasions like this. The man I'm wholly interested in is about to see me in my most relaxed state. I'm not sure how I feel about this. With a twist of the door handle, I open the door to face Julius.

His head rises slowly, and a smile spreads across his face at a gradual pace. My knees go weak, forcing me to use the door to keep upright. How can a smile cause such a reaction?

"Hey," he says as I sag into the door for more stability. I thought I was smitten, but I'm not. I'm falling for him, and I'm not sure I can find a way to stop.

"Hey."

"I wanted to stop by and give you this."

Before I can ask what "this" is, he steps forward, cups my cheeks between his large hands, and presses his lips to mine. My mouth opens for him, beckoning him deeper. For some reason, my hand can't let go of the door, but my other one bunches his shirt into my fist, and I tug, wanting him to come in so I can close the door.

Julius pulls away, but only for a second before his lips are on mine again. I moan, needing more. He grins against my lips and chuckles. "I can't stay, but believe me, I want to."

"What? Why?" I sound desperate, and maybe I am. From the second I laid eyes on Julius, I've been attracted to him, even when he was a colossal jerk. The allure has only grown stronger the more time we spend together, and when he kisses me, I lose what's left of my self-resolve.

"I have a game tomorrow."

"And that means, what?"

He laughs again. "We have rules. They're odd but have to be followed nonetheless."

"Well, I, for one, am not following anything you're saying."

Julius looks confused. I'm not sure why since I'm not the one speaking in circles. "I guess I assumed Peyton had told you that the NFL requires us to stay in a hotel the night before a home game."

What on earth? "Why?"

"It's all part of our player agreement. We have funky rules. I don't make them, but I abide by them."

"Huh," is all I can manage to say. "So, you came over here to kiss me like that and leave?"

He looks at me oddly and scratches the back of his neck. "Yeah, I guess so. Want me to do it again?" Julius leans toward me. I put my hand on his chest to stop him. He smirks and pushes a bit but finally gives up.

"You're mean," I tell him.

"I'm sorry. Can I make it up to you?"

"How?"

He shrugs. "Come to the game tomorrow?"

"How is me coming to your game making it up?"

Julius shrugs again and decides that batting his eyelashes might get him his desired answer. He's right, it probably will, but I need to find the strength to ignore his wily ways.

"It's not. It's a way for me to see you again tomorrow. I'm going to be honest here. I'd like to see you at my game. I can leave a ticket for you at will call."

"I have to work tomorrow, but I'll keep it in mind."

"Okay," he says as he places his hand on my waist. He pulls me in for a kiss. It's short but full of intent. There's no question in my mind about how we feel toward one another. "If I don't see you tomorrow, I'll call you when I get home."

"Good luck."

"Thanks." Julius kisses me again and then rushes down the hall. I stand in the doorway, watching him. When he gets to the elevator, he yells, "Get back inside before I come back there."

I shake my head and close the door. I stay here, leaning against it with my fingers touching my lips. Julius's scruff has left a little bit of razor burn, and I like it probably more than I should.

Now that I'm up and thinking about Julius, I'm too wired to sit back and down to read. I start to get ready for dinner by doing my make-up and hair, all while creating a list in my mind of things I want to ask Peyton about the team. I'm curious now since Julius mentioned the rules. I hadn't ever thought about them before.

Peyton and I are meeting halfway between our places. It's a three-block walk, but the evening air is chilly, and I hate that it's dark out, but am very thankful for the street-lights and the open businesses. I'm still a bit wary of my surroundings, and Aiden's words still replay in my mind when I'm out at night.

When I reach the restaurant, Peyton is sitting on the bench in the vestibule. Along with her brother and Noah's dad.

Cue massive freak out.

"Hey," she says as she stands. "You remember my brother, Quinn, and my father-in-law, Liam?"

"How could I forget?" Literally, there is no forgetting that my one friend here is music royalty. I extend my hand, and we all shake. "It's nice to see you again. In town for the game?"

"Yes, it's not often that we miss them," Liam says.

"Noah must love having you there."

"He does," Peyton says.

Her brother excuses himself and goes to the podium to let the restaurant know we're here for our reservation. Peyton chose an American bar and grill type place for us to have dinner. The eatery looks packed, and it's loud. A million things run through my mind right now, mostly will we have an enjoyable conversation, or will the noise level make us yell?

Quinn motions for us to follow him and the hostess. Instantly, I notice how he walks—with his head down. I turn and look over my shoulder and find Liam doing the same. I also see they're both wearing ball caps to try and hide their identity. I wonder if I would've recognized them if they hadn't been sitting with Peyton? I'm not sure I would have. But I'm also not looking for celebrities.

As we walk to the table, I hear my name. There is some finger-pointing, but I ignore it. When a little boy waves at me, I wave back. I had some of this in North Dakota, but not to this extent. Leon Woolworth has gone above and beyond to introduce me to the Rose City, and people have taken notice.

After we sit and the host has left the table, Liam starts laughing. I look at him quickly and then to Peyton, wondering what inside joke I've missed. "I must've missed something."

"Not at all," Liam says. "It's nice not being the one cat-called and pointed at for once."

"Oh." I look around the table, only to see everyone staring at me. "The ratings say I'm popular."

"She's fabulous," Peyton adds. "Noah says the guys talk about the weather all the time now. She's giving men a reason to pay attention."

"You're making me sound like some sort of sex symbol."

Everyone laughs. "It's a hard life, but someone has to do it," Quinn says as Peyton elbows him.

"Not what I mean at all. I'm just saying that people are taking notice of the changes Leon has made. When anchors are retiring, he's bringing in fresh, young faces. He's trying to revitalize the news, and he's doing it in ways that are making people take notice."

"Believe me," Liam interjects. "It's a good thing."

"Unless you want to have a drink," Quinn adds. "Inevitably, someone will have their cell phone out, taking pictures and video because it's important to them. It's something you learn to live with."

"Well, I'm going to have wine with dinner. I walked, and I'm not working tonight. If someone wants to post a picture of me being an adult, so be it. I swear people have too much time on their hands lately," I say.

"I'll order the bottle." Liam flags down our server and orders not only a very expensive bottle of wine but five different appetizers.

"Are you going to eat all of the food you just ordered?" Peyton asks.

Liam shrugs. "I couldn't decide what I wanted to try."

He couldn't decide. I've barely looked at the menu, and he's already found five things he wanted to try. The menu is small. American fare with flare is what I'd call it. I finally come across something that sounds enticing—a barbeque brisket and cheddar sandwich. I haven't had a good brisket in a long time and find that I'm craving it a bit. When the server returns with our wine, Liam is the focal point of the taste test. I watch with rapt attention as he swirls, sniffs, and finally sips the wine. He nods, and the waiter pours the wine into our glasses. The temptation to ask how come the rest of us haven't sampled is there, but I know it's not proper. Liam is paying. He's the decision-maker. Besides, I don't care that much about wine, and I'm not confident I could tell what is considered a good red or not.

By the time the server finishes with the wine pouring, the food runner sets down a tray filled with the appetizers—my mouth waters. I'm hungry but torn. I could eat a few of the items ordered, or I could wait for my dinner—such a dilemma. Before I can even decide, Liam sets a plate in front of me, with one of everything on it, and tells me to eat up. Liam tells our server that we'll be ready to order dinner in a bit. It's then that I realize this isn't just a dinner. It's an event for the four of us. Liam is in no hurry to go anywhere. He wants us to enjoy our time. I finally relax, take a sip of the wine, and dig in.

The conversation never stalls. Quinn and Liam ask questions about my work, and while I'm curious about theirs, they don't allow me to ask. They're forthcoming with information and liken their rockstar lives to mine. In my world, the two don't even come close to correlating.

"Did you always want to be in music?" I ask Quinn.

"I don't know," he says. "I've only known music, and playing comes naturally to me, as does songwriting. Unlike my Uncle Liam, I didn't dream of being anything else. I also didn't dream of being in a band or living on the road. It's weird. It's a thing I do, and while I love it, if someone told me I had to walk away tomorrow, I'd be okay with that too."

"With me," Liam adds. "My father told me what I was going to do, where I was going to go to college. I wanted none of that. I wanted to be able to make my own decisions and definitely make my own mistakes. I chose a college I didn't want to be at, hated everything about school, and pretty much started resenting everyone in my life."

"My dad wanted me to be a lawyer, follow in his footsteps and all that. He was sad when I decided on North-western over Northeastern."

"I think my parents thought I was going to go into coaching," Peyton adds.

"Didn't you, though?" Quinn asks.

Peyton shrugs. "Sometimes, I miss talking about the game to other people. It's why I fill in for Aiden when he's out because being in front of the camera feels good. It's comfortable."

"Leon speaks very highly of you."

"As he does you," she says. Her words bring a smile to my face, and honestly, the compliment warms me. I want to succeed at my job and someday be like Camden—on national television, where I'm a household name.

We're on our second bottle of wine when we finally order dinner. Usually, I'm in a rush. Sit down, order, eat and get the hell out of places, but tonight is different. It's casual, no fuss, no muss. I'm relaxed, and when I should be freaking the hell out because Liam Page is sitting next to me —close enough to touch and smell—and Quinn James is across from me—for most women, this is paradise. It's odd because while they're celebrities and everything about this situation tells me I should be anxious, I'm not.

"Peyton, I have a question for you. Earlier, I was with Julius, and he told me he had to sleep in a hotel the night before a game. I'm confused because they're home tomorrow."

"The NFLPA has some odd rules," Liam says.

"The what?"

"The players association," Peyton answers. "The day before a home game, the players must be at the field for a walk-through. It takes an hour. If the player doesn't show, they don't play tomorrow. The night before the game, they're in a hotel, regardless of whether it's a home game or not. All the players need to be together, and they'll be bussed to the stadium in the morning."

"But Julius was with me this morning. Reggie had a game," I say.

"The walk-through was at six a.m.," she says.

My mouth makes the "oh" sound without me saying anything. "I never realized how structured football was."

"It really is," Liam adds. "The NFL is working hard on cleaning up their image after a few incidents. Things used to be stricter, but they've eased up for the past couple of years."

"I'd like to go back to where you said you were with Julius this morning." Peyton looks at me with her eyebrow raised.

"Um . . ."

"Ooh, gossip. I'm here for this," Quinn says as he leans forward. Liam and Peyton bust up laughing while I stare at him. He waggles his eyebrows and motions for me to start talking. I finish off my half-empty glass of wine and let the words tumble out of my mouth.

TWENTY-TWO

JULIUS

I t's been a long time since I've had a sleepless night before a game. If we were playing in the Superbowl, I would expect to spend the night staring at the ceiling, but we're not. It's a typical game. One we must win to keep a two-game lead over our opponents. And one we're expected to win. Noah Westbury is having a career season and is one of the top-rated quarterbacks in the league. I shouldn't be anxious or nervous about our game. Yet, something is on my mind, and I can't pinpoint what it is. I want to blame everything on Elena, and I probably should. Each time she calls, she makes more of a mess of our lives than they were before she calls, and I'm left picking up the pieces of the kids' broken hearts. Mine is well past the point of breaking. It's on the path of healing and finding happiness again, thanks to Autumn.

Autumn.

Saying her name makes my heart race and my palms sweat. These feelings are supposed to be good, the type I should embrace, but the thought of her and me together is somewhat terrifying. There's something there that I can't put my finger on. I like her, and I do not doubt that she wants me—even though she shouldn't after the way I treated her. Autumn is a forgiving person. That much is true. And as much as I want to be with her, I'm hesitant to pull the trigger. Each time I'm with her, I feel comfortable, and that scares me. I'm still married, and starting another relationship before I've even filed the paperwork on my divorce seems wrong.

The alarm on my phone goes off. I blink at the ceiling a few times before mustering the strength to roll over and shut the piercing sound off. Today is going to be a long day. It was vital for me to get a good night's sleep to be focused on the field. I don't need another replay of my epically shitty game like last time.

My eyes adjust to the bright light on my phone. I have texts from my parents, Elena and Autumn. I stare at Elena's name on my phone. When she walked out, I changed her name in my contacts from **My Wife** to **Elena White**. White being her maiden name. I couldn't stomach seeing **Cunningham** after her name, not after she did what she did. I open Elena's first because I already feel off today. I might as well let whatever she has to say to me make things worse and have my parents and Autumn build me up.

Elena White: I want to finish discussing this new girlfriend of yours.

There's nothing to discuss.

It's too early in the morning for her to be awake. I close this chat window and go to the message from my parents. It's a video of the kids wishing me good luck today. Seeing them, happy and with smiles on their faces, brings tears to my eyes. I love them more than I love life and want them to be happy. I don't know if I'm doing a good job or not. I don't know if I'm on the right path to being a successful parent and guiding them through a divorce. I honestly don't know much about anything except how to love them whole-heartedly.

I'll see you at the game – I text my parents. I'm forever grateful that they gave up their retirement to come live near me. I don't know what I'd do without them. More so, since they've become my go-to for babysitting, especially during overnights and away games. Sure, the kids have Miss Meghan, but she's young and deserves a life as well.

I finally allow myself to look at Autumn's text. It's one line: **I should be able to make it by half-time.** I open the message to reply and am saddened when I see that's the only thing she sent. I don't know what I was expecting, especially since I didn't text her after leaving last night. I wanted to, and I thought about it a lot. I wanted her to send me a flirty message like before. I suppose if I wanted something like that, I could've initiated it. I respond with: *I'll leave the ticket at Will Call. I hope you had a good night with Peyton. I'll ask her to make sure you have a press pass.* I'm excited Autumn will be at the game, albeit slightly nervous. The last time she was there, I laid a giant egg on the field and played the worst game of my life. Of course, in my infinite wisdom, I blamed her. Everything from the moment I met Autumn was her fault. It was easy to blame her than myself and the shit that's going on with Elena and my joke of a marriage.

My alarm sounds again. It's time to get moving. I take my phone into the bathroom and turn on the self-help podcast I found. For some reason, listening to people talk about their problems and how they've solved them is sooth-ing. It shows that I'm not such a fuck up. When the temper-ature is decent, I step in and let the water run down my back. It won't be until later, when I'm at the stadium or home, that I'll get a powerful spray that I need to loosen up my muscles. These hotels aren't designed to help us athletes ease our aches and pains.

After dressing in sweats, I make my way down to the conference room where breakfast is. This is the most essential part of my day, and the only time I'll eat until dinner tonight. Once I get to the field, the last thing on my mind is food. Water and Gatorade are all I'll have later. Right now is my only chance to add all the necessary fuel to my body so I can outperform everyone determined to bring me down today.

Noah raises his hand when he sees me. I nod, signaling I'll be over after I make my way through the buffet line. Thankfully, the hotel provides staff to help us carry our plates to the table. Because us football players see a buffet and it's game on. It's a challenge to see how many plates we can fill on our first trip through.

The unlucky employee who helps carry my food follows me to where Noah is sitting. Players usually sit wherever they want. Sometimes the coaches want to have impromptu meetings while eating breakfast and will beckon a player over, and sometimes this is just like the cafeteria. Breakfast can totally turn into a popularity contest. You can fully expect a rookie receiver or running back to try and sit with Noah to plead their case that they need the ball when they're in there. Unless they're a first or second-round pick, these rookies are likely filling in for a down to give people like me a break.

I sit down across from Noah, who moves a couple of the empty plates he has in front of him to give the hotel employee more room to set my copious amounts of food down. Noah looks at me and then down at the table and back at me. He grimaces and then laughs. "Are you seriously going to eat all of this?" he picks a piece of bacon off one of the plates and sticks it in his mouth.

I shrug. "Maybe. I don't want to have to get back in line with the defensive backs."

Noah nods in agreement. "You ready for today?"

It's a question Noah asks most of us on game day. He's trying to get a feel for where his teammates heads are before we get onto the field. It's his job to lead us, but we won't be in sync on the field if we're not on the same page.

"I am. I feel good. Slept like shit though."

"I rarely sleep well the night before a game. I hate hotel beds, and I hate being away from Peyton, especially when I know she's at home. At least she's not by herself."

"Parents in town?"

He nods. "Quinn too. He and my dad went out to dinner with Peyton and Autumn last night. My dad went all out, according to my wife, and they ended up staying at the restaurant until closing."

"Great, so what you're telling me is your uber-famous dad is trying to woo the woman I'm trying to woo?"

Noah leans forward and asks quietly, "Are you and Autumn a thing?"

I shake my head slightly. "No. Maybe? I don't know. I like her a lot, but there's a nagging voice in the back of my head telling me I need to take a step back and let this relationship, or whatever it is, germinate a bit longer. I haven't even filed for divorce yet. Elena is already on my ass about my 'new girlfriend' and I have a feeling she's going to try and use this against me."

"Can she?"

"I don't know. I've put off the attorney talks this entire time. In hindsight, I should've spoken to one the second

Elena walked out, but I think there was a part of me that hoped she would come back. That was until I found out she was having an affair."

"Affairs are hard to get over," he says. "I know my emotional affair with Peyton wasn't fair to Dessie."

"The whole situation with Dessie, and what she did—that was messed up."

Noah sets his napkin down onto the table. "That was my fault. I should've ended the relationship long before it started. But I agree, the actions she took when everything started falling apart were very bothersome. She really could've messed up a lot of lives with her antics."

"What's she doing now?" I ask.

Noah shrugs. "Don't know, and I don't care. I'm married to the woman I'm supposed to be with. It took a near-fatal accident to realize I don't care what people think about our age difference. I've been in love with Peyton for as long as I can remember."

"Is it weird with your dad being her uncle?"

Noah shakes his head. "It's not like they're related. It's the life-long friendship thing. No different than our mothers. I grew up calling her mom Aunt Katelyn, and now she's my mother-in-law, but I still refer to her as my aunt."

"It's definitely weird," I tell him.

He picks up his napkin and throws it at me. "It's why we don't talk about it. Only our closest friends know. People judge others too much."

"That, they do," I say in agreement.

Noah waits with me while I finish breakfast. A few of the other guys come to the table to shoot the shit and whatnot. None of the rookies stop by, which is good. I don't want to tease anyone today. Honestly, the rookies we have are promising and will be a great asset next year.

After I finish and head back to my room to change, I'm on the bus with the rest of the team. The sun is shining, but it's cold out—a typical fall day in the Pacific Northwest. I'm not looking forward to the winter though. Lately, with climate change, our calm—no snow winters—have been anything but. A couple of years back, the team ended up stranded at the stadium because of icy roads. For two days, we couldn't leave. Elena freaked out, and rightly so. Growing up in the South, she rarely dealt with ice or freezing temperatures. It's partly the reason she wanted to be in Los Angeles all the time, especially in the off-season. She craves the heat. The hotter, the better. Give me four seasons, and I'm happy, except when it's below zero. No one likes to be that cold.

I'm not surprised when we pull into the parking lot to find people already tailgating. The smell of lighter fluid and briquettes fills the air, as does loud music. We have die-hards, those fans who are here the moment the gates open to get their favorite parking spot. This one time, when I was injured and couldn't play, I came out here to check things out. Being on the other side of things really puts my job into perspective. I got to see firsthand what goes into a Sunday game. Fans love their sports teams and their favorite players. When we can give a little of ourselves back to them—they love us even more.

Inside the locker room, my gear is hanging and ready for me. I strip out of my suit and hang it up nicely. I learned a long time ago to make sure I'm wearing my supportive gear under my slacks. One too many towel whips to my ass were enough to teach me a lesson. I dress in my workout gear before heading over to the trainer to get my ankles and wrists taped. I'm old for this game and probably have a good five years left, assuming I don't have any injuries derailing my career. It's hard to imagine I'll be retired or no longer able to play in my late thirties. Football is hard on the body.

Once taped and ready, I head out to the field. I like to start with a good stretch and meet with one of the trainers on the sideline. He works my hamstrings, checks my knees, and then helps me stretch. When he moves on to the next guy, I head out onto the field and run the snake, but only a quarter of it. I'm not looking to get tired before the game starts, but I want my legs as warmed up as they can be. When Noah wants to practice throwing the ball, I volunteer. Each and every time. There is no better way to get ready than to take a toss from your quarterback.

Noah gives me a hand signal, and I run the route. He hits me in stride, right in the center of my chest, with every throw. This is, of course, unrealistic because there will be a defender or two—or five, trying to prevent me from catching it. Football might be a physical game, but it's a mind game as well. And some defensive specialists really know how to fuck with your mind.

The stands start to fill up, and the media outlets are either setting up or already on air. I have no idea how many times the cameras are on me. We're given the signal that we need to get ready for the game. We head back into the locker room, where we dress in our pads and full uniform. The vibe around the locker room is different than when we first arrived. It was chill and relaxed, and now we're focused and hyping each other up. Coach gives us a quick pep talk. This isn't like high school, where we only see our coach for two hours a night, and he has to use the time before the game to go over strategy. We've done that all week and again yesterday morning. We're ready.

We head out to the field after the team introduction. The stands are full, and everyone is on their feet. I run to the bench and look up, spotting Reggie, Roxy, and my parents right away. I wave and blow them a kiss before slipping my helmet on. It's time for the coin toss. My teammates and I go out to the center of the fifty-yard line. Handshakes happen with our opponent, and the head official tosses the coin, with me yelling, "tails."

"Tails it is."

"We'll receive," I say, and the official makes the catching motion and points to which direction we'll start. I'm halfway toward the bench when our special teams take the field. Each guy that passes by, I either bump chests with or grab their helmet and tell them to run like the wind. I'd love to start this game off with a run back.

Sadly, the run back doesn't happen.

Noah and I run out together. In the huddle, he tells us what play we're starting with. I line up on the left and watch him. As soon as the ball is in his hands, I'm down the field, juking my defender as much as I can until I cut across the field, poised and ready for the pigskin to land in my arms. As soon as I see the perfect spiral, I raise my hands and leap. The ball touches my fingertips, and I curl them to pull the ball into my palms. The moment my foot touches the ground, I'm in stride, running toward the end zone.

I glance over my shoulder to where my defender is. His hands reach for me, but I veer. *Not today,* I repeat in my head. What I forget to do is look to my right. The safety comes out of nowhere and takes me to the ground. As much as I want that touchdown, we're on the ten-yard line, and I couldn't be happier.

The next play goes to the running back. He wiggles through the melee of men and comes out the victor on the other end. I'm happy because we're on the board but pissed I didn't get the call.

At half-time, we have a two-touchdown lead, with Noah scoring the second one.

When I come out of the locker room, I spot Autumn at once. She's standing with Peyton, wearing the Portland Pioneers shirt she wore to her first game. Damn, she's beautiful. Her long dark hair is in a braid, which I'm learning is her favorite hairstyle when she's not working, and she's wearing a Pioneers trucker cap. Autumn looks every bit a fan. As I approach the bench, she sees me and smiles. Instead of going up to her, I pick up a football and lob it to her. I fully expect her to catch it, but she doesn't. She steps to the side, and Peyton takes it easily out of the air. She sends it back to me, the ball whizzing in the air.

"Damn, Peyton. I'll never understand why you don't play football."

Noah laughs and shakes his head. "She would need to put on about a hundred pounds and grow at least a foot."

"You're lucky I don't have a ball in my hand, Westbury," she yells back.

"How the hell did she hear you?" I ask him.

He points to his helmet. "Mic'd up."

"Oh," I mouth.

We start the second half with the same play we started the game with. This time though, I make it to the end zone for six. After I cross the line, I wait for my teammates to congratulate me and then hand the football to the referee. I've never been one to celebrate in any other fashion. Some of my teammates like to dance, while others like to spike the ball. Me—I like to keep things simple.

TWENTY-THREE

AUTUMN

This is the first time I pay attention to the game. The last time I was here, I watched occasionally but mostly chatted with Peyton, Aiden, and anyone who stopped to talk to me. I have a purpose this time. He's on the field, running routes, cutting across the field, and dodging defenders—all terms I pick up from Peyton. I still don't know much of anything about the game, but by the smile on her face, the roar of the crowd, and the cheering coming from the sidelines, whatever Julius is doing must be good. As I stand next to Peyton, I realize that if Julius and I are going to be a couple or whatever the proper term is these days, I'm going to have to learn about the game of football. He's asked me a lot of questions about reporting the weather. At first, I thought he did this because he had mocked me, but now I know it's because he's genuinely interested in what I do.

After the game, Peyton invites us over. I like that she assumes Julius and I will be together. I sort of love her for that. She shows me to the locker room, pointing to where I can stand and wait for Julius. I hadn't planned this, but I like the idea of surprising him. She tells me he's in a press conference but will come out this door after he's showered. Peyton also warned me that Julius is slow. He likes to take his time and be the last one out.

"Duly noted," I tell her before she leaves me in the hall. People stroll by, some carrying arms full of equipment and other things. They nod or wave if their hand is free, and I do the same in return. Right now, I feel like a high schooler waiting for her boyfriend to come out of gym class, but I want to be here. From everything Peyton said, Julius had a good game, and I want to be the first non-member of his football world to congratulate him.

Team members come through the door. I smile at each one and chat with Noah when he appears. "Congrats on the win," I tell him.

"Thanks. Glad you could make it out."

"Me too. I'm happy Julius invited me."

"You know," he says. "You always have a ticket on standby. Say the word, and Peyton will make sure you have a pass."

"I know, but honestly, it feels awkward. I don't want to assume."

Noah lets out a hearty chuckle. "Assume away. Since your arrival, you've made my wife smile. You've given her a friend who wants nothing but friendship in return. If you want to come to a game, so be it. Hell, if you want to move to our building, I'll put in a good word with the board."

"Okay, now that's pushing it. Have you seen where I live?"

He shakes his head.

"Walk out the main door, and I'm at the water. Granted, the water is the best, but I also love being so close to the park."

"A couple of the guys live in that complex. They all like it."

"Oh really? I guess I never assumed more of the team would live there aside from Julius."

"The owners are good friends with the owner of the Pioneers—they cut the players a deal." Someone down the corridor calls Noah's name. He nods and tells me to have a good night and that he hopes to see me at his place later.

It's getting late, and I start to think Peyton is wrong about Julius. I know there are a lot of men on a football team, but I swear at least a hundred have already come out of the locker room. A few even offered to take me home, while one who I don't know asked if I wanted him to get Julius. As tempting as his offer was, I passed. But now, I'm second-guessing my decision. I think I've held this wall up for at least an hour, if not longer. How long can it take someone to do a press conference and take a shower? What in the hell is he doing in there?

I push away from the wall and step toward the door, only for it to fly open. I startle and jump back. A little "oof" escapes, and I cover my mouth.

"Hey," he says, with a grin so wide and bright it could melt the snow. "What are you doing here?"

"Peyton showed me where to wait?"

"Were you about to come into the locker room?" he asks as he looks over his shoulder.

Busted. I nod and feel the heat in my cheeks rise. "I thought maybe you left through a different door. I was going to open it and holler inside for you."

"Do you want to have a look around?" Julius reaches for the handle on the door and opens it, propping it with his foot. He motions for me to enter. Each step I take is hesitant, almost as if I'm afraid I'm going to get into trouble. Or worse, become a locker room cliché.

This is the first time I've ever been in a locker room that wasn't at the gym or school. I'm pleasantly surprised by how clean it is and am shocked by the space. The room is massive, with a giant Pioneer logo on the floor. The lockers themselves look like cabinets, with shelves, hangers, and cubby holes. Julius leads me over to his space, and inside there are pictures of Roxy and Reggie and one of his parents.

"Wow, this place is huge."

"It has to be when you have forty-six men trying to get dressed at the same time, plus staff and about fifteen coaches moving about. It can get a little cramped in here." We continue to walk around. "Once the room is clean, staff will shut the doors. When we return for our next home game, we'll come in, and all our equipment will be ready to go."

"What about practice?" I ask.

"We have a practice facility. The equipment manager will make sure our pads, helmets, and other necessities are in our lockers there for our next practice."

"There are so many logistics that go into this sport. I had no idea."

Julius nods. "It's weird because growing up, my parents had to buy my equipment. My mom used to complain about the smell of my pads or the grass stains on my pants. When I got to college, they had managers to take care of everything. It was a nice change, almost like a reward for doing well in high school. Now, it's ten times more than in college. If I don't like how something fits, the manager takes care of it."

"And you just show up and play?"

He shrugs. "More or less. Each guy has a different philosophy. Noah and I are close, and in the off-season, we hang out together, mainly in California. The warmer weather helps with muscle aches and pains. We workout, train, run, do everything we can to stay in shape for preseason. Other guys sit on the couch from whenever the season ends until July, and then it's a mad dash to get ready."

Julius guides me into another room. It looks like a spa but isn't. "This is where we come if we have an on-field injury or need to recoup after a game."

"Ice baths?"

"Yep, ever had one?"

"No," I say. "But I've seen the commercials. They don't appeal to me."

"You get used to them," Julius tells me. "This is also where we get stim before a game if we need it, and where we get our wrists and ankles taped. Then when the game starts, the training staff is on the sidelines, making sure we're good through the entire game."

"I saw them on the sidelines, and one was in the tent thingy."

"Yes, that's where we go if the injury is minor. Mostly to keep the media away from what we're doing and to protect the spectators from seeing our blood gush."

I set my hand over my stomach, feeling queasy. "I'm happy never to see anything like that."

Julius takes me to another room. "This is where we shower. We have a schedule. Noah is always first, and the rookies are last. The rest of us fall in line."

I don't tell him what Peyton told me—that he likes to take his time. I'm sure if he felt it was important information, he'd share it. I turn to leave, but strong hands on my waist stop me. Julius pulls me to his chest and walks backward until we're straddling on a wooden bench. It's wider than the ones at the gym and a bit more comfortable.

"We're in the room where you boys shower," I point out.

Julius nods. "I wanted to be alone for a minute."

"You're the last one here."

"The staff is still here and the cleaning crew. People are always around, lurking behind corners and hiding in the shadows."

I decide to move closer, our knees touching. Julius's dark hair is combed back, and he smells like clean linen with a hint of Old Spice mixed with his everyday woodsy scent. His baby blue eyes watch me for a sign . . . of what, I don't know. He doesn't need my permission to kiss me or put his hands on me. Instead of waiting for him to make a move, I push my fingers through his dark hair and watch as his cheeks turn a light shade of red. His hands are gentle as they cup the back of my legs, gripping the back of my knees. Julius tugs me forward until my legs are wrapped around his waist, and I'm no longer on the bench but straddling him. Those rough hands of his press into my backside, pushing me closer to him.

It's me who makes the next move. Tilting, I press my lips to his. Soft at first until I feel his mouth open against mine and his tongue tasting mine. I sit up higher on him, feeling his hardness through my jeans. Julius holds me tightly as he kisses me. He tugs at my shirt, and I nod, letting him know he can do whatever he wants. He lifts it and places his hands against my skin, his finger digging into my flesh while I move against him. We both moan, and he breaks away, kissing a path of desire down my neck and across my chest. When his hand cups my breast, my head falls back, and I push harder into him. I want him. I have since he pierced me with his soulful eyes on Peyton's balcony.

"Julius," I whisper his name. It's my way of consenting for more. I want . . . no, I *need* for him to touch me, to put his lips in places he has yet to explore. But he doesn't. He continues to kiss me, ignoring the burning I feel deep within. His arm hugs me to his body, and my hips jerk, creating some much-needed friction. Julius groans and his hand finds purchase on my hip, moving me back and forth.

A door slams shut, and he pushes me away. I tuck my head and wipe my face with the back of my hand. It takes me a moment to calm my beating heart and to regain my breathing. Was I really going to have sex with him in the shower room of the stadium? Honestly, I don't want to know the answer to that question.

I crave him.

Every part of Julius sets my body on fire. His smoldering eyes, big hands, and the way he tilts his head to the side and looks at me like I'm the most beautiful woman he's ever seen. Which I know isn't true. I've seen the cheerleaders and his ex. Elena is gorgeous. And let's be honest, Julius Cunningham could have any woman he wanted.

Yet, I'm the one in the locker room, making out with him. This alone should be enough for me.

"I don't think anyone is coming in," he says quietly.

"Will you get in trouble for having me in here?"

"No," he says while shaking his head. He keeps his eyes focused on the entrance and not on me. I reach for his hand and lock our fingers together. "Are you okay?" he asks.

I look at him in surprise. "I'm perfect."

He moves toward me and kisses me. "What are you doing tonight?"

"We," I pause and let the word linger between us, "were invited over to Peyton and Noah's."

"Yeah?"

I nod. "I don't have any plans if you want to go."

"My family and I usually go out to dinner after a home game."

"You go," I say, not wanting to keep him from his children. "And when you get back, if you want, come over to Noah's or stop by my place."

"I will," he says before kissing me again. We make out a little bit longer but nothing like before. The tension between us is intense and whatever is growing between us feels incredibly real.

Julius walks me to my car, where he gives me a goodbye kiss. "I'll call you later," he tells me and then helps me in my vehicle.

"Do you want me to drive you to your car?"

He shakes his head and holds out his phone. "I need to make a call."

"Okay, talk to you later." I watch him walk away and hold the phone to his ear. I suspect he's calling his ex, and for some reason, it irritates me. I tell myself to chill. They have children and need to talk about their care, but why not do it when he's in the car and driving home? Why not spend a few more minutes with me?

TWENTY-FOUR

JULIUS

The entire drive to the restaurant to meet my parents and kids, I think about Autumn and what could've easily happened in the shower room. I knew taking her in there was a mistake, but I wanted her to see where I spend my Sundays. It probably would've been better had I done it when I knew more staff would be around. I'm not worried about the cleaning crew, but if one of the coaches walked in or one of my teammates, I'd get a ton of shit.

Elena's name pops up on my console and I groan. During the game, she called and I tried to call her back, but she sent me to voicemail. I want to do the same now, but it'll do me no good to ignore her.

"What?" I bark out as I answer.

"Is that any way to greet your wife?"

"Soon to be *ex*-wife," I remind her. "Besides, we're separated. I'm not sure you can refer to yourself as my wife anymore."

"Legally, we're still married, Julius. If something were to happen to you, I'd be the first one they call. I'd decide the best care for you." Her words turn my stomach. I can see it now, me in a wheelchair, unable to speak for myself, and her dictating my care. I need to change all my paperwork tomorrow. I can't put it off any longer.

"Thanks for reminding me to change all my paperwork with the league."

"Whatever," she says. "Are the kids in the car?"

"You know they're with my parents, and Reggie has his phone if you need to talk to him."

"How would I know the kids are with your parents? I don't know your schedule, Julius."

My mouth drops open. Is this woman for real? "For as long as you've known me, Elena, you know where I spend my time between mid-July and February if I'm lucky. My schedule has never changed. It's not like I switch jobs often."

"Well, I forgot."

I sigh and rub my face with my free hand. Traffic is heavy for a Sunday. I had hoped most people would be home by now, which is the main reason I like leaving the stadium so late. I loathe traffic.

"So, what did you need?"

She huffs, and I fear the worst is about to come out of her mouth. "The movie I signed on for is having budget issues, and I'm wondering—"

"No," I say, cutting her off.

"No? You don't even know what I was going to ask."

"Let's see, you're either going to ask for money or ask me to finance this side job of yours. The answer is no."

"Julius, you still have to support me."

"I do. I pay for the house you live in, and I pay for your car, as well as your insurance."

Elena huffs again. "Listen, I'm trying to do things the

right way here. I've spoken to a lawyer, and he's assured me there are loopholes in the prenup. He said it'd be easier if we work out some sort of support deal instead of dragging this out in court."

My teeth grind against each other, and my pulse races. The grip I have on my steering wheel causes my hand to cramp. It's taking every bit of self-control not to hang up on her. Part of me wants to give her the money she wants so she'll go away. The thing is, she'll never be gone because of the kids, and I'm not keeping their mother away from them. I'm not that kind of person. The other half of me wants to fight this out in court. I know the prenup is ironclad. I insisted on it because I heard so many horror stories of college athletes getting taken by their wives. When I suggested Elena sign one, she didn't even balk. I never questioned why Elena didn't have a problem with signing one because at the time I thought she was in this marriage for the long haul.

"I really don't know what you want me to say, Elena. You had an affair and documented it through social media. You didn't try to hide the fact, and never mind what I witnessed the last time I was in our home in L.A. I'm at a loss here, so help me figure things out."

"I want what's due to me, Julius. It's not fair. You have all this money, and you're being a prick about it. Why can't you just pay me off like the other guys do?" She's getting heated. I can sense the frustration in her voice.

"You know, if you had come and told me you weren't happy, and we decided to separate, I'd be more amenable. But you cheated. You brought another man into our bed without any consideration of how that would make me feel. You flaunted your new relationship right under my nose and somehow thought I wouldn't find out, which blows my mind. Did you really think someone wouldn't tag me in a picture of my wife making out with another man?"

"You don't need to yell."

"I'm not yelling." Except I am. I can't help it. She infuriates me.

"I need the money to survive."

"Then get a job, Elena. Sell the house. I don't know what to tell you. But I'm done having this conversation. Send me the name of your lawyer so I can give their information to mine. Tomorrow, I'll take care of all of this. You don't even have to pay for the divorce. I'll do that. You're on your own for lawyer fees though."

"Julius—"

I hang up. I'm done listening to her and whatever excuse she can muster. I expect she'll end up getting her way, though. Elena will drag me to court, and it'll be my luck that we end up with a sympathetic judge who doesn't like pro athletes.

MY PARENTS AGREE to take Roxy and Reggie back to their place for a sleepover. I need some adult time after the conversation with Elena. I promise to be at my parents in the morning for breakfast, with clean clothes, school supplies, and a ride to school. As I drive back to my place, I think about Autumn and what she's doing at Noah and Peyton's. Is she thinking about me? Missing me? Or is someone there monopolizing her time? Thinking about her talking to someone else gets my blood boiling. I've never been the jealous type, but all this shit with Elena has me on edge and questioning everything. Deep down, I know not all women are like my ex, but her actions aren't helping me think otherwise.

I pull into the garage of my complex and drive to my parking spot. After I shut my SUV off, I sit there for a minute, contemplating my future. I see nothing but lawyers fighting over my kids and my bank account. All Elena had to do was ask for a divorce, but no. She had to go and cheat.

Noise from the outside has me looking through my rear-view mirror. There's a group of women, four or five of them, heading toward the elevator. They help make up my mind on what I'm doing and that's staying in the car, at least for the time being. I lean my head back and close my eyes. Only to have my conversation with Elena replay in my mind. My life is a freaking nightmare, except when it comes to Autumn. I don't know what it is about her, but she definitely knows how to bring a smile to my face. As I sit here, I wonder if I would've looked twice at her if things weren't sour between Elena and me? I don't want to think any woman could pull me away from my wife because I've never looked sideways at another woman since I met Elena. But something in my gut tells me Autumn would've been the one to get me to look. I hate that feeling. I'm not the sort of man who does those things to his family. Maybe this is part of the reason why I couldn't stand being around Autumn when I first met her.

"And now you can't stand to be away from her," I say to my reflection.

I get out of the SUV, make my way to the elevator and take it to the lobby, where I exit and walk toward Noah's place. Autumn will be there, and I want to see her. I'm past the point of caring whether people think I'm doing something wrong because I'm not divorced yet. Elena doesn't seem to care, so why should I?

My thoughts cause me to stop. People behind me bump into me, muttering obscenities because they're in a rush to get somewhere, and I've made them detour. That's probably the first lesson I learned when I moved here; if you need to stop, move over to the side so people can continue with their journey.

"What am I doing?" I ask aloud.

"Blocking the sidewalk," someone says as they pass by.

I ignore them and look in the direction of Noah's building and then back to mine. I feel like I'm at a fork in the road. If I go right, my future could be waiting for me there, and if I go left—well, all I see is darkness. Why can't I see the other path? Why do I only see darkness? Most importantly, why am I overthinking everything?

"Fuck it." I continue toward Noah's. I deserve to be happy, and if it's Autumn or someone else down the road who will make me happy, then so be it. I can't live in the past or let Elena's decisions to break up our family mess with my life any longer.

The doorman holds the door for me. I check-in at the front desk, thankful Noah has me on his approved guest list. I'm given a passcode for the elevator and sent on my way. I think about texting Autumn to let her know I'm almost there but decide I want to see her face when I walk in.

I knock once and then open the door to Noah and Peyton's apartment. The scene is somewhat lively. A few of my teammates are here, and Noah's parents and little sister. I scan the room for Autumn and find her on the balcony with Quinn, Noah's best friend. I wait for a spark of jealously to hit me, but it doesn't. When Elena and I would come to one of Noah's get-togethers, Elena would attach herself to Liam, Harrison, and Quinn. Even Elle if she came. I should've seen the writing on the wall then. After I grab a drink, I head out there to say hi.

"Hey, man, good game." Quinn and I shake hands and hug, and then I place my hand on Autumn's hip and lean in to kiss her cheek. "Hi," I whisper. I feel her cheek rise and assume she's smiling.

"No gigs this weekend?" I ask after greeting Autumn.

He shakes his head. "Nah. Soon though. We just finished recording an album. The producers need to do their thing, and then it'll be released."

"How's Nola?"

"She's good. She's working and planning a wedding."

"Yours?" I ask, laughing.

Quinn laughs as well and nods.

"Congratulations," Autumn says. "Do you have a date?"

"Not yet. We gotta figure out the tour dates. We'll get married in South Carolina. Her mother wants a spring wedding. Nola wants a fall one. I'm trying not to get in the way of planning."

"You don't want to have a say?" Autumn asks.

"It's not that," Quinn says. "Nola and I are on the same page; we agree on what we want. It's the timing. She wants to graduate from college, and I respect that. And we also have to make sure I'm not on tour because I want to take her on a honeymoon. I don't want her to feel like my career is in the way of having a traditional wedding. The spring to fall thing is a weather thing. We don't want to do it when it's too hot or during storm season."

"Autumn knows all about the weather," I say as I elbow her gently. She smiles, but it doesn't reach her eyes. I don't know what I said wrong, but clearly something. The three of us continue to talk until Autumn steps away to answer her phone, and Quinn excuses himself, leaving me feeling a bit awkward. I try not to watch Autumn as she looks at her phone, but I can't take my eyes off of her. She seems upset or maybe even sad. Autumn pockets her phone and continues to stare out into the darkness. I wait a long moment before walking over to her.

"Everything okay?" I ask.

She startles and looks at me. "Yes, things are good." Autumn rises onto her toes and kisses me quickly, and then she shies away. "Sorry, I probably shouldn't have done that."

"Why?"

Autumn looks toward the sliding glass door and then back at me. "I don't know," she says as she shrugs. "I feel like you wouldn't want your teammates seeing us like that."

She's right, but probably not for the reasons she's thinking. My teammates are a bunch of adolescent men who like to tease and say stupid shit. "Don't worry about them." I pull her long braid forward just so I can touch her hair. "Roxy wants to grow her hair long so she can do this to her hair."

"I can do it now to her hair. It's very easy."

"She'd like that."

"Do you want to get out here?" she asks. "Go to my place for a bit?"

TWENTY-FIVE

AUTUMN

Julius and I walk back to our complex. I have my arm wrapped around his, and my head rests on his shoulder whenever we have to stop at the crosswalk. It's then that he kisses my forehead or rests his head on top of mine. These moments are sweet and tender but a prelude to what's coming or at least what I hope will happen when we get back to my place. I'm past ready to take the next step with Julius. I don't mind the kissing part of our relationship. In fact, I love it. But I want to feel his strong hands on my body, tugging and pulling at my heated flesh. When he pulled me onto his lap earlier, I thought I was going to lose my mind. I was ready to become the locker room cliché.

When we arrive at our apartment building, I let go of him. Everyone inside knows who he is, and I don't want rumors to start. Only, Julius isn't having any of it and pulls me to his side and places his arm around my shoulder. I like this show of affection, out in public, where people are watching. It's odd because I've never been the type to flaunt anything, mostly due to my job, but right now, I want his arm around me. I want people to know he's getting into the elevator with me. I want them to assume. I want people to see how lucky I am because I do feel blessed.

Inside the elevator, Julius presses the button for my floor. As much as I'd love to go to his place, I suspect that his children are home, and I don't want him to feel awkward. I know I want more privacy than what his place can offer right now. The bell chimes, signaling we've arrived on the fifth floor. My heartbeat picks up the pace and starts thumping harder. Julius takes my hand in his and steps out of the elevator. I fall in step behind him as he walks us toward my place. When he reaches my door, for a moment, I wish he had a key and could let us in. Instead, I have to let go of his hand to pull my key out of my pocket. I step in front of Julius and start to slide the key into the lock. His hands are on my hips. He's so close I can feel his breath on my neck.

"I've never seen a woman carry only one key on her keyring," he quietly says as one hand glides from my hip to my stomach and the other rests on the waistband of my jeans.

"I didn't want to take my purse to Peyton's, so I took my house key off the ring." My words come out in a stutter, likely caused by the uptick in anticipation of what could happen once I open the door. The lock clicks, and all that's left is for me to push the lever down and open the door. I don't know why I pause. It could be to catch my breath, to steady myself, or maybe my subconscious needs a moment to reflect where I'm at right now. Behind me, one of the most handsome men I've ever met wants to take me into my apartment and do God knows what with my body, and I want that. One thousand percent, I want to be with Julius Cunningham.

Julius decides for us and pushes my door open. He guides us into the room and shuts the door once we're clear. It's dark in here, with only the lights from the riverwalk illuminating some of the space. I find it peaceful and can only imagine what the view from Julius's apartment looks like from the top floor. My view must pale in comparison to his.

"Would you like something to drink?" I ask as I step away. I unzip my jacket and take it off. For some reason, I'm afraid to look at him. Fearful he might see how desperately I want to be with him.

"No," he says, breaking the silence in the room. "The only thing I want is you, Autumn." He turns me toward him, and a small gasp escapes as Julius's hand cups my cheek. He looks into my eyes and then rests his forehead against mine. I think we're both nervous and excited right now. Our breathing increases. Our chests are rising and falling together. My hand trails up his arm until I get to his neck, and then my fingers are in his hair, pulling him closer to me.

Finally, our lips touch, and it's like the first time all over again. Julius's arm wraps around my waist, hugging me to his chest. My breath catches in anticipation of what is to come. My mouth opens slightly, beckoning him. Julius's tongue touches mine, and it's like we are back in the locker room. My hand goes to his shirt and tugs the hem. Julius steps back, and the loss I feel from not touching him is heartbreaking. Even though he's standing in front of me, looking at me with his lustful eyes, I want to touch him. He watches me watch him, as he pulls the collar of his shirt. In one fell swoop, his bare chest is before me, and all I can do is swallow. My fingers itch to trace the lines of his pecs. My tongue darts out, wetting my lips when I see his happy trail. The waistband of his briefs shows slightly above his jeans, and it's like a prelude to what's hidden behind the denim he's wearing.

I step forward with thoughts of kissing every inch of his chest, but then decide if he's taking off his shirt, I might as well remove mine. My arms cross in front of my chest, and I grip the ends of my top, pulling until it's off and laying on the floor. I keep staring at it while I work the clasp of my bra, only to have Julius stop me.

"You're unwrapping my gift without me," he says as his fingers undo the back of my bra.

His words make my knees weak. He sees me as a gift. I glance at him and start to pull my arms away. He stares intently and tosses my bra onto the growing pile of our mingled clothing. Without another thought, we're kissing, and his hands are on my body, cupping my breasts. I push into him, needing the friction of our bodies touching.

Before I can register what is happening, he's popped the button on my jeans and has them around my ankles. I help kick them off and relish in the way his mouth feels as he kisses and nips at my skin. I giggle as he picks me up, which makes him smile. I wrap my legs around his waist, and he carries me to the couch. I fully expect him to lay me down, but he doesn't. He sits and leans back. It's like he knows what I want. His fingers dig into my flesh, guiding me closer to where the bulge of his pants is. Julius sits up, cups my breast, and sets his mouth over my nipple. My head falls back, and in an instant, I'm grinding against him, moaning like a woman who hasn't been touched in years.

His mouth is magical. And so are his fingers. He sucks and licks while his fingers twist and pull. Each action from him causes me to buck wildly against him. I haven't had this much desire build within me in years. The need for him to be inside of me is urgent, but he doesn't seem to want to move any faster. So I decide to take matters into my own hands. I reach between our bodies and start working the button on his jeans. As soon as the zipper is free, the bulge turns into a full-blown erection. I have no choice but to lean into him, to give me the angle I need to touch him. My hand slides into his boxers, and he smiles against my skin.

"So eager," he says.

"So horny," I retort. "I've wanted you from the first time I saw you."

"Me too." Julius does everything he can to get his jeans off without me having to take my hand away from his shaft. I stroke, he fumbles, and then makes up for it by rubbing me between my legs.

"Oh . . ." I start to moan, but he stops what he's doing. I look at him, wondering what happened.

He shakes his head slightly. "I want to feel you," he tells me. I think I understand what he's saying but am somewhat confused. Do I move? Do I stay? My hand is still pumping his shaft, and while I think I should stop, I don't.

Julius reaches for his jeans, and the movement is awkward. I'm still on his lap, with his erect cock in my hand. I start to move away.

"Don't move."

"Okay." It's then that I realize he's getting a condom. Julius is back in his earlier position, looking at me. I move my hand, and he slides the rubber over his erection. I stand and shimmy out of my panties, waiting for him.

He beckons me to come toward him. "I want to watch you," he tells me as he helps guide me onto his lap. I grip him, not afraid to show him that I can take control. I don't care if he's some big-time football player. I know how to satisfy myself.

And that's precisely what I do.

JULIUS and I lay on our sides. Our legs are intertwined, and his arms are wrapped around me. Visions of what took place on my couch replay in my mind. The firm grip he had on my hips, moving me up and down on his erection. His eyes closing, and the way he moaned and called out my name. Julius, angling his body just right to help give me the relief my body craved. The way he took control and flipped me onto my back and pounded into me because he could no longer wait to make me his. Us, looking deep into each other's eyes while our bodies did what comes naturally.

I think that is what I'll remember most about this moment. The two of us, lying on our sides, with my leg hitched over his hip. We were effortless, fitting together like our bodies had been designed for each other. Julius moved slowly, never taking his eyes off mine. He read me, knew exactly what I needed, and delivered. I have never had a more intense orgasm than I did with him in that moment.

"What are you thinking about?" he asks.

"Nothing and everything," I tell him.

"Same. I can't believe this happened."

"What do you mean?"

He adjusts and pulls me a little closer. He's starting to harden again, and my lady bits begin to cheer. "We started off so rocky. I never would've imagined us being like this. You're so beautiful and smart, and I treated you so poorly."

"I like to find the good in people," I tell him. "I wanted to hate you, but I couldn't. The universe put us in each other's path for a reason."

He flexes his hips toward mine. "Is this the reason?" he asks, and I laugh.

"I don't know about that. But I do enjoy that particular reason."

"Can I ask you a weird question?"

I nod.

He thinks for a moment and then finally asks. "Are you adventurous when it comes to sex?"

"Why do you want to tie me up?"

Julius smiles. "Not necessarily, but I'd like to know the rules, so to speak."

I look at him questioningly.

"Like, if you're in the kitchen, are you game for a quickie? Do you like sex in the shower? In the car? Or are you a 'we have to plan to have sex' type person?"

"No, I don't think we have to plan. If the mood is right, it's right. As far as the car—I haven't done that since high school."

His eyes go wide, and then he grins widely. "Naughty, Weather Girl."

"You know, I used to hate it when you called me that. I thought it was disparaging and rude, but now when you say it . . . well," I move closer, put my leg over his hip, grab his growing erection and rub it against me. "I really, really like it."

TWENTY-SIX

JULIUS

It's Tuesday, and I'm sitting in this tiny waiting room while waiting for my first therapy appointment. My phone rests in my hand, and the screen shows messages from Autumn, Elena, and a slew of other people. The only people I've spoken to in the last twenty-four hours have been my parents, my children, and a few of my teammates. I don't know what I'm doing or what's going on in my head, except I'm beyond confused about life right now.

The door opens, and a woman, no taller than five feet, smiles warmly at me and asks me to follow her. I stand, unfolding myself from the crouched position I put myself in, and follow her. If she's intimidated by my size, she doesn't show it. The door shuts behind me with a loud click that causes me to jump. In reality, it probably isn't as bad as my mind is making it out to be.

"Have a seat," she says, pointing to the blue sofa resting against the wall. I do as instructed and immediately look out the large window. The view isn't much. We are three stories up and surrounded by old buildings that have been converted into office space.

"I'm Dr. Eileen O'Donnell. It's nice to meet you, Julius. You can call me Eileen."

"You as well," I say. "Thank you for seeing me on short notice." This morning, I woke up and went right to a lawyer my agent knows to take care of the paperwork needed to file for divorce. My agent's office had done most of the work but needed someone local to look things over. According to my agent and this lawyer, Scott, everything seems cut and dry, as I expected. I signed the papers, and they assured me Elena would be served by the end of the day. I should've felt relief, but a sense of longing, sadness, and anger washed over me. How did my life and marriage come to this? A five-sheet packet of paper detailing our prenup agreement, her transgression, and the terms of what I want for custody.

"I've known Scott Perrigo for a long time. He said it was important that we talk. I'm here to help," Eileen says. "Why don't you start talking about how you're feeling, and we'll go from there."

"I'm not sure what to say."

She looks down at a piece of paper, and I wonder what Scott told her or what my agent told Scott. Eileen glances up and says, "Filing for divorce can be a hard thing to process, especially when you're not ready."

"I'm ready." As soon as I say the words, my chest seizes. I shake my head slightly, angry with myself. I *am* ready, so why does it feel like I'm making a mistake?

"I understand that you have two children?"

"Yes, my son, Reggie, he's eight, and my daughter Roxy is three."

"And how are they doing with their mother being gone?"

"Reggie struggles. He misses her and is angry. As much as I try to block social media on his phone, his classmates share what they hear from their parents, so he knows his mom has a boyfriend. He feels like she's chosen her boyfriend over him."

"And what do you think?"

"I think he's right. I believe my wife," I pause at the sourness that comes from calling Elena, my wife. "My soon to be ex-wife is absent from the children's lives. She's trying to find her big break into acting and uses it as an excuse to stay away. But, when Reggie asks, I tell him his mom is working. He doesn't buy it though. He's smart. He knows what's going on."

"Probably a lot to take on for an eight-year-old."

"It is," I agree.

"And your daughter?"

"Still just a baby," I say. "She doesn't really talk about her mom a whole lot. Roxy will talk to Elena when she calls, but even the calls are sporadic. At first, I made it a point for the kids to call their mother each night before bed, but Elena wouldn't always answer, and I found that to be extremely hurtful to them, so I stopped forcing it."

Dr. O'Donnell writes something down and then sets her pen down. "What about you, Julius?"

I smirk. *What about me?* I shrug. "I never thought my wife would cheat on me, and I definitely never thought I'd file for divorce. I guess I thought I'd beat the odds and have a long marriage like my parents. I know Elena isn't the only one to blame, but I'm putting all the blame on her. She signed up for this NFL wife reality show. It was a hit, but suddenly, we had drama, and we were fighting. We hadn't fought before. We spent the season here and then the off-season in Los Angeles. I thought we were a strong couple. Then, these cameras start following us around, and producers are saying shit, causing issues. I tried to make her see this, but she felt I was overreacting, and accused me of stifling her passion for acting. Which only started after the reality show. When it was time to return to Portland, she told me she had a part in a movie and I should take the kids with me. I didn't balk because I'm trying to support her career and whatnot. Turns out, she had started dating someone behind my back—a guy she met on the set. I thought the images I saw on social media were from the movie set. When I confronted her about it, she asked for a divorce. I reminded her that our prenup has an adultery clause, meaning she doesn't get a cent of alimony if she cheats. At first, she denied it, but when I went to talk to her, her boyfriend showed up and all but confirmed they are in a relationship."

"Have you ever cheated on your wife?"

The question angers me. Is she assuming because I'm a professional athlete that I've cheated because others have? I start to shake my head but quickly stop myself. "I feel like I have," I tell her.

"Care to elaborate?"

Not really. "I met a woman. We've spent time together, and I've introduced her to the kids."

"Has Elena's boyfriend met the children?"

I look out the window. It's raining, and the only thing I can see outside is cars and an array of different colors moving down the sidewalk. If you find yourself caught in the rain in Portland, there is no one to blame but yourself. It's guaranteed to rain. You might as well carry an umbrella with you. Or start watching the weather reports, as I have.

"He hasn't, and I never intended for the woman I'm seeing to meet them as well. It just happened."

"Let's go back to why you feel like you're cheating."

I sigh and rub the front of my jeans, and then readjust

the way I'm sitting. "I feel like just because Elena asked for a divorce doesn't mean we are divorced or separated. I don't know. I'm having a hard time wrapping my brain around it."

"How did you start seeing this new woman?"

"We have the same friends, and she won me in a charity auction. Since the night I met her, I've been attracted to her —which also happened to be the day I returned from seeing Elena and met her boyfriend. I was angry at my wife, the world, everything. Then this beautiful, drop-dead gorgeous woman walks in, and instantly I wanted to know her. I wanted to be with her." I look down at my lap and brush some imaginary lint away. "I can't help but wonder if I would've cheated on my wife with this woman. Thinking like that makes me sick to my stomach. I tried to stay away from her. Found every excuse I could. I accused her of using my friends to get places in her career, but none of it mattered because the first moment we were alone, I kissed her."

"And that makes you feel like you cheated?"

I shake my head. "The other night, we slept together, and ever since, I have felt like I've disrespected my marriage. I hadn't even filed for divorce yet and already slept with another woman. I can't wrap my head around how this makes me any different from Elena."

"Unfortunately, I'm not the person to tell you that your feelings should be different. You're the only one who can. Everyone is going to have a different opinion. Some will say you're separated. Others will say you're not. It's not something anyone can decide except for you. Does the woman you're with feel the same way?"

Once again, I look out the window. The rain hasn't stopped, and according to Autumn, it's going to rain all day or at least drizzle, tapering off in the evening, only to pick up again overnight. I watched her broadcast last night because I needed to see her but I am too much of a coward to knock on her door and face the music.

"I don't know how she feels. I don't want to tarnish the night we had together. It seems mean to go to her and say I feel like I'm cheating on my wife, especially since we've been dating and whatnot. Are you suggesting I step back from her?"

"No, I'm not suggesting anything. We just met, and we're establishing a baseline. I think you have a lot to work through, starting with your feelings. I've gathered you feel like you're cheating, but also feel like you would've done so once you met this new woman. Am I correct?"

I nod because she's right, and I hate myself for it. "Autumn is her name," I tell Eileen. "She's amazing, and I've never been so attracted to someone that all I do is think about them. With Elena—we had been caught up in a tornado, and our relationship went from there. With Autumn—we locked eyes, and I knew right off that she was dangerous. Which again, is so incredibly stupid because she's harmless." I stand and start to pace around the room. There are bookshelves along the wall, each shelf filled with books, photos, and knickknacks. On the next wall over, it's painted dark blue, while the rest of the room is a cream color. But hanging on this wall are the diplomas Eileen has received. Her bachelors, masters, and her Ph.D. are all encased in ornate frames.

Eileen stays in her chair, with the pad of paper resting on her knee. Each time I look at her, she's watching me, observing my every move. What does she see? Does she see me as a football player or some messed-up dad and husband needing advice? Or something else?

"You've convinced yourself that you would've acted on

your attraction with Autumn. Do you know if she would've reciprocated once she found out you were married?"

I'm on the other side of the room now, looking at the inspirational posters hanging on the wall. "No, she would not have done anything. When she found out I had kids, she asked right off if I was married. Plus, my situation is easy enough to look up online, or she could've asked our mutual friend. Autumn has a lot to risk by getting involved with a married man—and I don't think she would've taken the gamble."

I finally make it back to the sofa and sit down. "How do I get past what I'm feeling?"

"Only you can answer that, Julius. I can't tell you how to feel."

"Am I wrong to feel this way?"

Eileen sets her tablet on the coffee table and then folds her hands in her lap. "Your wife asked for a divorce. You didn't go to counseling or try to work things out. To you, the marriage was over. You moved on, which you're allowed to do. Whether you date one person or many, sleep with one or all, it's your business. You answer to you at the end of the night. If you feel like you're in the wrong, stop and take a step back. Do you want to know what I think?"

I chuckle. "That's why I'm here, right?"

Eileen smiles. "Yes, in a nutshell." She leans forward, resting her elbows on her knees. "I think you look at Autumn and are afraid she's going to be like Elena. In the back of your mind, she's going to cheat if you get too serious and you've put a mental block up to protect yourself. You don't want to get hurt."

"No, I don't."

"Tell me, have you cried since all of this happened with Elena?"

I shake my head.

"I have an assignment for you. I want you to go home, stand in front of the mirror and talk about how you feel...and I want you to cry. Just let it out. Crying is good for the soul. It helps us heal."

"*Cry?*" I question.

"Yes, I want you to at least try. And I want you to talk to Autumn, let her know what you're going through. It's important to be upfront with her or anyone else you're involved with."

"Yeah, I should probably call her. I've been avoiding her since we slept together. I know she's worried."

Eileen stands and ushers me to the door. "Communication is key, Julius. I'll see you next week."

"Thanks, Eileen." I step out into the waiting room and then out into the hall. I pull my phone out of my pocket and text Autumn. **I hope you forgive me for being absent these past two days. I had some things to deal with.** I send the text and put my phone away without waiting for a response. If I were her, I wouldn't respond.

AUTUMN

I feel stupid for sleeping with Julius. For letting my physical attraction take over. I should've listened to my mind and heart because deep down, I knew neither of us was ready. It's one thing to have a one-night stand, but it's entirely another thing to *think* you have a connection with someone, do the deed, only to have them ghost you. This is exactly what Julius has done. He's playing the part of Casper like a Hollywood A-Lister, and I'm just along for the ride.

I pick up my phone and look at the text from Camden. When I received it the other night, I thought my eyes were deceiving me. **Weather channel has an opening. I gave your name to my boss. Send resume ASAP! The job is all but yours!!!!** I don't want to believe this can be real. There is no way the job of my absolute dreams is dangling in front of me. It's been my goal from the start to make it to the national level, to be in front of millions of people, broadcasting worldwide. I'm young, I'm not tied down to anything, and this job would be a dream come true.

My phone rings, startling me. Camden's face fills the

screen. It's a picture I took at graduation, the last day I saw him. We went our separate ways that day and had long since broken up .but remained close. We both knew he wouldn't be able to commit to a relationship with how much traveling his job required. At first, it hurt. When we started dating, I thought we'd be in it for the long haul. But even when I saw the signs that he wasn't, I stayed, which was dumb on my part.

"Hey," I say after I press the accept button and turn on the speakerphone. I'm in my dressing room, with the door closed, and don't expect any interruptions.

"Hey yourself," he says. "How's Portland?"

"I love it." Although, after Julius left the other night, not so much. I don't know why I expected him to spend the night, but I did. I wanted to move from the couch to my bedroom and make love to him again. But when I asked him to come to bed, he told me he had to leave. "Why do I sense hesitation in your voice?"

I glance up and look at my reflection. There are bags under my eyes, something I will have to hide with a copious amount of concealer and foundation. These are from a lack of sleep and energy. I didn't run yesterday or today because my mind is hosting its own marathon, and I couldn't drag my sorry ass out of bed.

"You don't," I tell Camden. "Just surprised to hear your voice."

"Well, when you didn't text me back right away, I started to worry. Then, before too much panic set in, I figured you were busy and had an erratic schedule being the new person on set. However, it's been a few days, and I'm starting to worry. Is everything okay?"

I close my eyes and drop my head toward my chest. Camden has always been preceptive, except when it came to our relationship. He always knew when something bothered me but had the hardest time figuring out why we were breaking up when we meshed so well.

"Everything is good. I was at a cocktail party when your text came in, and honestly, I just forgot to respond when I got home that night."

"Party with the bigwigs?" he asks with a hint of humor in his voice.

"Peyton Westbury," I tell him. "We've grown close since I moved here, and she and her husband have me over often."

"See, I knew Portland would be good for you. How's the rain?"

I look around my walled-in dressing room, wishing I could see the outside. "It's been raining for days, but I honestly don't mind it. It's better than snow."

"And what's Portland like?"

"The fall has been beautiful. When I arrived, everything was still in bloom. My apartment is right on the waterfront, and there's a paved path for people to use—lots of green space, food vendors, and a ton of artists. Portland has a great vibe. I stay close to my apartment. I've walked to work a few times, but like with any city, there needs to be a massive clean-up."

"So, about this job?"

"Yeah, what can you tell me about it?" While this would be my dream job, when I received his text message the other night, I wasn't interested because I let my feelings for Julius cloud my judgement, but now . . . Now, I feel like I need to do what's best for my career and ignore my heart. It was a mistake getting involved with a recently separated man. Camden goes on to tell me about the job. The most enticing part is I'd be working with him. We'd travel to most of the locations together, setting up on opposite sides of the cities we're in to give viewers a broad scope of whatever weather phenomenon is happening. The only thing he can't tell me is what I'd be paid, which I knew. Camden would not know that.

"What do you think?"

"I think," I say, then pause to inhale. "It's exactly what I've dreamed of."

"Yes!" I imagine Camden doing some sort of fist bump when he says this. His enthusiasm makes me smile.

"I'll send my resume over in a few minutes. Thank you, Cam."

"Of course. When I saw the posting, I told my boss that I knew the right person for the job. I swear, it's yours if you want it."

"I do want it, although I hate to leave here. Leon has been so amazing to me, but I also don't want to pass up the opportunity."

"I know what you mean," Camden says. "But I think Leon would understand if you took a national job. These don't come along too often."

I agree with him, and after a few more minutes of chatter, we hang up. I chance another look in the mirror and notice there's some life to my face. My cheeks are pinker, and my eyes seem brighter. The bags are still beacons though, reminding me why I feel the way I do.

After hanging up with Camden, I send my resume off without any hesitation. I'd hate to leave Leon after everything he's done for me, but Cam is right—a job like this doesn't come along very often, and I need to seize the opportunity presented. Being a national weather correspondent is what I want. I want to be where the storms are, standing in the parking lot while a category four pushes toward the mainland.

I head over to Lisette's office and ask her to come to my dressing room, telling her I need some assistance with my make-up. She comes over and tells me to sit, and starts working on my face.

"I've never seen you like this. Are you ill?"

With a broken heart, yes. "I haven't slept well the past few nights."

"Drink some tea before you go to bed and take a long hot bath. The hours you keep aren't always good for your body and definitely not for the soul. Leon keeps all of you so busy with appearances, fundraisers, and charity events. He needs to cool his jets on the marketing."

Oh, how I wish I could tell her my extra job duties didn't bother me and that I allowed my heart to get involved with the wrong man. "I'll be fine tomorrow," I tell her as she works on my face.

Lisette has me look in the mirror. She covered my bags flawlessly, and I look like a whole new person. Too bad, I don't feel that way. "The ratings for last week are in," she says as she stands behind me, playing with my hair. "We have more viewership in the eleven o'clock hour than we've had in years. It's because of you."

"I doubt that. The team is good. We work well together."

She isn't buying it, though, and frowns. "Know your value, Autumn. Once you start accepting your worth, you'll go far in this world." Lisette leaves me with those words lingering in the air. Does she know about the job at the Weather Channel? It wouldn't surprise me if she did.

I finally make my way into the computer room where I start putting my segment together. I've printed all the reports for the weather, not only tonight but also for next week, and piece them all together with my production manager.

"Nothing but rain," he says with a sigh.

"You live in the Pacific Northwest," I remind him. "Do you expect anything different?"

He chuckles. "Good point."

I do point out that the rain will subside by the weekend and that we'll have a small heatwave before the weather turns dreary for the remainder of fall and into winter. He, too, echoes my sentiments on how rain is better than snow, and as long as it doesn't get too cold, he'll be happy.

Leon comes into the room cheerful and with a beaming smile. "Listen up," he shouts to get everyone's attention. "This evening, we are trying something new. We will be live for the viewers." He says this as if we aren't live every night. No one responds, and the only sound in the room is the hum of the computers.

He must find this funny because he starts laughing. "Oh, I forgot. We'll be live on social media. I don't know what I was thinking." He continues to chuckle at his blunder. "We are going to give the viewers a chance to chime in and ask questions or make statements. During the segment, each anchor will read comments to the television viewers and answer questions."

"Seems like you're setting us up to fail," Selene says from behind her computer. I happen to agree with her. I've seen some of the comments posted on social media. I'd hate to read them aloud.

"Nah," Leon says as he waves her statement away. "Read what you want. Use sound judgment. Obviously, if someone has an issue, we don't need to repeat it. One of the producers will try to filter out anything rude, suggestive, or inflammatory.

What we are trying to do here is reach viewers on another level. Most people have chosen to get rid of cable and basic television packages, but we need to deliver our segments to them as people who bring the news. If this doesn't work, we'll stop it, but for right now, this is how we will do things moving forward. You'll share an iPad on set, you'll laugh right along with everyone else, and you'll do it with a smile." Leon exits, and the rest of us look around, wondering what the hell just happened.

"That man has lost his mind," Selene says a few seconds after the door shuts.

Others agree, but I keep my thoughts to myself. It's not a bad idea, but one that should probably have a bit more insight before it's thrust out into the wild. After I finish putting my segment together, I head back to my dressing room to change. My phone vibrates in my hand with an incoming text. My heart drops to the floor and stays there for a long moment before bouncing back into place. How can one person make me feel this way? I hold my breath as I slide my finger across the screen to open his message.

Julius Cunningham: **I hope you forgive me for being absent these past two days. I had some things to deal with.**

Really? He's been ignoring my calls and texts but wants forgiveness? Nah, I can't. I won't. I deserve someone who is going to give me the courtesy of communication and worry about my feelings along with his own. I close the app and go about my business. He can wait two days for my response.

TWENTY-EIGHT

JULIUS

Roxy pats her bed. The sight of her doing so gives me pause. She looks so tiny in her big girl bed, yet I can see her growing like a wildflower in front of my eyes. I take the spot next to her, cross my ankles and wait for her to snuggle into my side. The book we are reading tonight, *Rugby and Rosie*, was a favorite of mine growing up. The pages are old, tattered, and the tape my mom added to fix a ripped page has yellowed with age. I start reading the story about two dogs, both Labradors. One is older. The other is a puppy. To some, the story is sad because a family brings a puppy home, but it's only there to learn how to be a guide dog. I find the story heartwarming and genuine.

By the time I finish reading, Roxy is asleep on my chest with her mouth open and likely drooling. I stay there for a moment, relishing in her warmth and the love she has for me. I can't imagine not seeing her every day and don't understand how Elena can stay away from her children. It doesn't make sense. I'm a wreck when I'm gone for an away game, checking in as often as I can, using every piece of modern technology offered so that I don't miss anything with my kids. Yet, their mother doesn't call every day or get on video chat. Days will go by until she reaches out or calls them back, and yet she expects me to hand them over to her. There is no way in hell I'm going to allow my kids to live anywhere but my home. I don't know what I have to do to make this happen, but I'll do it.

I slide out from under Roxy and place her teddy bear under her arm where I was. I'm shocked when she doesn't wake up but also thankful. Sometime in the wee hours of the morning, she'll climb into my bed and suction cup herself to my side. I'm not sure I'll ever get used to her sleeping with me, but at this point, her comfort is far more important than my own.

Out in the living room, I sit down on the couch and flip the channels until I decide to leave the television on ESPN. I have hours until the news comes on again, having missed Autumn's earlier segment. She doesn't want to talk to me. I've gathered this much by her lack of response to my text message earlier. I deserve the cold shoulder, the silence she's giving me. I haven't handled myself very well since we slept together, and I know my actions make it seem like I used her. I didn't, but I'm not sure how to convey this to her.

My phone vibrates, and my heart skips a beat, thinking it might be Autumn. With a quick glance, I see that it's Noah. **I'm at your door. Let me in.**

"Hey," I say as I open the door. "What are you doing here?"

Noah holds up a six-pack of beer and two bags, which smell like grease. "Peyton is at her group meeting tonight, and I thought I'd come to hang." He walks in and heads right to the kitchen. I follow and place my hand over my stomach as it growls. Noah laughs.

"I gotta say, this is a surprise, but I'm damn thankful you brought Killer Burger."

"The only thing that sucks about take-out is we don't get bottomless fries."

"I don't care at this point." Noah pushes the bag toward me while he twists the caps off two beers and I rip the bag of fries open, stuffing one in my mouth. The only thing missing is a chocolate shake. Noah takes the seat next to me, opens the other bag, and hands me my burger.

"What do I owe you?"

"Nothing," he says.

I nod and take a few bites before setting it down. "So, why are you really here?"

Noah says nothing until he's swallowed his food. "No reason. I went out for a burger, saw your building, and thought, what the hell? It's been a while since we've done this."

"And that's it?" I'm certain Autumn told Peyton something.

"Yep," he says. "Just came to chill and to see how you're doing and to see how things went today."

I need some liquid courage to get through the drama of the day. Noah is probably the only person I'd ever confide in about anything personal because I know he won't say anything to anyone, aside from Peyton. He's told me from day one he'll never keep a secret from her. I admire that about him. Truthfully, I want what he and Peyton have. They're so aware of each other. Anytime you're in a room with them, you can sense their connection. Noah always knows where his wife is and is by her side if he feels she needs something. Elena and I were never in tune with each other like that.

"Well, I filed. Elena will get the papers tomorrow. I'd

like to think she'll sign and send it back, but I know her. This is going to set off a shit storm. I asked for full custody, with reasonable visitation. No alimony. She can keep the house in Los Angeles. And then after I filed, I went to therapy and talked about my feelings and how frustrated I am, and Autumn."

"Autumn, why? Are you guys serious?"

I shrug and take another drink. "I suppose we could be if I weren't an idiot. I sort of left her in limbo for a few days and didn't return any of her calls or texts."

Noah looks at me and shakes his head. "Peyton is going to whack you upside your head."

"I know, and I deserve it. Autumn is amazing, and I've probably lost her."

"You think so?"

My shoulder lifts again. "Would you pursue a relationship with a woman who isn't divorced and raising two kids, who can't be bothered to call you after you've slept . . ." I let my words trail off. I never intended to tell Noah about Autumn and I taking our relationship to the next level.

"Dude, you didn't?"

The up and down motion of my head is so slight, I'm not sure he notices until he gives me the most exaggerated eye-roll. "You ignored her calls."

"Let me grab you some salt to pour in my wounds," I say.

"Peyton isn't going to slap you. She's going to flat out beat your ass."

"Believe me, I'm doing a fine job of that on my own."

There's a noise in the hall, causing Noah and me to halt our conversation. Reggie walks into the kitchen, surprised to see Noah sitting there. "Oh, hey, Mr. Westbury," Reggie says as he pads toward us. As close as Noah and I are, I'm trying to teach my children to respect adults. Noah has told the kids they can call him by his first name, which I appreciate, but I have told the kids they can only do that on game day.

"What's up, Bud?"

"Nothing. I heard some talking, thought I'd come to investigate."

"Want some fries?" Noah pushes the bag toward Reggie, who happily takes a few.

"Do we have any ice cream?" my son asks. I shrug and tell him to look in the freezer. He does and pulls out a half-gallon of something. "Can I make a milkshake?"

"Of course. Do you want my help?"

Reggie shakes his head and proceeds to grab the things he needs. Noah nods toward him and says quietly, "How is he taking everything?"

Another lift of my shoulder. "Some days are really good. Others, not so much. He knows his mom is seeing someone, but he also knows I've been dating Autumn. He seems to like her, though. He's hard on Elena; calls her out on her bullshit. He tries to call his mom almost every day and maybe speaks to her every third day."

"I can't imagine. After I met my dad and he had to go back to L.A. for work, we talked every day, sometimes multiple times a day. I don't remember exactly how long it was, but I think he moved back to Beaumont within a month of meeting me. And now, I talk to him and my mom every day. I can't imagine not speaking to them, especially at Reggie's age."

"He talks to my parents more than he talks to his mother. I hate it." I see Reggie struggling with the ice cream and get up to help him. I don't take over but put my hand on his and help him scoop the rounds into the blender. I stand back while he measures the milk, and I tell him I think I'm going to make one after him.

"Mr. Westbury, do you want a milkshake?" Reggie asks.

"Yes, I think I do," he tells my son, who beams back at him. I take the scoop and carve out more rounds of ice cream and then head back to my seat. Reggie gives Noah the first shake and then goes back to make mine.

"This is really good, Reggie. Thank you," Noah says. "Is there a secret ingredient?"

"Miss Meghan adds a dash of vanilla."

A dash of vanilla? Who is this boy in my kitchen?

"Well, it's very good. I'm going to have to tell Miss Peyton to do the same next time."

Reggie brings my shake over. His smile is so bright he looks like he doesn't have a care in the world. I hate that this divorce shit has dimmed his light. He should be happy and carefree all the time.

After Reggie makes his milkshake, he puts the ice cream and milk away and then comes to sit down between Noah and me. Instantly, he takes a fry and dips it into his shake. "So good."

I take my son's lead, as does Noah. Before we know it, the large bag of fries is gone, as are the shakes, and the three of us are sitting back, rubbing our bellies. Reggie lets out a burp—one that rivals anything I could've done—and starts laughing as he covers his mouth. I look at him in horror, but Noah follows up with his own, impressive belch.

"What is wrong with the two of you?" I ask, acting completely horrified. I move away from my disgusting mates and start to clean up the mess, shaking my head as I go. I'm not mad at Reggie, although I am slightly taken back by his actions. He is usually very civilized. Noah, on the other hand, not so much. When Peyton isn't around, he's as crass as the next guy. Reggie apologizes and begins to help me clean up.

"I should get going," Noah says as he throws his wrapper away. "Peyton's group will be done shortly, and I want to be home when she returns."

"I meant to ask you earlier," I say as we walk toward the door. "I thought she finished up with the group before you guys got married?"

"She had, but sometimes she needs their support. She works to avoid triggers but saw some wreckage on the news the other day and had some trouble decompressing."

"Damn, trauma like that never goes away, does it?"

Noah shakes his head. "Nope, but at least she recognizes when she needs to talk to others and doesn't hold her feelings in. I'd rather her go to her group than bottle her emotions up."

"Makes sense."

Noah and I say goodbye, and I tell him I'll see him at the facility tomorrow for practice. I head to Reggie's room, knocking quietly on his door before opening it. I find him sitting on his bed with a smile on his face.

"I'm glad you came out to visit," I tell him as I go in and sit down next to him.

"I think we should have people over more often."

"I do too." I pull my son toward me and kiss the top of his head.

"When can Miss Autumn come over?" he asks.

I don't have the heart to tell him she and I haven't spoken in a few days. I don't want him to think she is like his mother, and I don't want him to be mad at me for my stupidity. "When she's not working, you're in school."

"Yeah, that sucks. Career day is coming up. Maybe I can invite her."

"What about me?" I ask.

Reggie looks at me and says, "Let's be real, Dad. The likelihood of going to the NFL is slim. Miss Autumn's job is more realistic."

"When did you become so smart?"

He shrugs. "I have a pretty great Dad to teach me things."

I pull him forward again and kiss him. "Thanks, bud. And thanks for the milkshakes. We definitely needed those tonight."

Reggie tells me he's going to read for a little bit before he goes to bed. I don't know how long I sit on the edge of his bed, but his asking about Autumn really put her at the fore-front of my mind.

"I'm going to go down to Autumn's apartment and leave her a note. I won't be gone for more than ten minutes. Think you can take care of things?" He doesn't have to do anything but be present if Roxy were to wake up. We have a state-of-the-art alarm system in place.

"Are you inviting her over?" he asks. His question makes me wonder if he thinks she'll spend the night or if he's trying to parent me and is subtly telling me it's too late.

"I am, but only for a bit. I don't want to leave you and your sister alone, so it's easier for her to come over when she gets off work."

"Okay. Let me know when you're back." And just like that, my son has become my parent for a few minutes while I run a quick errand. I have no idea if Autumn will come over when she gets home, but I'm hoping. I really want to talk to her face-to-face, and I want to do it tonight.

TWENTY-NINE

AUTUMN

I'm exhausted, emotionally and physically, by the time I reach my door. Since I went off the air and the entire drive back to my place, I ignored my phone. Julius texted, and at last count, I think there were five or maybe six notifications from him. Perhaps I'm being childish by not looking at them to see what he has to say, but my feelings are hurt, and I need a few more minutes and the comfort of my home before I read what he has to say. Deep down, I know there's an apology followed by the classic "we're better off as friends" line. The thing is, I knew better than to get involved. His demeanor when we first met should've been a clear sign that we aren't right for each other.

But he's so damn hot.

"Looks aren't everything," I mutter to myself as I walk toward my door. With my key poised, I pause and look at the folded piece of paper taped to my door. I don't know why, but I look up and down the hall, almost as if I'm going to catch the culprit who dared to leave whatever this is for me.

My heart races, and I have a slight issue swallowing. What if I have a stalker? I've seen some of the comments left on ChatGram. They're lewd and somewhat troubling. I've heard stories of stalkers finding out where people live and how presents start showing up at your place. Personal safety is one of the first things they teach us—never give out personal information. But with the internet the way it is, you can find just about anyone these days. This stupid piece of paper, which could be harmless, makes me wish I had a fake name, something I chose not to do because I like the puns that came along with Autumn being a weather anchor.

"Pull up your big girl panties, Autumn."

Except my pep talk does nothing for the lack of courage I feel right now. If this note is threatening, there are video cameras in the halls and by every entrance. For the most part, my building is very secure, and I can't imagine someone would risk coming in here to leave me a stupid note.

Slowly, as if the paper is going to bite me, I lift the edge and bend to read the words. "Can you . . ." is all I can make out until I lift it more. Inhaling deeply, I hold my breath and move the flap higher. "To my apartment when you get home. The code is 54845—Julius."

I exhale in a loud, obnoxious way. "I'm going to kill him," I say to the empty hallway. Why would he do this to me?

Because he wants to see you.

I open the door, close it behind me, and pull my phone out to read his messages. The first one is a lengthy, heartfelt apology, or at least it seems that way. The couple that follows is him asking me to call or text back, and the last is him saying he left a note on my door and not be afraid when I see it.

He knew how I'd feel.

I don't know why, but my heart swells with this knowledge. Julius is looking out for my well-being, despite everything. I don't change my clothes or text him back. He doesn't need to know I'm on my way up because I might change my mind halfway there. I also don't know what the hell I'm doing right now, except this amazing man, who I'm crazy for, wants to see me. Never mind that it's almost midnight, and he has children sleeping in his apartment who have school in the morning. He, himself, should be sleeping since I know he gets up with them and takes Reggie to school before going to practice. He shouldn't wait up for me. But he has because he wants to talk, and that says volumes to me. He meant his apology—I can feel this in my gut.

My nerves are on edge as I raise my hand to knock on his door. My knuckles never make it to the wood, though, because the door swings open, and I jump.

"Hey," Julius says with a smile that makes my knees weak, and I have to place my hand on the door jamb to keep myself upright. He reaches for me and puts his hand on my hip. "Sorry for scaring you."

He did scare me, but I feel like my heart needed a reset so I could see what's in front of me. Is Julius worth the headache he gave me the past few days? I think he might be.

"Come in." He opens the door wider and sweeps his arm out. At first glance, his apartment doesn't seem like it should be in this building. Gone are the basic off-white walls and the beige-colored carpet. Julius takes my hand and gives me a tour. His walls are rich with color. Blues and reds dominate the living area, while a soft yellow with hints of lavender makes his kitchen feel like sunshine and warmth. Down the hall, the walls are adorned with pictures of his family. From floor to ceiling, nothing but smiling faces, funny poses, and poignant moments.

"This wall is amazing."

"I wish I could take credit for it. Elena did it."

The mention of his wife, rather ex-wife, gives me pause. I don't know the rules for dating a married man that is going to file for divorce. *Is going to but hasn't.* What am I doing here? I shouldn't be with a man who can't decide on whether he wants a divorce or not, and I don't . . . no, I refuse to be the other woman. He has children he needs to think about.

I glance at Julius and smile softly. It's not forced, but it also doesn't come easy because I have a knot in my stomach the size of Texas. "You said you wanted to talk," I remind him.

"Let's go sit." With his hand on my back, he guides me into the living room. His sectional is massive and takes up most of the space. In my apartment, I'd have to put pieces in my bedroom, and there still wouldn't be enough room for it. The open portion of the sofa faces the large glass door and balcony. From Julius's apartment, you can see the skyline of the city. Red, blue and white lights from the tall buildings flash—a beacon to airplanes coming and going. Up here, it's peaceful. You can't hear the traffic down below or the voice that carries when people are out, walking back to their place after a night at the bar. On the wall is a large painting of Reggie and Roxy. They're hugging and have wide, toothless grins. On the other wall, extensive cabinetry, which I'm guessing houses a television. Everything about this living room screams comfort, and I can easily see myself curled up on the couch, reading a book to Roxy.

I shouldn't think thoughts like that though. It's not my

place, nor do I want the pain I felt yesterday to have a permanent spot in my heart. Roxy is another woman's child, and the man a few feet from me is her husband. It's best I remember my place.

Julius sits, and I make sure to put some space between us. My wall is up. I need to protect my heart when it comes to Julius. He clears his throat and looks at me. "I'm sorry for the lack of communication these past couple of days. Monday got away from me, between practice and the kids, and then I had a lot of stuff to deal with. I regret not answering your texts yesterday."

"Apology accepted," I tell him.

He moves closer to me, only for me to add distance between us. I hold my hand up and shake my head. "I like you, Julius. Lord knows I shouldn't, but I do. However, this has been eye-opening for me. I know you're busy, but I need a guy who will respond when I text or call, especially after we've been together for the first time. Not hearing from you was a gut punch. I've never been a one-night-stand type of person, and that's what you made me feel like."

"I'm terribly sorry, Autumn."

"I've given us, this thing between us, some thought, and I'm not sure there can be an us until you get divorced. I don't want to be in limbo, wondering where I stand in your life. I mean . . . you haven't even filed yet, and we've slept together. The situation is making me feel very uneasy."

"I understand," Julius says as he moves closer. He reaches for my hand and picks it up. Our fingers thread together, and while my head is saying pull back, my heart is like, get it, girl. Damn, I want to get it, but the risk isn't worth it.

"One of the reasons I didn't text you earlier today is

because I met with a lawyer here, who finalized my papers and sent them to a process server in California. I'm serving Elena with papers. We've dragged our feet long enough on this, and it's not helping either of us. She's moved on, and I want to move on. Being with you—it's shown me that I've been hanging on by a thread to a marriage that has been broken for a while. I didn't want to admit it until I met you."

Julius studies me while I let his words sink in. I believe I've heard everything he said, but what sticks out is that he's filed for divorce. I don't know why, but I feel like a tremendous amount of weight has been lifted off my shoulders with this revelation.

"How do you feel about the filing?" I ask him.

"After I filed, I went and saw a therapist. I had put this off for some time, but she could squeeze me in, so I took advantage." Julius shrugs. "We talked about Elena and everything that's happened since she told me she wanted a divorce. We talked about the kids and how they're coping, and we talked about you. It felt really good to talk to someone who doesn't know Elena or me and who just listens and asks questions. At first, I didn't think I'd be able to open up about everything, but after a few minutes, I let it all out. To answer your question, I feel relieved. It's hard to grasp that your marriage is over, but this therapist said I'm doing everything right, and I'm approaching the situation without blinders. I know I'm not the perfect man or husband, but I didn't deserve to be cheated on, and it's taken me a long time to accept that."

"No one deserves to be cheated on. I've never understood why people do that. Why not just tell the other person you don't want to be with them and move on."

"Because breakups are messy."

"So is cheating," I say. "I'm glad you told me that you

filed though, because I was starting to feel like what we were doing could be considered cheating."

"Me too." This time when Julius moves closer, I don't move back. "I really like you, Autumn, and after Sunday, the only thing that kept going through my mind was that I'm no better than Elena. I've dragged my feet on filing, but no more. This divorce needs to happen for many reasons."

"Well, I'm happy you did. I don't want to feel like we're doing something wrong. Do the kids know?"

Julius shakes his head. "There isn't much to tell them. Roxy is too little to understand, and Reggie understands too much. He knows his mom has a boyfriend, and he knows that I like you. Anything more will just hurt or confuse him. Besides, Elena is going to make a big stink about the filing. She'll play the victim and try to turn him against me because he's at an impressionable age. To combat this, I've already set him and Roxy up with some therapy appointments. We'll go as a family," he pauses and then corrects himself, "the three of us and the kids will have individual appointments. I want to make sure they're well-adjusted through all of this."

"You're a good dad, Julius."

"I'm trying. Those two are the most important people in my life, and I need to make sure they're happy."

A yawn takes me by surprise, forcing me to cover my mouth. "I should get home. It's late, and you have to be up with the kids." I stand, not giving him a chance to protest. I could easily fall asleep on the couch right now—that's how tired I am.

Julius follows me to the door. He opens it and leans against it. As I pass, he reaches for my hand and pulls me to him. The kiss is chaste, but the desire is there. "Thank you."

"For what?"

"For forgiving me. I don't deserve it. Hell, I don't deserve anything from you. I'm like night and day when it comes to you."

"Yeah, the back-and-forth game is a bit tiresome." I wink, letting him know I'm joking. Only, I'm not, really. As much as I'd love for this relationship to take off, I'm going to tread a little bit more carefully. For all I know what happened this week is a hiccup and may never happen again, or it's an omen and something I need to heed.

"Goodnight, Julius."

"Goodnight, Weather Girl."

THE REST of my week went like I was back in school with my nose stuck in a textbook. Do your assignment, flip the page, meet with your peers, do another project, flip the page, and so forth. Only the pages are text messages with Julius, my peers are my co-workers, and the main assignment I must do is to be at Julius's apartment on Sunday to watch the game with his parents and children. I couldn't even say no because Julius knows my weakness—Roxy. He made her ask, and with her sweet little voice and those doey eyes of hers, there was no way I'd tell her no. I, however, wanted to strangle her father because I'm not ready to spend the day with his parents. The kids, I can handle, but parents are a whole different story. They're the last chapter of the book—the review portion—before you take the final exam. Sure, I've seen them in the stands, but an introduction done by Reggie and Roxy, without Julius being home, is putting a bigger knot in my stomach than I had when Julius asked me to come to his apartment earlier in the week.

Now, I stand outside his door. I raise my hand to knock,

only to drop it and turn around, and then I go back and do it again, only for the same result. In my other hand, I have a seven-layer dip that I love but realize others may not enjoy it as much as me, and I should've brought something else. Although Julius told me to just bring myself and that his mother has everything taken care of. But my mind insisted I bring something.

"Flowers—that's what you should've brought." I look down at the dish in my hand and wonder if I have time to go back to my apartment to drop this off and then head to the nearest flower stand. There is one on almost every corner, especially near the waterfront. Surely, I can find a lovely bouquet on a Sunday afternoon.

"Are you going to come in?" I hear Reggie's voice before I see him. I whip around and almost lose the dip. I grab a hold with my free hand and try to steady myself.

"How'd you know I was out here?" I ask, remembering that his father did the same thing to me.

"We have a camera that tells us when someone gets off the elevator."

"But there are other apartments up here," I point out.

"You used our code," Reggie says as his eyes roll. It seems I should know all of this already.

"Huh," is all I can muster. Reggie holds the door wider and welcomes me, much like his father. He's wearing a mini version of his dad's jersey, and so is the tornado running toward my legs, except Roxy's is pink.

"Autumn," she says, except my name comes out more like Au-um, but who really cares. She can call me whatever she wants because she's cute. Reggie takes the dip from my hands which allows me to crouch down and visit with his sister.

"Aren't you the cutest thing ever," I say as I tug on one of her pigtails.

"I wanna braids like you, but no one do dem for me." She shrugs.

"I can braid your hair for you." Her eyes go wide, and she reaches for my hand. I give it willingly. She tugs me into the other room where Julius's parents are standing. They look as awkward as I feel right now.

"Hello," they say, stepping forward. "I'm Susan, and this is my husband, Roger." There is no mistaking that Julius is their son. Staring at his parents, I find it hard to pinpoint who he looks like most. Julius has his mother's smile, nose, and cheekbones, but his height and build definitely comes from his father. If I didn't know any better, I'd say Roger and Julius are twins and not father and son. They have the same dark hair, blue eyes, and olive skin tone.

"Dat's not yous name," Roxy says. "Yous gamma and dats gampa." She crosses her arms for emphasis.

"It's nice to meet you," I say, extending my hand to shake theirs. "I'm Autumn. Thank you for having me over today."

Susan waves my words away. "We are happy you could join us." She motions for me to follow her into the living room, where now, instead of the area in front of the sectional being clear, there's a table there—filled with food. "Are you hungry?"

"Of course." Roxy pulls me to the sofa and demands I sit next to her. Reggie returns with a glass and a can of Sprite for me.

"This is what you had when we went out to dinner," he says as he hands it to me.

"Thank you for remembering."

Susan and Roger take turns asking me questions. Some

of which Roxy answers for me. I'm surprised she remembers things so clearly. When they ask about working at the station, I tell them that I love it and love being in Portland.

"Where are you from?" Susan asks.

"Texas, but I went to school in Chicago."

"Your parents?" she asks.

The question catches me off guard. "Um, my dad is from Boston, and my mom, New York."

"How'd they end up in Texas?" Roger asks.

"My dad took a job with NASA, and they moved him to Texas. I was born there. Julius tells me that you live in Michigan?"

Susan nods. "We do, normally. With everything going on right now, we rented a place not far from here. We'll go back once the season is over."

"I know Julius appreciates you being here."

"There isn't any other place we'd rather be," Susan says.

"Except at the U of M games," Roger adds, earning a hard eye roll from Susan.

By the time halftime starts, I've stuffed my face so much that I'm ready for a nap. Roxy's curled into my side, fast asleep. But I did manage to braid her pigtails for her. She told me she plans to grow her hair as long as mine so we can be twins because our hair is the same color. According to her, we almost match.

The Pioneers are up by two touchdowns, per Reggie, when a voice echoes through the house, "Guest arriving."

"Who's here?" Roger asks.

"How would I know?" Susan says as she gets up. I'm trying to focus on the game, but my mind is too curious about who might be here. Would Julius's friends come over, uninvited? I know it's not Peyton because she travels with the team.

"Oh, dear," I hear Susan say from the hall. I don't know who I expect to walk in, but the person who enters is a woman wearing Julius's jersey, with her blonde hair all done up, and a pair of tight white pants.

"Mommy," Reggie yells from the couch. He trips over his own feet trying to get to his mother, while every nerve in my body seizes. I haven't moved a muscle by the time she comes toward me with Reggie attached at her side.

"You can leave now. Their mother is home. Your services won't be needed anymore."

"I'm not the sitter," I say, but she doesn't seem to care. "I'm—" I stop talking when Roxy stirs. Elena goes to her, jabs her elbow in my side, and picks her daughter up. Roxy cries out.

"Elena, maybe let Roxy wake up a bit before you hurt her," Susan suggests calmly.

Roxy rubs the sleep from her eyes and looks at me, and then she looks at her mother. "Down," she says, but Elena ignores her. "I want down." This time she starts kicking until Elena has no choice but to set Roxy onto her feet. She comes running to me and throws herself onto my lap. I don't look at Elena because I can feel the daggers piercing my skin.

"It's okay, Roxy." I pick her up and set her next to Susan. "I gotta go home, but I'll see you at the park in a couple of days, okay?"

"No, stay," Roxy cries.

Susan holds onto Roxy as she starts to cry. If I don't leave now, I'm going to say something that could likely hurt Julius's divorce case. I tell Reggie I'll see him later, but he doesn't respond. I don't really expect him to with his mom in the room.

No sooner does the door shut behind me, I hear it open

again. Stupidly, I turn and look only to find Elena coming toward me. "I'm back now, so whatever you have going on with my husband, it ends now." She turns and walks back into the house. The door clicks shut, and I expect silence. Yet, all I hear is screaming.

THIRTY

JULIUS

The game was brutal. There is no other word to describe it. The hit I took late in the fourth has made it hard to breathe. There isn't a doubt in my mind that my chest guard protected me tonight. If it wasn't for the pads, I think my chest would've caved in. What makes this pain I'm feeling worse is that the referee didn't even throw a flag. Even the instant replay, which was for the benefit of the hometown crowd, showed the severity of it, and yet nothing. I can only hope there is a fine coming down from the league, but I won't hold my breath. Not that I can right now anyway.

We have an hour from when the game is over to get showered, changed, and on the bus to go to the airport. It's late here, and I'm ready to be in my own bed. The past two nights at the hotel yielded very little sleep for me.

After I shower, I dress quickly and head out of the locker room. Fans are waiting when a bunch of us exit the building, asking for autographs. I give mine freely because you never know when I might be traded to this team or another, and if the fans have waited for you to come out, you might as well reward them. I'm not fooled though. I'm sure these people rooted against the Pioneers and me for four quarters, but I'm not holding that against them. Everyone makes mistakes.

Once I'm on the bus, I turn my phone on, and while I wait for it to come to life, I rest my head on the tinted glass and close my eyes. All I want to do is sleep, lay in bed for the next two or three days while my body heals. I'm thankful we have tomorrow, as well as Tuesday off, because I need time.

My phone vibrates in my hand. The notifications are non-stop. I watch as the text messages come in, all from my mom, Reggie, and Elena. Scrolling, I look for the one from Autumn and find nothing. I try not to let that bother me, but it does. I know I messed up, but I thought she had forgiven me. The last I knew, she was coming over to watch the game with my parents and kids. I suppose there is a chance she changed her mind or was called into work, but I think she would've texted me or something. At least, I hope she would've.

Noah sits down across from me and sighs heavily. He took a beating too but managed to survive long enough to give us the victory. There were times during the game when I thought our offensive line was playing for the other team. Too many open holes left Noah vulnerable. I know everyone has an off-game. Hell, I've had many, but for the whole line, whose purpose is to protect the quarterback, to fail at their job is unheard of.

"I'm ready for vacation," Noah says. His eyes are closed, and his head is resting against the seat.

"I'd like to start in February if you don't mind. Preferably starting the second or third week."

Noah laughs. "I hear ya. That's my plan as well, although Peyton may have to ask for time off."

"Wouldn't that be a shit? We win the Super Bowl, and your wife still has to work."

Noah hums in agreement. "I'd tell her to quit or take time off without pay. There is no way in hell I'm missing DisneyWorld if we win the big one."

Now I'm the one laughing. "I'm sure everyone in the organization would go if we win."

"When we win," he reminds me. His eyes are still closed, and I think about doing the same, except my phone is still blowing up. I look down at the notifications. There isn't anything new, just my phone reminding me that I have a slew of messages. I scroll, once again looking for Autumn's name, hoping I just missed it in my early search. Still not there. Now comes the time when I decide who I want to hear from first. The twisting in my gut tells me Elena has done something, which is why my mom has texted so much. That or there is something wrong with the kids, which could be why Elena is texting. The sheer amount of anxiety I'm feeling right now is making me sick. I finally open the messages from my mom. Of course, the last one is the most damning and sets my mood right off. I don't even desire to read the previous ones she sent because I'm so angry. My eyes focus on the last one.

Mom: Elena is back, and by back, I mean she's unpacked clothes in your room.

What the fuck?

I exit her window and go to Reggie's. Of course, he's also telling me his mom is there, but he says his mom is home. She's home. To him, everything is right in his world because this is everything he wants, for his parents to be back together. I finally click on Elena's message, and the anger I felt after reading my mom's message increases tenfold.

Elena: I'm home for good.

Why does she think this is okay? Did her boyfriend break up with her once he found out she isn't getting any money out of me?

"Hey, man, you okay?" Noah's voice rings out. I look at my hands. My knuckles are white, and it's like I'm trying to squeeze the shit out of my phone. Or break it. If it broke, I could play stupid when I get home, and no one would be the wiser.

"Yeah. It seems Elena decided to move home."

"As in back to Portland?"

I shake my head, slowly back and forth, until I look at him. "Back to the apartment." I go back to reading the messages from my mom. I give Noah a summary of what I read. "It seems Elena showed sometime during the fourth, interrupting everyone's game watching, and she suggested Autumn leave."

"Oh, shit."

"Yeah. And here I am, encouraging her to go to my place and spend some time with my parents and the kids, and Elena shows up? I can't even imagine what went down."

"You should call Autumn. She's likely the only one to give you the truth. Your mom's view is skewed, as is Elena's. Autumn is literally the only one who can tell you exactly what happened. Not that I think your mom would lie to you."

"No, I know what you're saying." I press her name and bring my phone to my ear. The other line rings until it goes to voicemail. I don't leave a message. Instead, I hang up and redial her number, only to have my call go to voicemail again. This time, I leave a message. "Hey, I'm on my way to the airport. If you get this, text me." After I hang up, I stare at my phone. I should probably call my mom, but I don't want to hear about the drama. Not right now. I send her a text, letting her know that we are about to get on the plane.

BY THE TIME the plane lands, I'm exhausted. Usually, I sleep, but with everything going on in my head, there was no way I could close my eyes long enough without seeing images of Elena being a shit to my parents. My mom won't say boo in front of Elena, especially if the children are around. My dad won't hold back. He's never been a fan of Elena and tolerated her until she asked for a divorce.

We are on a charter bus once again, and this time, I try to keep my eyes closed. I have no idea what to expect when I get home, other than knowing Elena is there and my parents are back at their rental. In the slew of text messages from my mom, she had concerns about leaving the children with Elena, but being as we're not divorced, there isn't much my mom could do. Elena wouldn't take the children—this much, I know.

I say goodbye to my teammates and drag my tired ass to my SUV. As soon as my CarPlay comes on, my playlist starts playing. I look at the time and know it's too late to call Autumn. I wish she had texted or called me back. I want to talk to her, get a feel for what exactly happened at my place tonight. Right now, I feel like I'm walking into a firestorm without any protection.

The drive back to my apartment takes hardly any time because of the lack of traffic. The one time I need the drive to be prolonged, it's short, and I'm pulling into the garage in no time. My bag feels heavy. Almost like it's carrying the weight of the world in it.

When I get to my floor, I hesitate outside the elevator doors. The temptation to go down to Autumn's floor and knock on her door is pressing. It's late, though, and she works tomorrow. I don't want to wake her. The truth is, she may not even want to see me. I already messed up earlier in the week, and while I worked to fix the gap I created, adding Elena to the mix is enough to scare anyone away.

When I come around the corner, the door to my apartment is open. Elena stands there in a T-shirt that is meant to look like my jersey. She reaches for my bag, but I hold onto it. "What are you doing here?" I ask her. To my knowledge, she received the divorce papers, and while I can hope she will just sign them, I'm not stupid. She wants money. The money I'm not willing to give her. I might need to rethink my stance on this because if she goes away with a cash payout, it'll be worth it.

"I'm home."

I tilt my head slightly. "I thought we agreed you'd give me notice when you wanted to come to visit the children, and I would get a hotel. Showing up in the middle of my game, when I'm out of town, is a bit . . ." I pause to seek out the right word. "Dare I say, rude?"

"It's rude to come home to my children and husband?"

I push past her. "Ex," I remind her. "I've filed for a divorce, Elena. I know you've received the papers."

"I did," she says as she follows me into my bedroom. "But then I sat there and read what had become of our marriage, and I realized I didn't want this. That we owed it to ourselves and our babies to try again."

Her words make my stomach roll.

"Boyfriend break up with you?" I look at her, sitting on my bed, and wait for her answer.

"We were never really together, Julius. And he was never my boyfriend."

"Just your fuck buddy? Got it." I leave the closet and head into the bathroom. Unfortunately, she follows. "What happened here earlier?"

"Nothing, why?"

"No, not nothing, Elena. What did you say to my parents and to Autumn?"

Elena blanches. "I would never say anything to your parents. We sat here and watched the rest of your game. I braided Roxy's hair, and Reggie called out the plays as Noah did them. Everything was perfect."

"And Autumn?"

"What about her? She was on her way out the door when I arrived." Elena moves into the bathroom and sits on the countertop. "I know you've been seeing her, and I get it, but I'm back now, and I'd really like to work on our marriage, Julius. You should've seen how excited the kids were when I walked in. Reggie is so happy, and Roxy fell asleep in my arms. I didn't realize how much I missed them until now."

"I've moved on, Elena."

"Well, unmove on, Julius. We owe it to each other to give our marriage another shot."

I pop some Tylenol and drink from the faucet. "I'll take the couch," I tell her as I exit the bathroom.

"What's wrong with the bedroom?"

"Not if you're in there, Elena. I told you. I'm done." I

shut the bedroom door behind me and head back into the living room. I go to my pile of stuff, pull my phone out, and scroll to Autumn's number. **Call me when you wake up. I need to talk to you. I missed you, Weather Girl.**

THIRTY-ONE

AUTUMN

As soon as the elevator door closes, I feel relieved. I half expected Elena to continue to follow me, but she turned back to the apartment—the one she has shared with Julius since they moved here. If that isn't a deterrent for this relationship with him, I don't know what is. My mind is racing with everything that just occurred in that apartment. One minute, we're all sitting there rooting on the Pioneers, and then the next—a straight-up hurricane. Pint-sized too. Julius and I are close in height, but Elena is tiny, which means Julius towers over her. Still, her personality and demeanor are anything but small. She's fierce, demanding, and scary. More so, she's a mama bear asserting her claim on her cubs. I can't fault her for being aggressive toward me. What bothers me the most is I feel like I'm innocent in all of this. I'm not the other woman. At least I hadn't looked at myself that way until this past week. However, Elena made me feel like I am one in a matter of seconds.

When the elevator reaches my floor, I don't step off. It takes me until the door starts to close to realize what I need —a drink. I hit the button for the lobby, and once I'm there, I walk into the restaurant adjacent to the entrance. I'm guessing that the game is over because of the lack of people here and easily find a spot at the bar.

"What can I get you?" the bartender asks as he wipes the spot in front of me and sets a coaster down. He rests his hands on the bar, waiting for me to give his order. If I'm drinking, my usual is wine or something fruity, but I feel like this situation calls for a more potent drink.

"Whiskey."

He looks at me oddly, waits a beat, nods, and then walks away. I've never had whiskey in my life, and I suspect he knows this. This guy is probably so good at his job. He knows what people like me drink, and it's definitely not whiskey.

When he returns, he sets a small glass of amber-colored liquid down in front of me, along with a bottle of beer and a glass of water. I look at him expectantly, and once again, he places his hands on the bar and leans down. "You'll want the beer chaser and then the water to wash it down. Trust me."

Trust me. Famous last words, right? I glance around the bar, looking for some distinguished gentlemen or someone similar to who I have pictured in my head, to see how they're drinking their whiskey. I pick the glass up, swirl and sniff—my stomach rolls at the powerful odor.

"Gah, how do people drink this?"

"It's an acquired taste." I look up to find the bartender cleaning the spot next to me. "Many start like you, one sip at a time."

"I've never had one," I tell him.

"I could tell, which is why I brought you the extras. Whatever made you decide to order *that*," he pauses and tilts his head toward my glass, "must've really upset you."

She did. He did. I can't decide who I'm more upset with. Julius. Elena. Or myself.

"Maybe I wanted to try something new?"

He chuckles. "Yeah, maybe. But I doubt it." He walks away toward the end of the bar, where he spends time helping the other customers. A few football fans are still lingering, but most of the patrons in here seem to be residents of the building or people who happened to pass by and wanted a place to eat.

I finally convince myself to taste the whiskey. When the glass touches my lips, my phone rings, and Cam's name lights up my screen. Setting the glass down, I stare at my phone, wondering if I should answer or not. I give in and answer. "Hey."

"Hey, yourself. What are you doing?"

I sigh and contemplate telling him the truth. At the end of the day, I consider him my friend. "I'm sitting in a bar, about to try my first whiskey."

"Why? Someone break your heart?" he asks with a slight laugh.

"Yes," I tell him.

"Wait, what?"

Another sigh emits. "I started seeing someone, and I just don't think things are going to work out. My heart isn't broken, but I'm sad. I really like him."

"The football player, right?"

"How did—oh never mind, you probably saw it on the internet or whatever. But yes, him. He's a great guy. He's just going through a major life change, and I don't want to be a complication or get too far deep only to have him end things."

"Come visit me," Camden suggests. "I'm heading to Texas because there's a hurricane in the Gulf. You can see your parents, do an on-air test, and just storm watch with me."

"I just started my job, Cam. I don't have vacation time yet."

"Don't tell Leon it's a vacation. Tell him you want to cover the story because Portland could, potentially, have a hurricane someday, and you want to be prepared."

I laugh at his absurdity. "I doubt Leon will go for it."

"Eh," he says. I know he's shrugging his shoulders. He does it every time he brushes something off. He makes life sound so easy. Maybe his is, but mine feels like a complicated mess. "Call Leon, and then call me back." Camden hangs up, leaving my protest hanging in the air. I pull my phone away in disbelief and find myself smiling at the text message from him.

Camden Porter: Call him. Call me. Let's meet in Texas!

He's crazy, and as tempted as I am, I won't do it. I don't want to rock the boat with Leon. What I have here—what I'm building here—it's a solid foundation for my future.

"Still trying to decide if you want to burn your throat?" the bartender asks.

"Something like that." He laughs and walks away.

I ordered the stupid drink. I might as well try it. I pick up the tumbler and bring the rim to my mouth and tip my head back. As soon as the whiskey touches my tongue, I know it's not for me and quickly pull the glass away. I hear laughter and glance at the bartender, who is shaking his head. *Wise guy.*

THE FOLLOWING DAY, I find myself in Leon's office, sitting across from him. He called me in and said he had an urgent matter to discuss with me. Instant fear and excitement washed over me. These two emotions do not complement each other. At all.

To make matters worse, I've ignored the text messages and phone calls from Julius. I purposely didn't run this morning out of fear he'd be outside my door, or he'd catch up with me on the path and force me to talk to him when I'm not ready. I don't know what to say or how to tell him what I'm feeling. I don't want to be a side chick or the woman that tore a family apart. But I also feel like what Julius and I started to build had the potential to be amazing.

When Leon requested we meet, I almost asked him if we could FaceTime so that I could continue to hide from Julius. I know I'm being ridiculous and need to grow up. I need to be an adult about things, but I honestly don't know what to say to Julius. First, he hates me, then he likes me, then we sleep together, and then he disappears for a few days. When I think we're on the same page, his wife returns. Now what? I honestly don't know where I fit when it comes to Julius. z

Leon Woolworth is not a big man, but his presence is massive. I tower over him, without my heels on, and right now, I feel like I'm two feet tall by the way he stares at me. I swallow hard, waiting for him to say something. In my opinion, he's a bit dramatic. He picks up a piece of paper, sets it down, picks it up again with a heavy sigh, and swivels back and forth in his chair.

"You applied for another job," he finally says. If I thought there was tension in the room before, it thickened my one hundred percent with those words. I open my mouth to say something, but words fail. Leon sets the piece of paper he's holding down. I crane my neck to see what it is and find that it's blank.

What in the hell!

"I get it," he says. "National TV. It makes sense. But I have one question."

"Okay?" My question comes out meekly, and I have to clear my throat.

"What is wrong here?"

"Nothing," I tell him instantly. "Absolutely nothing, Mr. Woolworth. The only reason I applied was to see if they'd even consider me. I love my job, the crew, everything. I simply had to appease my own curiosity."

"Do you need more money?"

I feel like when someone asks you this question—there is only one possible answer: yes!

"I will never decline more money, but my application wasn't about that. National has always been my goal, and when the opportunity presented itself, I submitted my resume. Nothing more. I honestly thought they'd skim over me for someone more seasoned."

Leon frowns. "Clearly, you don't know your worth. Let's work on that, okay?"

I nod, not clear on what's happening here.

"Anyway, they want to do a live interview."

"A live interview? What does that mean?"

"They'd like you to come on location with them. It seems Mr. Camden Porter requested to have you shadow him. Normally, with these types of interviews, you'd fill in for someone who is going on vacation or leave, so this one seems out of the ordinary. I'm inclined to tell them no because I don't want to lose you, but I've never been the type of person to hold people back. I'm here to help you grow, Ms. LaRosa." Leon pauses and folds his hands together. "However, I'm not letting you go without a fight. You are a valuable asset to my station, and I want to keep you. So, I suggest you go on this assignment, fail and come back where you are loved, cherished, and needed. Am I clear?"

His words sink in slowly. From the mention of Cam's name to Leon's love for me, I find myself stumbling over my thoughts. What is going on in my world right now?

"Are you just going to sit there?" Leon asks.

"I'm sorry, I'm just confused."

Leon smiles brightly. "Go home and pack, Ms. LaRosa. You're going on assignment."

I leave Leon's office and head to mine. I'm not going home because I have work to do, and I need to ask Camden what the hell is going on. By the time I reach my dressing room, my phone chimes with an incoming text. It's from the Weather Channel with my itinerary and flight information.

"How is this my life right now?"

The next chime is a text from Peyton: **Are you on your way?**

Shit. I forgot about lunch. I text her that I'm running late but will be there shortly. It's a good thing I'm going to see her because I need some advice.

THE DRIVE toward the restaurant takes a bit longer than GPS tells me because of traffic and because I thought I could find the restaurant myself. I'm directionally challenged when it comes to driving, and I usually walk. As luck would have it, which seems to be on my side today, there's a parking spot across from where Peyton and I are meeting. Since moving to Portland, I've mastered the art of parallel parking and zip my car in without any issues.

"I'm meeting someone," I say as I pass the hostess station. Peyton sees me and raises her hand. "I'm so sorry. Leon called me into his office first thing this morning."

"What's going on?"

Before I can tell her, the server is at our table taking our order. Once he leaves, I spill everything to Peyton, who listens to what I have to say without interruption.

"Wow."

"I know. I'm nervous, scared, and honestly don't know what to do."

"What did Julius say?"

"Honestly, I don't know what's going on with him. One minute we're great, the next, he's absent, and then when I think we're finally on the same page, Elena's back, and I don't know where I fit."

"Yeah, Noah mentioned something about Elena returning."

"Do you like her?" I ask.

Peyton shakes her head. "Not really. My sister calls her a stage five clinger. We see them a lot in California during the off-season, and we've had them over when my family is there. She's like static to my dad, Liam, or my brother. She likes to name drop, which really bothers me. But, I don't say anything because Noah and Julius are best friends."

"Elena definitely acted like she and Julius are not headed to Divorce Court. She just made me feel so icky for being there."

"Are you going to talk to Julius?"

I shrug. "I know I should, but I have a feeling he'll tell me nothing has changed, and I don't know what to do with that." Peyton and I continue to discuss my love life over lunch. She tells me she's excited about my opportunity and asks me to text her when I'm about to go live so she can tune in.

When I get home, Julius is waiting outside my apartment door with a bouquet of roses. He sees me and straightens. "I got tired of you not responding, so I thought I'd wait here until you came back."

"You could've been here for days."

"It's a risk I was willing to take."

I laugh and open my door. Julius follows me in and into the kitchen with the roses. "Thank you. They're beautiful."

"They're not enough," he says. "I know Elena was nasty to you the other night, and I figure that is why you're ignoring me. I'm sorry about what she said."

My lips go into a thin line. I don't know what to say. The way she acts isn't his fault, but I can't help but feel like the situation is. "You guys have a lot to work out."

He grimaces. "Not really. She's in a panic because the finality of her actions is closing in on her. I think she thought I wouldn't file, and when she received the notice, she saw the money start to disappear. As long as she's my wife, I'm responsible for things like the house and her car. Once we're divorced, she's on the hook, and I think she freaked out."

"Did she go back to L.A.?"

Julius shakes his head. "No, she's moving back apparently, which is good for the kids. She's out looking for a place right now."

"Oh." I turn my back and start to clean my kitchen a bit. I can feel his presence when he steps closer. Does he think I'm going to carry on a relationship with him? That I'm going to be the other woman? He's right. The children need their mother, but I don't need Elena and her volatile disposition when it comes to me, and I have a feeling she's not going away quietly.

"The divorce is going to happen, Autumn. Elena knows this."

I turn to face him and can see the pain in his eyes. "That's good. I, uh..." I swallow my words. I don't know what to say to him. "I should probably get ready and head to the station. I have a ton of work to do."

Julius's expression falls. He wanted me to say something else, but I just don't have it in me. I need time to think about what I want. I'm too young to be mixed up with a messy divorce. He steps forward and kisses me on my cheek. "I'll watch your broadcast tonight," he tells me. "Let me know when you get home?"

I nod, and he backs away. When he gets to the door, he says, "Nothing has to change between us, Autumn. You're the one I want to be with." Julius closes the door quietly behind him.

"Things have already changed," I say into my empty apartment.

THIRTY-TWO

JULIUS

It's been two days since I've seen Autumn, and the empty feeling I have growing in my gut is very unsettling. We've texted a couple of times. Short, to-the-point words that leave me with a lot of questions. The flirting conversations I've grown accustomed to are missing, and I have an overall sense of dread that things aren't the way I want them. The gap I feel between us is my fault, and I can accept responsibility for my actions, especially when I dragged my feet when it came to filing for divorce. The minute I realized Autumn was someone I wanted to spend all my time with, I should've been in the lawyer's office. Hell, the second I found out Elena had an affair was when I should've done something. I procrastinated, and now I think I'm going to end up paying in the long run.

After our forty-five-minute weight training session, we make our way to the cafeteria to grab breakfast before our nine a.m. team meeting. Because we won on Sunday, Coach had our breakfast catered this morning. It's a reward and one we strive for each week. It's Coach's way of showing appreciation, and since we're football players who like to eat, he goes all out for us. After I get a couple of plates of food, I take a spot next to Noah. Alex Moore and Chase Montgomery are already seated and stuffing their faces. I can't say I blame them. I'm starving.

"Hey," Alex says as I sit down. He looks forlorn, an unusual sight for Alex. He's the happiest guy I know, aside from Noah.

"What's eating you?" I ask him.

He shrugs, and I glance to Noah and Chase, who offer no help at all. Alex sighs heavily and then emits some low groan, which is so exaggerated you'd think he's spent time with Roxy and asked how to get what she wants from me.

"Dude, you're acting like my kid. Spill."

"Maggie was offered a job in England." Maggie is Alex's girlfriend or, more aptly known around the team as the perfect woman because she not only puts up with Alex but makes sure the Pioneers are included in the best events to give us optimum publicity. Unbeknownst to the fans, the sports teams fight for the spotlight. Professional athletes get a bad rap because, let's be honest, we do some stupid shit. That stupid shit can make it so businesses don't want us around even though we can bring many people. Maggie, though, she always turns a blind eye and wants us at all her events. She runs the Children's Museum, and when she took the job, it was some rinky-dink playroom. Now, it's this fantastic, interactive experience for children, and it's all because of her. So, I'm not surprised other organizations want her.

"Is she going to take it?" Chase asks.

Alex shrugs.

"It's what? An eight-hour time difference?" Noah asks.

"Yeah, something like that. I don't know." He shakes his head. "I feel like I'm losing her."

"Maybe she's ready to settle down, and this is your wake-up call," Chase, the perpetual bachelor adds.

"There aren't many times in life when I will agree with Montgomery, but this is one of them," I say to Alex. "You and Maggie have been together for as long as I've known you. She probably wants to get married and have children."

"So, I should ask her to marry me?"

"Is that what you want?" Noah asks. "Do you see yourself married to Maggie?"

Alex shrugs. "I don't know. I've never thought about it. I thought we were content with owning a house and just living life."

"Content is not a good thing," Noah tells us. "Content means you stopped trying. I'm happily married. I love my wife more than my own life, but nothing brings me more pleasure than knowing I did something to make her day better or made her smile. I work hard to make sure she knows how much she means to me. I plan dates and fly her mom up here when I think Peyton needs her and buy her flowers because I walked by the florist when I was out. It's the little things just to remind her that she's the love of my life."

"You and Peyton don't count in this mess," Alex says. "You have like this once-in-a-lifetime love affair."

Noah laughs, but I happen to agree with Alex.

"That may be true, but it doesn't work unless we work. No one should count on love carrying their relationship. You can fall out of love with someone because no one is putting in an effort."

"Or you end up like me," I say. "With a looming divorce and a woman who won't return your text messages because your ex-wife said some shit she shouldn't have."

"Your life has too much drama for me," Chase says. "It's why I date."

"You date because no one wants to put up with your ass after a week," Alex says to Chase. "What dating app are you currently using to troll for women?"

Chase throws his napkin at Alex. Chase is constantly on the hunt for someone who doesn't know who he is. Usually, he finds someone, but once he tells them, they accuse him of lying. It's an endless battle for him. There are times when I feel sorry for him, but he brings a lot of drama to himself. We've told him time and time again there is nothing wrong with dating someone who knows you're a professional football player.

"I've decided to give up on dating during the season. I'm in bed by nine most nights, and these women I met want to text until midnight, and I'm not up for that."

"Make sense," Noah says. "A lot of people don't understand the schedule we keep during the season, and according to some fans, we need more practice."

The three of us laugh. If we listened to half the stuff we saw on social media, we'd either be out of a job or the best team ever to grace a football field.

"Look, I can't give you any advice," I say, "because I'm dealing with my own drama. All I can say is, don't wait. If Maggie is who you want to be with, then show her. Dragging your feet digs you a hole, and some holes are too deep to get out of." With that said, I pick up my fork and start eating. The others follow, and the conversation changes from relationships to sports. Chase is excited for the upcoming college basketball season, while Noah says he's heard scuttle that Portland is looking at adding a Major League Baseball team. This sparks a more in-depth conversation on whether the owners would build a stadium or see about piggybacking with ours, much like the Oakland A's and Raiders used to do. Regardless, adding more revenue to the city is always a good thing, and making Portland a professional sports hotspot would put Oregon truly on the map as a place to be.

After breakfast, we head into our team meeting. Noah and I sit down next to each other, and I study him for a bit while he looks at his wife. Her cheeks blush when they make eye contact, and it makes me realize this is the type of reaction I want from Autumn when I look at her. It also makes me wonder what the hell she's thinking or what he did to cause her response. Damn, to have a love like theirs would be a blessing.

Every so often, during the meeting, I catch Noah and Peyton staring at each other. It's like they're carrying on a secret conversation with their eyes. Something tells me if I tried this with Elena, she'd get extremely irritated with me, and if I tried it with Autumn, confusion would set in. It's a hard slap in the face when you realize you don't know either of the women in your life, past and present. If I'm going to make things with Autumn work, I need to be better at communicating. And I need to convince Noah to write a book for us clueless guys.

ΦΦΦ

I'M BEAT when I get home from practice, and thankful the house is quiet. Elena moved into an apartment a few floors down. It's not what she wants, but I'm honestly tired of being the one who caves to her demands. She walked out and left this life behind. I know I told her I'd give up my apartment to her, but I don't want to. Elena called me child-ish, and she's right, but damn it if I haven't earned the right to be. I'm not the one who fucked up. She is. However, having her in town gives the kids a chance to spend some time with her, and I think that's important for them. They're not staying over but are with her until dinner, and then they'll be home. The few hours from practice until they come home, is time for me to relax.

I startle awake when the sound of my A.I. alerts me that someone has used my elevator code. As much as I hope it's Autumn, I know it's the kids returning from their mom's. Miss Meghan walks in with her hands full of book bags and art projects. My son is behind her, not carrying a damn thing.

"Why aren't you carrying your bag?" I ask Reggie.

He shrugs. "Mom says it's Miss Meghan's job."

I look at Meghan and then back at my son. Irritation fills me. "Miss Meghan is responsible for taking care of you and your sister when I'm not around. She's not your servant. You carry your own things unless she volunteers. Do I make myself clear?" My voice is stern. I give him and Meghan a pointed look.

"Yes, sir," Reggie says. He takes his stuff from Meghan's hand and then heads to his bedroom. Once his door closes, I peer down at Roxy with her jutted lip. It's hard for me to punish her because she's three and only doing what her mother tells her. Reggie knows better.

"Miss Meghan can only carry your stuff if she offers, okay?"

She nods. "Okay, Daddy."

"Take your backpack to your room, please." Roxy turns, hugs Meghan, and then runs to her room with her bag dragging on the ground. "I'm sorry about Elena. Don't let her bully you."

"I won't. I'll stand my ground next time."

"How was everything?"

"It was fine. The kids mostly watched television."

"Where was Elena?"

"On her phone."

The earlier irritation has increased to a boiling point. I can't tell Elena how to parent, but her lack of interest proves that I'm a much better fit for custody than she is.

After the kids have their bath and shower, I snuggle with Roxy in bed and read *Rugby and Rosie* to her. "Daddy, can we has a doggie?"

"I'd love to, but we live in an apartment. Dogs need a place to run."

"Can we moob to a house?"

A house would be ideal. I haven't thought about leaving the apartment life and getting a home with a yard. Everything is so convenient where we live now, but having a yard and some pets would be nice. "Maybe," I tell her. I kiss her nose. "I'll think about it." We finish the story, and I tuck her in. When I get to Reggie's room, he's already asleep. I make sure he's tucked in and tell him I love him.

I walk back into the living room and hear Autumn's voice. I know I'm hearing things because it's not time for her segment. I grab the remote and turn the volume up on the T.V. There's a woman who looks identical to Autumn, standing in the rain.

"What the hell?" I listen as she tells viewers about a hurricane bearing down on Houston, Texas. She's standing next to another reporter. The man comes into the camera, and by the way, he looks at her, I just know. He places his arm around her and then speaks to the camera.

"Autumn, what do you think about your first storm coverage?"

"It's amazing, Camden. I'm so happy to be back in my

home state. I'm praying Hurricane Wanda doesn't do any severe damage when it makes landfall."

"I think everyone is praying for that right now. Skip, back to you."

"Thank you, Camden and Autumn. We're praying for you."

My eyes deceive me. There is no way this segment is live. I saw Autumn two days ago. I know a lot can happen in forty-eight hours, but I'd like to think she would tell me if she planned to leave.

Did she move away and not tell me?

I reach for my phone and call Noah, who picks up on the second ring. "Hey, did Autumn move?" My question is blunt. There is just no way to sugarcoat this.

"I'll let you talk to Peyton."

"Hi, Julius."

"Hey," I say. "What's going on?"

Peyton sighs. "The Weather Channel is interested in Autumn. She's in Texas covering the storm for them."

"And the guy she's with—that's her ex, right?"

Peyton is quiet for a moment. "Yeah, Camden Porter. He got her the gig."

"Fuck," I mutter and then apologize to Peyton for cursing. "This is all my fault. If I had—"

"Nothing's your fault, Julius. An opportunity came up, and she took it. You should really talk to her about it though."

"I won't tell her you told me."

"It's okay if you do. Leon knows she's there. It's not a big secret."

It may not be a secret to everyone else, but she kept it from me. "Thanks, Peyton." We hang up, and I start to pace. There are two ways to approach this, guns blazing with the woe-is-me- factor, or I can be the not-your-boyfriend-but-wants-to-be-supportive-guy. The latter because I need Autumn to know I fully support her, even if it means she's leaving town.

"Fuck," I say aloud. "Why did I wait so long to move things forward?" There isn't anything I can do about my actions; I can only make better decisions moving forward.

Instead of texting Autumn, I decide to call her. Chances are, she won't answer, but whatever. It's worth a shot. By the fifth ring, I'm ready to hang up.

"Hello?" she's breathless, and my heart sinks because all the wrong thoughts are going through my mind right now.

"Hey, Weather Girl. I just saw you on television."

"Oh my, I'm a mess. Did I look okay?"

"You're beautiful, Autumn. When are you coming back?"

"Miss me already?" she asks.

"I do." As much as I want to ask her why she didn't tell me she was leaving, I don't say anything. I'm going to play it cool. There could be several reasons why and each one is likely valid to her. Hell, maybe she forgot or thought she did or figured I'm too stuck in my head to pay attention.

"Once the storm passes. It's slow-moving so probably a few more days."

"Please be safe. I worry about you out there in that mess."

"I will . . ." she fumbles with her phone, and I hear a male voice in the background.

"Ah, my competition is there," I say jokingly, even though I'm far from joking.

Autumn laughs. "No one can compete with you, Julius. I gotta go back on air. Watch me, okay?"

"I will. Text me when you can chat again."

"I will. Good night, Julius." Autumn hangs up but her words linger in my mind. What did she mean when she said no one can compete with me? Does that mean what I want it to mean? That she wants to be with me or is it some other reference because of who I am. Either way, it's going to plague me until I can get a solid answer.

THIRTY-THREE

AUTUMN

When I come down the escalator and into the luggage area, I hear my name. I turn and see a bouquet of balloons rushing toward me. At the speed the balloons are moving, I expect to see bodies flying, but people are moving out of the way for the tiny bulldozer heading my way. When Roxy breaks through the crowd, tears well, and I crouch down, waiting for impact. I didn't expect Julius to come to the airport to pick me up. Last night when we spoke, he asked what time I was due in, and I told him because it's not a secret, and with the way things have been between us lately, I honestly have no idea where we stand. We both have some communication issues we need to work out.

"Ah-um," she says my name as clearly as she can. Her tiny arms wrap around my neck, and I inhale the scent of her strawberry shampoo. Until now, I didn't know I missed her, which is stupid because she's owned my heart from the day I met her in the park. There's something about Roxy that just stays with you.

After a long moment, I finally tell her that I missed her.

I'm honest with Roxy about my feelings. She has my heart wrapped around her little finger. I spent so much time worrying about her father that I completely opened my heart to her, and now I'm probably in trouble. I realized, while in Texas, my clock is ticking. I know I still have time. I'm young, and my career is taking off, but if I'm going to pursue something with Julius, we need to discuss future children.

I set her down and make eye contact with her father. *Damn.* My mouth waters at the sight of him. He looks hot in his black slacks, and his naturally tanned skin is like a beacon against the white untucked button-down shirt. Instant flashes of our one night together flash in my mind. How can one night stay with me for so long? My fingers twitch, forcing me to make a fist, or else I'm going to reach for the hem of his shirt and pull him to me. I've missed the way his body feels against mine. I didn't know how much until I saw Camden. As soon as he hugged me, I knew I was in love with Julius Cunningham.

Days ago, I had it in my mind that I was going to become a travel weather person like Camden. This was my dream job, and it dangled in front of me like a piece of cake. Only Julius and the kids weren't there. I broke down and told Cam about Julius on my first night there over dinner when he tried to hold my hand. Cam's expression told me everything I needed to know. He wanted me there because he wanted to be with me when I wanted to be in Portland, curled up on the couch with the cutest little girl I know, sleeping in my arms. Once I started talking about the Cunninghams, I couldn't stop.

Julius leans in, wraps both arms around me, and we hug. As much as I want to resist, I can't. I breathe him in and get lost in the scent of his cologne. Spice, woodsy, and clean. He makes me weak and fogs my mind up, and that's a serious problem. I'm already in too deep but need to find a way to pull back until Julius has his life figured out. It pains me to think this because I want to be with him, but not at the expense of my sanity. The baggage he carries—it's a lot. It's more than someone my age should get involved with. The thing is, I'm not sure I can walk away with my heart intact.

"I'm happy you're back," he whispers. His lips linger against my skin, and I shiver.

I test the waters to see where he's at. "I missed you, Julius."

His arms tighten, and he lifts me off the ground. He buries his face in my neck, and his hand cradles my head. "I'm so sorry, Weather Girl." He's sorry for what, exactly? Elena? The ghosting? The entire situation? "We'll talk later, okay?"

I nod against him, and he sets me down. Julius takes my bags from me, and without hesitation, I reach for Roxy's hand.

"Do you have other luggage?" he asks.

"No, only my carry-ons." Roxy skips next to me, laughing each time a balloon hits her dad's head. I try to wrangle the bouquet in my free hand to keep them from hitting other people. Thankfully, most of the travelers are giving us a wide berth. I'm surprised people aren't pointing and saying Julius's name or bugging him for his autograph.

We make it to Julius's SUV without any run-ins with fans, and we didn't lose any of the balloons. He takes them from Roxy and tells her to climb into the back seat while trying to get the mylar assortment tucked safely in the back cargo space.

"When Roxy suggested balloons, I thought they were a

good idea. I regret my decision making," he says with a shake of his head.

"I can sit in the back and hold them down so you can drive," I offer, but Julius shakes his head.

"I want you next to me."

"Julius," I pause after saying his name. I'm not sure what I want to say or what needs to be said. I had no idea he planned to pick me up, which I love, by the way. But I don't know where we stand. I don't have a clue as to what's going on in his head. I want to know. I want him to be an open book and tell me everything, so we're on the same page.

"Don't," he says as he steps forward. He curls his fingers around mine and brings my hand to his mouth. "If you're going to tell me to take a hike—which I deserve—please wait until we're back at the apartment. I don't want that tension to be between us on the ride downtown. If you're willing to hear me out—which I hope you are—just know that I plan to tell you everything once we're home. The kids and I would like to have dinner with you, and if you're up for it, I'd like for us to talk after they've gone to bed. I suspect you're probably tired, so I promise not to keep you long."

Julius and I make eye contact, and I can feel the sincerity in his words. I close the small gap that exists between us and press my lips to his. "I meant it when I said I missed you."

"I missed you more," he says. Julius guides me to the passenger side of his car and holds the door for me until I'm safely inside. I turn and rest my elbow on the console. Roxy is swinging her legs back and forth, her little ankles hitting the edge of her car seat.

"What's for dinner?" I ask her.

She smiles and then lets out the cutest giggle. "Chicky nuggies."

"My favorite," I tell her.

The entire drive to the complex is a full-on karaoke session of little kid songs. Most of them I know from watching various programs while growing up and happily join in, but some are new to me. Julius surprises the hell out of me when he belts those out.

After a quick pit-stop to drop my bags and balloons off, Roxy dubs my apartment the best place ever. I happen to like where I live and love the view, but this little girl lives in a freaking penthouse. I suppose when you see your own place, day in and day out, something different is like a shiny new toy.

When we get to Julius's, I'm shocked to find out that Reggie isn't there. Julius shrugs and says, "He's staying at his mom's." I can hear the hurt in his voice and know there is more to the story and figure Julius will tell me if it's something he wants me to know.

In the kitchen, he busies himself with cooking the dinosaur chicken nuggets and a tray of fries. It's not my ideal dinner, but Roxy loves it. Besides, I ate so many tacos while in Houston, I honestly can't stomach much more food. While Julius tends to the food, I follow Roxy to her room. It's as big as mine with a white four-poster bed, light pink canopy, and matching comforter. In the corner, there is a life-size cutout of her father, carrying a football.

"Dat Daddy," she says, pointing to him.

"Did he buy it for you?"

She nods and laughs. "He funny."

"Yeah, he is."

Roxy continues to show me around her room. After she points out all her toys, she tells me to sit at her table and pours me a glass of tea. She scolds me when I pick my cup up though, because my tea is very hot, and I'm going to burn myself. I wait for what I think is an appropriate toddler time before picking it up again.

"This is delicious," I tell her.

"I make it."

"Your tea skills are perfect."

"Fanks," she blushes. "Hab dis." Roxy hands me a plastic chocolate chip cookie. I take my pretend bite and tell myself to think that it's real. Maybe if I do this, I can kick my sugar addiction.

"Ahem," Julius clears his throat from the doorway. He stands there, leaning against the jamb, with his hands in his pockets and one ankle crossed over the other. His once buttoned-up shirt is now partially open, with one side of the shirt dipping just enough that his pec is showing. I swallow that hard plastic pretend lump of a cookie and try to force a smile, but I probably look like some drool bucket trying not to get caught staring at the man in front of me.

"I hate to interrupt your party, but dinner is ready, and Miss Roxy needs to go to bed soon."

She groans but grabs my hand and does her best to try and help me up from the chair. I'm going to have to work on my core strength if I'm going to have any more tea parties. Roxy holds my hand until we're in the kitchen at their four-person table. It's small, but I know Julius has a bigger, more formal one in the other room.

Formal.

The word plays in my mind. Everything about now feels incredibly formal. Almost like Roxy is putting on a show. To give me a glimpse of what life would be like here. Did Julius put her up to this? Or is she doing this because she likes me and I'm a guest in her home? I'm going with the latter because I can't imagine Julius using his child to get my attention.

The three of us sit around the table, sharing a plate of nuggets and fries. Julius set out different dipping sauces and gave Roxy her very own bowl of Ranch. When I looked at it questioningly, he shook his head and said, "double-dipper." That's all I needed to know.

While Julius bathes Roxy and puts her to bed, I sit on his balcony with a glass of wine in my hand. I check my phone for the first time since I landed. Camden has called twice and texted twice as much. He wants me to take the job and is confident I'll have an offer by tomorrow morning. As enticing as the opportunity is, I don't know if I'm ready. For one, it means moving. My mom texted to see if I made it home safely. She is another person I needed to check in with, and finally, Peyton, she wants to know if I've spoken to Julius. I'm about to reply to everyone when Julius steps out onto his balcony, only now, the white shirt that looks so good against his skin is completely undone.

"Sweet Jesus," I mutter and quickly take a sip of my wine in hopes Julius didn't hear me correctly and will have forgotten to ask me to repeat myself.

"We should talk," he says and motions toward the living room. He waits for me to step inside and then closes the door behind us. "It's a nice night, but the neighbors like to eavesdrop, and I'd rather keep my personal life personal."

"I understand," I tell him.

Julius sits down beside me and takes my hand in his. "I'm just going to talk because I have so many thoughts running through my head right now."

"Okay." I turn to face him and pull my legs up onto the couch.

"Elena and I are getting a divorce. I'm not interested in rekindling anything with her. She showed up here because she saw the writing on the wall when the process server handed her the papers, and she thought she could sweet-talk her way back in. The shit she pulled when you were here, unacceptable. I've told her to apologize, but don't hold your breath."

"It's not just Elena," I say and then shake my head. "I'm sorry, please continue."

"No, you're right. It's not. It's me too and the panic I felt. At first, I thought everything going on was second-guessing, when in fact, it was relief. I wasn't nervous about filing for divorce. I was nervous because I didn't want you to think I wasn't worth this headache. It seems that's all I've been, and I couldn't change it. I should've never gone two days without talking to you, especially after we spent the night together. That was the biggest mistake I've made in a long time. Complete stupidity. If I could get that week back, I would. If I could make it so Elena didn't randomly show up and say shit to you, believe me, I'd erase it all. I'm an idiot. There really isn't another way to sum this up.

"I'm not sure how I can make any of this up to you, but I'm willing to try. I want you, Autumn. I want us to walk down the street, holding hands. I want people to know we're together. I want our families to have Christmas together. Most importantly, I want you in my life as my girlfriend. I know we have this age difference. The guys on the team tease me, calling me your grandfather, but I'm not that much older. You were just in high school when I graduated college. It's a doable difference."

I laugh at his hang up when it comes to our age.

"What I'm saying is, if you're with me, there's this role you'll fall into. Roxy loves you and she'll start seeing you as a parent if we're going to be together. If that's not something you want, please tell me. I don't want to hurt her. Her mother is doing enough of that."

"What do you mean?"

Julius sighs heavily. "Elena wants to take Reggie back to California with her."

"And not Roxy?"

He nods and my mouth drops open. "I'm not even okay with Reggie going but he wants to, and I told him he could choose. Elena . . . she's not doing this in his best interest, only hers. If she has him, I have to pay her child support. Because she had an affair, she doesn't receive any other support from me. This is the only way."

"And she'll use her son to get it?"

Julius shrugs. "She's desperate and right now my lawyer says I should let Reggie go. I'll make sure he has a nanny available because I'm not confident his mom will take care of him."

"What about his football team?"

"Elena told him they'd stay here until the season is over and then they'll go back. Elena is living a few floors down, which by the way, is not to her standards. We have a mediation appointment tomorrow to hammer out some details of the divorce settlement."

"I'm really sorry Reggie wants to leave."

"Me too," he says. "I'm hoping by the end of the year, he'll change his mind. Right now, Elena is doting on him and he's eating it up. He's eight and thinks his mom walks on water. Even though last week he hated her."

I rest my head on his shoulder and listen to his heartbeat. He curls his arm around me. "Am I too late?" he asks. I don't need him to elaborate, I know exactly what he's talking about. I saw the footage and the way Camden looked at me on camera. Hell, everyone I know sent messages asking when Camden and I were going to get married. He may feel something for me, but I'm all about this certain football player.

"That depends."

"On what?"

"If Roxy loves me, how does her daddy feel?"

Julius leans back so he can look into my eyes. He smiles brightly. "Her daddy is definitely falling in love with the new weather girl."

"That's good because this weather girl is definitely falling for this wide receiver."

Julius leans toward me but pauses. "Spend the night with me. Before you say yes, let me tell you how the night is going to go. We're going to go into my room and then into the shower where I'm going to fuck you against the wall. Then we're going to go to bed where I'll make love to you. And once we're asleep, a three-year old is going to crawl into bed with us. She's going to put her feet in your face, lay on top of you, and then stare at you until you wake up, fearing for your life."

"Wow, I don't know what to say about this offer." I try to laugh, but it's a bit hard knowing in detail what's going to happen.

"Say yes. Or at least come to bed with me now and if you want to leave later, I won't be mad. I know I'm asking a lot of you. If you're not comfortable with the Roxy thing. I understand, but before you make your decision, you should know, I told her you're my girlfriend. We had a tea party and had the most adultish conversation I could with her. She knows her mommy doesn't want to live here. She cries some and has meltdowns. But she had a place for you at the party and the balloons were her idea. Meghan was supposed to come babysit her while I went to surprise you, but Roxy insisted on going. I guess it's a preview of what life will be like with me. I have two kids, they're my priority."

"As they should be, Julius. I will not be the person that comes between you and your children."

"And you won't be. I'll find balance or proper separation if need be."

Something tells me Reggie will force the separation and that's something I'll have to deal with.

Julius cups my cheek and kisses me softly. "What do you think? Option A or B?"

"Option A," I say in between kisses. "Definitely need to shower."

Julius smiles against my mouth. He stands, takes my hand, and pulls me down the hallway to his bedroom, where he closes the door and makes good on his offer.

THIRTY-FOUR

JULIUS

Waking up next to Autumn has to be the single best thing I've experienced in a long time. Luck was on our side last night—no invasion of the three-year-old. At some point, I woke up a bit worried and had to check on Roxy. Ever since Elena left, she's been like clockwork, coming into my room at night. I'm starting to think she did this for my benefit so I wouldn't be alone and not so much for hers.

When Autumn left this morning, she told me she would see me later. The problem with later is I have no idea when it will occur. This morning, Elena and I are meeting with the mediator, and then it's off to practice. Coach is being gracious and moved practice time to later this afternoon. I'm grateful because if I miss the walk-through today, I can't play on Sunday. And Autumn has her segments which air starting at five until the news is over at eleven-thirty. Our hours suck, at least until February, when I have more freedom to do whatever. Still, not seeing her five nights a week is sort of a downer.

When I come into the kitchen, Roxy is sitting at the

table, eating breakfast, and Miss Meghan asks her what she wants to do. I think it's cute that Meghan gives Roxy options, even though it'll be the same routine most days. They'll go to the library for story time, go to the park, and then it's home for naptime. Meghan will pick up around the house, but it isn't a job requirement, and she'll write a grocery list of things she needs so I can make sure the house is fully stocked. When Roxy is up from her nap, they'll get Reggie from school. I really don't put too much pressure on Meghan. Her only responsibility is to keep my children safe.

The A.I. announces that someone is coming to the door. I wait a few seconds before going into the hallway. The tell-tale sound of a key sliding into the lock gets my blood boiling. As soon as Elena and Reggie enter, I kiss my son on the top of his head and tell him breakfast is on the table. Once he's out of earshot, I hold my hand out.

"What?" she asks.

"My key, I want it back."

"You've got to be joking, Julius."

"I'm not. Hand it over."

She does so but with great reluctance. This is no longer her house, and just because her children reside here doesn't mean she can come and go, as she pleases. More so, after the stunt she pulled with Autumn and my parents, I don't want Elena showing up unannounced anymore.

"I'm assuming it's okay if I ride with you to the lawyer's office?" she asks.

"I'm fine with that, but you have to get a cab back because I need to go to practice."

"You can't drop me off?"

"It's out of my way." I leave her in the hall and head

back into the kitchen. Reggie is sitting there, stuffing food into his mouth. "Slow down, Bud."

"I'm starving."

"What'd you have for dinner?"

He shrugs.

I know I'm not the best parent in the world, but I like to think I do a damn good job of keeping my kids fed. "Elena?"

"What?" She comes into the room and lets out an exaggerated sigh.

"What did Reggie have for dinner last night?"

Elena looks at our son and then at me. "Are you seriously monitoring me as a parent?"

"Yes," I state pointedly. "When I see our son eat like he hadn't eaten since lunch yesterday—yes, I'm going to ask what you fed him."

"Unbelievable."

I motion for her to follow me into the other room. She does so, but she's agitated. "I will always look out for his best interest, Elena. You know this. You also know I'm one-hundred percent against him living with you because of this exact thing. I'm going out on a limb here, but I bet he had cereal for dinner. Sometimes that is a great dinner, but he needs more, and you need to be able to recognize this. I don't know what's going on in your head or when our children didn't become a priority to you, but you need to figure it out. This is a fair warning—I'm going to tell the mediator that if Reggie is to go live with you—there needs to be a nanny, and the nanny's fee will be paid out of the child support. That money is to support him, not you."

"You can't dictate how I spend my money."

"I can, and I will. I didn't have to agree to mediation, yet here I am footing the bill for this as well."

"You're just angry because I want a divorce."

"No, Elena. I'm angry because you cheated. Had you come to me and said you weren't happy I would've done whatever was needed to fix that. But you stepped out on us. You chose to bring another man into our bed. You chose to disregard our vows. And then you expected me to pay you off. That's why I'm angry." I walk away and head toward my bedroom. Before I close the door, I shout, "I'm leaving in ten minutes if you want a ride."

Elena is still here when I come out. You'd think she would take a few moments and spend some time with her daughter, but Elena's sitting on the couch, scrolling through her phone while Roxy and Meghan clean up after breakfast.

"Thank you, Meghan," I say as I come into the kitchen. I kiss Roxy, tell Reggie to have a good day, and remind him that I have a late practice. There's a good chance he won't be home and will be at his mom's. Fewer rules there, I'm sure.

Elena follows me out the door and into the elevator. She sighs heavily, which I ignore, and finally, once we're in the car, she starts talking. "Do you remember the first day we met?"

"I do."

"I was so scared." She looks out the window. "Where did we go wrong, Julius?"

"I do believe we had this conversation, Elena. I'm not interested in rehashing it over and over."

She says nothing the rest of the drive to the lawyer's office. Once there, we go into a small conference room. My lawyer is sitting at the table behind a stack of papers. "Hello, Julius." We shake hands.

"This is Elena," I say to him. I thought I might slip up and call her my wife, but even my subconscious knows I've moved on. They shake hands, and then we all sit down.

Elena is across from me, and the lawyer is at the head of the table.

"Okay," he says. "We have a petition brought on by Julius to dissolve the marriage. Also on file is a prenuptial agreement signed by both parties. It is my understanding that we're going to follow the prenup?"

I nod and then look at Elena. She's looking down at the table and says nothing. "Elena," I prod. "If you're going to fight the prenup, then you need to hire someone to represent you. My lawyer is not going to go against my wishes of honoring the agreement."

"Well, I was doing some research."

This is not going to go well for me.

"And I discovered that Oregon is a no-fault state, so you can't use adultery for the divorce, and therefore the prenup allows for me to get a settlement."

"Yes, you're right, Mrs. Cunningham. However, we have substantial evidence of you committing adultery, and if we take this in front of a judge, they're likely to uphold the agreement."

I can see her wheels turning. "What do you want, Elena?"

"Money, Julius. I want the money, and the lifestyle promised to me when I married you."

"What are you talking about?"

"We live like we're running out of money. You make millions a year, and the only thing we have to show for it is a house in Huntington Beach. I want more. I deserve more."

"You do realize that the average span of my career is four years and that is without any injuries, or some younger, faster version of me entering the league. Every day I go out onto that field, I'm lucky I still have a career. But this can change at any time. I need to earn as much money as possible to live a life after my career is over and take care of my family. I have two kids to put through college. Where do you think that money is going to come from? And who is to say I'll even get a job after my career as a wide receiver is over? Do you think I want to sit on my ass at the age of thirty-five and feel sorry for myself because I didn't get a commentating job? The reason I don't spend money is so the money will be there when I'm older. I'm looking out for my future. And I never promised you anything other than to love you. I don't know where you got that in your head."

"I want what other wives have."

"What other wives? Are you looking at LeBron James's wife? Did you count how many endorsements he has when you looked at how they live? Hell, I'm just happy I get the occasional commercial, and Nike outfits me with shoes. Or are you looking at Gisele? Because she came into her marriage with Tom Brady as a freaking supermodel—what did you bring?"

"That's rude, Julius."

"Right, but you wanting to spend all the money I've earned so you can feel like you belong isn't. Got it."

The room is silent. Even my lawyer seems stunned by my ex. I wish I could live my life in hindsight because if I could, I would've never pursued anything with Elena.

"How much?" I throw it out there. Elena's eyes widen. "As much as I don't want to give you any money, I want out. I want to move on and have a healthy relationship with Autumn. I don't want this divorce looming over me anymore. So how much is it going to take, Elena?"

"Ten million," she says with a smirk.

"See you in court then," I tell her.

"You just asked me how much I wanted, and I gave you a number. Now you're playing games."

"No, I'm not. But if you think I'm giving you ten million, you're out of your mind." I glance at my lawyer, who is watching the back and forth between Elena and me. "One million," I throw back at her.

"Five."

I scoff. "For five million, I want full legal custody of the kids with the stipulation that you can visit anytime you want, provided you stay in your own hotel or apartment. The kids live with me, no matter where I end up or where I decide to retire. I make all their decisions—every single one. We can rotate holidays, not that I think you'll actually make time for them, but they need to know that they're spending Christmas with their mom as well. I will provide a nanny when they're with you to keep the kids in a routine. You're more than welcome to take them on vacation as long as it doesn't interrupt their schooling or any sports or activities they're participating in." I finish and look at my lawyer. "Am I forgetting anything?"

He shakes his head as his pen writes furiously across the paper.

"One condition," Elena states.

"What's that?"

"I want to formally meet your girlfriend. I get the impression she's going to be around for a while, and I want to know who is going to be mothering my children."

I let her words stew for a moment and make it seem like I'm pondering her request. I'm not. I'm fucking livid that she dares to act like she's mother of the year. "I have no doubt Autumn will be happy to meet you, especially considering your first encounter with her didn't go so well."

Elena has nothing to say.

I pull my phone out of my pocket and send Autumn a text, asking her if she's around to meet Elena. I don't want to prolong this divorce any longer. "Autumn is home and excited to meet you. Shall we go?" I stand, not giving Elena a chance to change her mind.

"I thought you had practice?" she asks, reminding me that I told her she had to take a cab back to her place.

"I do, but I'll take the fine if it means you'll sign the papers today and be done with this marriage."

I glance over at the lawyer, who nods. "I'll send the papers over today."

Elena says nothing during the drive back to the complex. I feel this meeting won't suffice Elena's curiosity about Autumn, but it's a start. I'm not going to hide my relationship with Autumn, and if Elena has questions, she can ask me.

Back at the apartments, we head to my penthouse. I told Autumn to meet us there. It's unlikely the kids will ever be at Autumn's place. Inside, soft music plays, and a sense of calm rushes over me. I like having Autumn here, but I know it's way too soon to ask her to move in with us. I don't want to rush this relationship at all.

"Hey," Autumn says as we round the corner into the living room. She stands to greet me. I kiss her. Not caring that Elena is there.

"Autumn, this is Elena."

Autumn steps forward and pulls Elena into her arms. The shocked look on Elena's face makes me laugh. As much as I want to monitor the conversation between them, it's not my place. Elena's going to say what she feels needs to be said, and Autumn will listen. I excuse myself and head into my bedroom. The pillow Autumn used last night still smells like her, and as I look around the room, I wonder what needs to change to make her feel at home. I know for sure we will need a lot of sleepovers before I ask her to move in, but I see it happening. I see her as a part of my future and a pivotal role in the children's lives.

Of course, things could change. Autumn's career could take her places I can't go. I've done the long-distance thing with Elena, and that definitely didn't work out in my favor. I could get traded, leaving Autumn behind. She loves her job, but she's young, and being a stepmom before you're thirty might not be something she wants.

The bedroom door opens, and Autumn strolls in. She sits down next to me and rests her head on my shoulder.

"How'd it go?"

"Awkward. She asked me my views on parenting, and I was honest with her. I told her I didn't have any because this was all very new to me, but her babies are important to me. Elena asked me to promise never to undermine her when it comes to the kids, and I told her I would never undermine you. I told her I'm in no way, shape, or form trying to replace her—that she will always be their mom."

"I caved and gave her money. It's all she's ever wanted from me. She's angry she's not living some elitist life because I refuse to live outside of my means. She doesn't understand that at any time, my career could be done, and then what? But the kids are staying here, even Reggie, who isn't going to be happy. So, I have to ask—are you okay with dating a single dad who plays professional football and may have to cancel a date or two if his kids need him?"

Autumn grimaces, and my heart sinks. Slowly, a smile forms on her lips. "If I had an issue, I wouldn't be here." She leans in, and her hand cups my cheek. Our lips meet. Our kiss is gentle, yet there's a sense of longing. Our mouths move slowly against each other's as my arm finds purchase around her waist. Autumn presses her body to mine, and everything within me ignites with fire. I want her. I want to make her mine over and over again until I'm spent, and there is nothing left to give.

She angles her body to move us to the bed, and I put on the brakes. "I can't," I say against her lips. The word "practice" is muttered, but it's incoherent. It takes great effort to pull away from her. Autumn opens her eyes slowly, and I can see the yearning. "I'm already late for practice," I tell her. "I desperately want you right now, but I have to go."

"Later, then?"

"The second you walk in tonight, you're mine."

"I suddenly hate that I'm on the evening news."

We both laugh at her statement. As much as I love watching her on TV, I too hate that she works until almost midnight. "I'll watch and fantasize about everything I get to do to you tonight."

Autumn walks with me to the parking garage, where we proceed to make out like horny teenagers. The thought of being with her in the backseat of my car overwhelms my senses. I push her away. There are cameras watching us, and the last thing either of us needs is for security to hone in on the rocking SUV. Comical as it might be, the embarrassment would be too much for either of us. With one last kiss goodbye, I climb into my car and start thinking of the most disgusting things I can. It would not bode well for me to show up at the practice facility with a hard-on.

THIRTY-FIVE

AUTUMN

For the first time ever, I hate my job. It's raining, and it's Sunday. In the world of football, these two things do not go hand-in-hand. On Friday, I promised clear skies for the game today. However, a shift in the weather pattern—that no one could predict—has the city of Portland under a constant drizzle. The rain cloud is content to hang over us all day, making for a very wet football game. Things probably wouldn't be so bad if I weren't dating the Pioneers wide receiver and planning to attend the game. Take those two things out of the equation, and you'd find me nestled on my couch, with a blanket over my legs and a good book in my hands.

Last night, instead of spending time with Julius and the kids, I gave myself a mini spa treatment. After a long soak in the tub, I did the whole self-care thing with an at-home mani and pedi, plucked, trimmed, and cut where needed, and put on the best mud mask I've ever used. I feel nights like this will be hard to come by once football is over. I'm not complaining at all, but I'm also unsure if I'm ready for the change. There is very little doubt in my mind that I'm in love with Julius. However, loving him means loving Reggie and Roxy, which is easy to do. I just don't know what my role is or should be. With Roxy, things are simple. We're already close, but Reggie—he's going through a lot, and at eight, I can't begin to comprehend how he must feel. He probably feels like his world is falling apart and doesn't see that his father is doing everything he can to protect him.

I'm putting on the last of my cold-weather gear when there's a knock at my door. I look through the peephole, and my heart jumps at the sight of two of my most favorite people. I open the door and squeal as I leap into my mother's waiting arms. When she lets me go, my father welcomes me into his.

"What are you guys doing here?" Even though I was in Texas, I couldn't see my parents. Leaving the approved area wasn't allowed, and since I was technically on a job interview, I couldn't go off on my own.

"We're here to visit," my dad says. I bring them into my apartment, and he sets their luggage down.

"Oh, sweetie, you have a view," mom says as she goes to the slider.

"It's not much, but I enjoy it." I open the door, and she steps out. The balcony is only wide enough for a small chair and table. Unlike Peyton and Noah's terrace or even Julius's, I won't be having any parties out here any time soon.

"Beautiful, but very cold." Mom crosses, rubs her arms, and then heads back inside. I give my parents the tour. It's small but homey, and I've done a lot to make it my own. When they finally settle on the couch, I ask again why they are here.

"Do you want us to leave?" my dad asks.

"No, not at all. I'm happy you're here," I tell them. "A

slight hint or notice would've been nice, though. I have plans today, but I'll cancel them, and we'll go sightseeing or something."

"Nonsense." My mom bats away my statement.

"I do believe tickets are waiting for us at will-call and a promise of a luxury box and tour of the stadium."

My mouth drops open. "I'm sorry, did you say tickets?" What the heck is going on?

Dad nods and has a big cheesy grin on his face. "Sure did. I've never sat in a suite before. Probably a good thing since it's raining out, and I didn't bring an umbrella."

"Wait," I say. "Can you please explain what's going on?" Before my parents can answer, my phone rings, and a picture I took of Julius, Reggie, and Roxy shows on the screen. "Excuse me for a minute." I take my phone and head into my bedroom. "Hey."

"Hi. How's your morning?"

"Well, it's turned out to be a pretty great one."

"Is that so?" he asks with a chuckle.

"Hmm, you wouldn't have anything to do with my parents being here, would you?"

Another laugh. "Thanksgiving is next week, and I thought it would be nice for your parents to spend it with you, and hopefully the kids and me."

"Wow, I don't know what to say other than thank you. I don't even want to know how you pulled this off or got a hold of my parents."

"Well, you can say you'll spend Thanksgiving with us. I promise delicious food, amazing company, and only two football games, followed by some college basketball. And yes, please don't ask. I don't want my source to get into trouble over this. It's all meant to make you smile."

"I'm smiling, and you know I'll be there. I want to warn

you, though, my father is a huge sports fan, so you probably have a best friend for life."

"I'm counting on it, Autumn. I've sent a car to pick you up. There's a luxury suite waiting for you and your parents. Plus, they can buy whatever they want at the fan stores inside the stadium. Everything is taken care of."

I sigh. "What about the kids? And your parents? I don't want to leave them out."

"Are you sure?" he asks.

"Julius, if we are going to do this relationship thing, I want to be in one-hundred percent. Are we moving fast? Yep, we are, but we're too deep to slow down now. Besides, you're going to meet my parents, and I've already met yours. You might as well make it one big happy family in the suite. And I want to be with Roxy and try to bond with Reggie."

"I don't know how I got so lucky, especially when I don't deserve you, Weather Girl."

"Just remember what you said when it downpours on you later."

Julius laughs. "I'll see you at the game."

❦❦❦

MY DAD IS giddy with excitement on our way to the stadium. Julius texted after we hung up that his parents and the kids would meet us at the suite and not to worry about them riding with us. It's a bummer because I think the kids and my dad would have a blast together as he's currently standing up through the sunroof.

"He's going to hurt himself," my mother says with a shake of her head. "He's such a child."

I can't help but laugh. "The hospital isn't far from the

stadium, and the team has an amazing medical staff if Dad needs something."

My mom stares at me for a minute, and I can't help but feel scrutinized. I straighten my jacket and brush my hand over my hair. It's an automatic response to someone gawking. After what feels like an eternity, I finally say, "What?" My tone is a bit harsher than I suspected.

"You're different," she tells me. "When I saw you in Dickinson, you seemed sad, withdrawn."

"I didn't like Dickinson a whole lot. It was depressing. Small town living is not for me."

"I thought it was because you missed Camden and still reeled from the break-up."

I shake my head slightly. "The break-up would've happened regardless. Cam and I are better off as friends. I used to think differently, but after the storm reporting I did with him, I realized he's not the one for me."

"And Julius is the one for you." It's not a question but stated as a fact. "He's the difference in your demeanor."

I want to tell her she's wrong, but I don't think she is. Even with everything that's happened since we met, I'd still take those days over not knowing Julius. "Maybe." I refuse to say otherwise out of fear I might jinx things. "We like each other, but his life is complicated right now."

"I read about him in People Magazine. More so, his ex. She seems," Mom pauses and then says, "busy."

"She's trying to make her mark in Hollywood." As much as I want to badmouth her for everything she's done, I can't. I won't. I promised myself I will always see the good in her because she's Reggie and Roxy's mother, and it's what they deserve. When they're older, they'll come to their own conclusions about their mother. Since she went back to

California, she's only called once, and as far as I know, she hadn't answered when Reggie phoned her.

Mom looks at me skeptically. She can probably see right through the bullshit but knows it's not her place to say anything. I'm sure, as a parent, the last thing she expected from me was to fall for a single dad going through a divorce and a high-profile one at that. The media is relentless when it comes to gossip, which only increased when *someone* leaked their divorce documents. I couldn't help it and looked to see what people said on social media. Most of Julius's loyal fans sided with him, while Elena's "wives" all took her side, who feel Julius should've paid Elena more money. I hope I am never like that or in a situation where money matters more than love and family.

When we pull up to the stadium, my dad hoots and hollers like he's some dedicated fan. I doubt he's ever watched a Pioneers game until I told him about Julius. The driver takes us around back. It's very cloak and dagger but saves us from having to stand in line and wait for tickets. I learned early that when Julius says will-call, he doesn't really mean for me to stand at the window while someone searches for my ticket. There is a private entrance for families at this stadium.

A Pioneer staff member meets us at the door and tells my parents they're getting a tour of the facility, and assures me they'll bring my parents to the suite when they're finished. Julius is giving them the royal treatment, which will definitely win my father over.

When I reach the suite, Reggie is standing outside the door, looking at his phone. Across from him is a security guard, watching him. "Hey, Reggie." I try to make my voice sound as upbeat and happy as possible, even though I know he's hurting.

"Hi, Miss Autumn."

I stand next to him. "Whatcha doing?"

He shrugs. "My mom won't answer."

"She's probably on set. I read somewhere that actors sometimes have to be on set from sunup until sundown, and most of the time, they can't have their phones with them because they don't want it to ring during filming." I'm trying —anything I can do to put a positive spin on things for him right now.

"Maybe," he says with a heavy sigh.

"Guess what?"

"What?"

"My parents are here, and I think my dad is a bigger football fan than you."

Reggie looks at me. There's a twinkle in his eyes. It's short-lived, but I saw it. "Not possible."

"Oh, I don't know. He might challenge your knowledge of the sport."

Reggie looks down the corridor. "Where is he?"

"Getting a tour and probably a hotdog. Oh, and probably one of those foam fingers that everyone has."

Reggie laughs. It's a deep belly chuckle that makes me smile. "That's silly. There are hotdogs inside."

"Yum! I'm starving. What do you say? Do you want to go in with me?"

He shrugs. "Okay."

I nod and hold my arm out for him. I signal to the security guard that I have Reggie now. With my hand on the door, he pauses. "Miss Autumn?"

I crouch down until I'm at eye level with him. "How about we stop the Miss Autumn stuff, and you just call me Autumn?"

"Okay," he says. "Thank you."

"For what?"

"For being my friend. You're starting to feel like a mom to me. At first, that scared me, but I think I like it."

Cue the tears. "Reggie, your words mean everything to me." I stand, pull him into my arms, and kiss his head. "I'll be whatever you need me to be. Whatever makes you happy." His little arms tighten around my waist.

"I'm so glad my dad found you."

Me too, bud. Me too!

THIRTY-SIX

JULIUS

The rest of November and all of December flew by. I swear I think I went to sleep Thanksgiving night and woke up days before Christmas. Whirlwind doesn't begin to describe my life right now. I'm still embattled with Elena and this ridiculous divorce. Instead of taking the offer on the table and agreeing, she listened to her "fans" on social media and the "wives" and decided to hire her own lawyer. Something she should've done from the beginning but didn't have the money. She still doesn't, but her counsel is willing to take payment once a settlement comes in. I've tried to tell her that means less money for her, but I'm wrong. I'm always wrong. I'm confident a judge will accept the prenuptial agreement as is. She won't be able to ask for custody of the children either. She's proven she can't effectively communicate with them. They haven't spoken to her since she left this last time.

The only thing Elena is doing is holding up my moving on with Autumn. We've talked about her moving in, but she won't until I'm divorced. She doesn't want Elena showing up and causing a scene and us having no recourse. As much as I agree with her, I hate it. I hate that Elena still controls my life.

Noah and I are at the jewelers. He's looking for a gift for Peyton but doesn't know what. Every time I say, "How about this?" he shakes his head. After the tenth time or so, he finally admitted he doesn't know what he wants to get her but wants it to be unique. He let it slip a few weeks ago, after one too many drinks, that they're struggling to get pregnant, and each time they find out they're not, Peyton begins to shut down. He's hoping that the trip they're taking to see family at Christmas will help her because he's afraid he's out of options.

It occurs to me that I might be able to help him. "Can I take you somewhere?" I ask him. He nods, and we head out and to my car. I drive us to a part of town I only visit when I can't get out of a funk, which happens after I've had to deal with Elena and her bullshit. I pull up to a row of stores and park along the curb.

"Where are we going?"

"I don't want you to laugh, but I started seeing this woman to help me with my stress. She's a healer."

"You brought me to a voodoo shop?"

I shrug. "Sort of. Just follow me." I open the door, and the bell chimes over the stop. The young salesclerk looks up, smiles, and then goes back to reading the magazine she holds. I take Noah over to the jewelry case and point. "Each stone represents what you need. For instance, I have an amethyst that I carry when I have to go to the lawyer or when I have to talk to Elena. I find that it helps, and I'm not angry all the time. Maybe it's my mindset or thinking the gem works, I don't know, but I wasn't a believer until I came here on a whim. I'm not saying this could help Peyton, but it might."

"Julius, hi. You brought a friend."

Madame Keisha steps out from behind the curtain. She eyes Noah for a long while and then shakes her head. "I have something that can help with that ache you're feeling."

"I'm sorry, what?" he asks after his head pops up. "I feel fine."

She nods and says, "Okay." Keisha disappears behind the curtain and then is back with a small jar of what looks like a white cream. "Put this on before bed. Nothing is wrong, but your body is telling you to stop and listen. This will help."

Noah takes it but does so with great reluctance.

"Now, you're looking for," she takes his hand in hers and smiles. "Baby. Do you desire to have children?"

He nods. "My wife is having trouble conceiving."

Still holding Noah's hand, her smile fades. "There was trauma. She's hurt."

Noah nods again. "She was in a bad accident. I almost lost her."

"You did lose her, but she came back."

I stand there in awe of Madame Keisha. Maybe people don't believe in her craft, but I do. She sets Noah's hand down and goes to her case. She starts putting gems together on a string and then slips them into a bag.

"Give this to your wife. She must wear it until the babies arrive."

Noah coughs. "Babies? What are you talking about? She's not pregnant."

"Yet," Madame Keisha winks. She looks at me and says, "Julius, I have something for you." She hands me another small bag. "Give this to your love. She will need it."

"What—"

"You'll find out in time." With that, she goes behind the

curtain and leaves us standing there until the clerk clears her throat. I direct Noah to the cash register where we cash out. Back in the car, Noah looks confused.

"Sorry for bringing you. I didn't think you'd freak out."

"It's not that. It's what she said about Peyton 'she's hurt.' She said it in the present tense like something is wrong with her now."

"The babies part doesn't freak you out?"

He shakes his head slowly. "No. Peyton's doctors have told her the chances of conceiving naturally would be hard. The damage from the car accident left her scarred. But we try. And we've talked about doing IVF or looking for a surrogate. The surrogate is out. She doesn't want to use one. Peyton's read too many horror stories where the surrogate wants more money or decides to keep the baby." He looks down at the bag in his hand and smirks. "This shit is just propaganda."

"Then how did she know that stuff about Peyton?"

He looks at me, and I swear he rolls his eyes. "I'm sure your friend there knows who I am, by way of you. If you look me up on the web, Peyton's story is well documented. It's not hard to fake it."

Noah's right, but I don't want to believe it. I drop him off at his place and tell him to have a good trip. He thanks me and asks that I not say anything to Autumn about the gems because it's unlikely he'll give them to Peyton.

"Does this mean you won't tell your mom about it?"

"Hell no," he says while standing on the curb. "She'd believe it and start rubbing the stones anywhere she can. Both moms are crazy for grandkids. No one is going to know about this little trip except for us. Got it?"

I salute him and pull away once he shuts the car door. I suppose he's right about keeping our excursion to the voodoo shop a secret. I haven't told anyone but him, even when Autumn has commented on the stone I keep in my pocket.

When I get to my apartment, Roxy comes running to me and tells me that Autumn is sleeping. "Autumn is at work, sweetie."

She shakes her head fast with her eyes wide. "Au-um has the ickies."

Autumn didn't say anything about staying home today. She spent the night last night and went for her run this morning and then took Roxy to the park after dropping Reggie off at school. She's taken over for Miss Meghan this week because she's on vacation, and Autumn wanted to help out.

I head down to my bedroom with Roxy on my hip. I open the door slowly and find a lump in my bed. "I'm going to set you down. Please don't jump on Autumn."

"I won't, Daddy."

Putting Roxy on the edge of the bed, I go to the side and place my hand on Autumn's shoulder. "Hey."

She moans.

"What can I get you?"

"Ginger ale," she whispers.

I pull my phone out and order groceries via an app. I request as much stuff as I can from Pedialyte to Pepto, including the ginger ale. Then I take Roxy out to the living room and set her up with a movie. When I get back to the bedroom, Autumn is rushing to the bathroom. I don't know what to do except offer to hold her hair back. She kneels in front of the toilet, expelling whatever contents she had left in her stomach.

"I have groceries coming. They should be here in a minute." I leave her side, grab a washcloth, and wet it down.

I set it to her forehead and hold it there. "Hopefully, it's just a bug, and it'll pass soon."

"Good thing you don't have a game this weekend."

She's right. We have another weekend off because of Christmas. It's rare when our schedules align, but I'll take it. "Stomach of steel right here. I'm more concerned about you right now."

Autumn tries to stand up. I help her and decide to pick her up to carry her back to bed. "I can walk," she says.

"I know, but I can carry you." I lay her down and pull the blankets back over her. "What can I get you?" I set my hand against her forehead to check for a fever.

"I'm not sick, Julius."

I look at her oddly. "I saw you get sick." I hate pointing out the obvious, but I *was* in the bathroom with her a moment ago.

"Julius," she says my name and then sighs. "I'm late."

"Give me your phone. I'll call Leon and let him know you're sick and can't come in. I'm sure someone can cover for you." I reach for her phone, but her hand stops me.

"I'm not that kind of sick."

"How many kinds of sicknesses are there?" I feel like Autumn is talking in riddles here.

"I'm the kind of sick that happens to women when their period doesn't show up on time," she pauses and looks at me. Autumn starts to cry. "I'm pregnant, Julius."

Pregnant.

My mouth opens to say something but closes when nothing comes out. I try again, but nothing.

"I know we haven't been together very long, and you're going through that mess with Elena. I don't know how it happened because we've been safe and—"

I press my lips against hers to silence her. She keeps her

mouth closed, which I'm thankful for because . . . well, she's been sick. When I pull away, I wipe her fallen tears. "I should've told you the second I realized this. I'm in love with you, Autumn. I love you so damn much. I planned to ask you to move in once my divorce is final, but I don't want to wait anymore." I move closer to her and take her hand in mine. "Autumn, will you move into this place and help me make a home?"

She nods and pulls me into her arms.

"Now, it seems like we had a little mishap with protection. Do you think I should sue the condom company?"

Autumn chokes out a laugh and shakes her head.

"So, tell me about this baby of mine growing in your tummy." I pull the blankets back and lift her shirt. "Hey there, baby. I'm going to be your dad." I kiss her belly a couple of times. "If you can do me a favor and not make your mommy sick, I would really appreciate it. I don't like to see your mommy hurting."

Autumn's hand goes through my hair, and I look at her. "I thought you'd be upset."

I maneuver until I'm lying next to her. "This isn't ideal, but it's not a dealbreaker. You're the one I want to be with no matter what. So, what if we're doing things a little backward. No one says we must follow their rules. We'll make our own."

Her hand cups my cheek. "I love you, Julius Cunningham."

"I love you, Weather Girl."

EPILOGUE

R eggie, Roxy, and I make our way into the stadium. The atmosphere is surreal, and according to Reggie, this is a once-in-a-lifetime opportunity. Every seat has a fan of football sitting in it. Every luxury box has a corporate sponsor, a celebrity, or some big shot, something or other. As a family, we chose to sit in the stands to be near the action. Because like Reggie says, we may only experience the Super Bowl once.

There are a few things in my life that I'm thankful for right now. One being, Reggie and I get along very well. For the first couple of weeks, after his mom left, he shut down. He reminded me that I'm not his mother and never will be. He would get angry with Julius if he invited me to dinner. Or when Reggie would wake up, and I was in the kitchen. The adjustment has been challenging for both of us, but I never stopped trying to be his friend. I never set out to replace his mother. Not then and not now. Elena is doing a stand-up job of separating herself from her children without any help. It took a picture of Elena on vacation, which she posted on social media, for Reggie to start seeing his mom in a new light. An unfortunate situation all around.

I'm also incredibly thankful for my job, for Leon, and the staff I work with. If someone told me six months ago, I was going to move to a vast city, fall in love with a professional athlete, and get pregnant, I would've died of laughter right in front of them. None of this was in my life plan—not that I had one to begin with. Thinking back, I feel as if I didn't have any direction. If it weren't for Leon, I wouldn't be here right now, which made my decision to stay in Portland ten times easier. Of course, Julius was a significant part of this. I knew from the start he was going to be someone special in my life.

I'm beyond appreciative of this life I live. I love my job, friends, family, and this little family unit I'm in with Julius and his children. Even though Roxy isn't mine, she's becoming my mini-me more and more each day. She's started doing her own weather reports in the living room each morning. Even though Julius still employs Miss Meghan, I take Roxy to the park each morning before heading to work. Meghan is there to take care of Roxy when neither Julius nor I are home, and she picks Reggie up from school. We plan to keep her when the new baby comes because I'm not ready to give up my career.

This baby growing inside of me is one of the best things to happen to me. At first, I didn't think I was ready. My career is just starting to take off. Julius and I haven't been together that long and the fact that when I told him about being pregnant, he was still married. The day his divorce became final was one of the happiest days of our new lives together. It's also the day I officially moved in. Once I told him about the pregnancy, he wanted me to treat his apartment as if it were mine. He gave me a key and full reign to redesign anything I wanted. His office will be the nursery, and we'll start on that once we tell people we're having a baby. It's still early, and I'd like to keep it a secret a bit longer. If it weren't for Julius, people would probably know already. My morning sickness kept me sidelined for the first week or so until he gave me the bracelet I wear constantly. He said it was given to him by a psychic and that he had no idea it was for me until I kept getting sick. Of course, once he said the word psychic, we had to have a long talk on why he went to one.

An usher shows us to our seats. All around us are Pioneer fans. Reggie has his foam finger, and we are wearing our Cunningham jerseys. As soon as Roxy sees Betty Paige Westbury, she begs to sit with her. Peyton's mom sits down next to me and hands over baby Oliver. Mrs. James is trying to rub baby fever on any unsuspecting wife and girlfriend on the team. Her reasoning is she's ready for grandchildren and figures if Peyton's friends are pregnant, she'll want to be as well. Oliver wears a Noah Westbury jersey, and it's the cutest thing I have ever seen. I only get to hold him for a few minutes because Elle shows up and takes him.

Nola sits down next to me, and I ask, "How are wedding plans?"

She lets out a huge sigh. "There are times when I think I want to elope or have a destination wedding, but then I think about my nieces and nephews in the wedding, and I want that too. I'm so torn. I just want to marry Quinn and start a family."

"I think Quinn's mother will be delighted with the last part."

Nola's eyes go wide. "You're telling me. She has baby fever worse than any of us."

Julius's parents and mine show up and take their seats. Reggie sits between my father and his grandfather, chatting about the game and the Pioneers' odds. All I know is that Julius is a ball of nerves. When they won their conference championship on a Hail Mary throw by Noah into Julius's arms, he said he almost crapped his pants on the field. I, for one, am happy he didn't do that.

I look out to the field and see the team warming up. My gut twists with excitement and nerves. I know once Liam Page starts singing the National Anthem, I'm going to start crying. It's pretty amazing that the NFL asked Noah's dad to sing. It's going to be an emotional day for the Westbury family.

Speaking of the Westburys, Noah's elderly grand-mother is coming up the stairs, with Mack escorting her. She takes a seat right at the railing. I've seen her at a couple of games, and let me tell you, the mouth on her would make a sailor blush.

"Who else is sitting with Noah's grandma?" I ask Nola. At our last playoff game, I had the chance to meet Mack. He came over with Noah and Peyton after the game, and it was then that Peyton told me about him and his connection with her family.

"Oh, that's Peyton's grandfather and Quinn's grandmother."

"Awe, their family is so blended."

Nola nods. "Literally one big happy family. Quinn told me one time that if it wasn't for Peyton and Elle's grandpa telling Katelyn to move on, their family might have never happened."

"Really?"

"Yeah, Katelyn and Mason—the twins' father—were high school sweethearts. Harrison met Katelyn months after

Mason's funeral. For Harrison, it was love at first sight, but for Katelyn, she was afraid people would judge her for moving on so quickly. Mr. Powell pushed Katelyn toward Harrison, and the rest is history. Harrison adopted the twins, and Katelyn adopted Quinn."

"Yet, they never married."

She shakes her head slowly. "Nope, and they won't. It's Goldie Hawn and Kurt Russell if you ask me."

"A true love story."

"Pretty much," Nola says. "I asked Quinn what he thought about his parents not being married, and he said it only bothered people who made it an issue. Growing up, they didn't know otherwise because they all had the same last name."

Peyton joins us from the field. She hugs her grandparents and Noah's grandma, and then her parents. She finally sits down in an empty seat near Nola and me and asks her sister to bring Oliver to her.

"Is Noah ready?" Elle asks.

Peyton shrugs. "It's a big stage. The biggest of his life. He's as ready as he's going to be."

"It's too bad you can't sit with us," Nola adds.

Peyton smiles, but I'm not sure if it's at us or the baby. "I'm right where I want to be."

"How's Uncle Liam? Did you see him before you came out?" Elle asks.

"No, he and Dad are in the dressing room."

"Uncle Jimmy is pissed that he's not here," Elle says. "Mom said Eden has some huge event in Australia tomorrow, and they had to fly there early to kill the jet lag."

Nola elbows me. "You look confused."

"I am. There's just so many in their family."

She laughs. "Not even gonna lie, I wrote everyone down

in a book and created a chart, so I knew. The worst part of all this—the only ones related to each other are the parents to the kids. The aunts and uncles are all long-time family friends."

"Yeah, Peyton tried to explain it to me. I just nodded along."

Elle snorts. "I love telling people that my sister married my aunt and uncle's son—that really gets people going."

Peyton slaps her sister. "You're a brat. Where's Ben?"

"He had to work. He's got a big project."

"A project that couldn't wait until Monday?" Peyton's face pinches as she stares at her sister.

Elle shrugs, signaling the end of that conversation. Peyton hands Oliver back to her sister and then tells us she will see us later. She talks to her mom quickly before heading back to the field, but not before taking Mack with her. It's then that everything shifts.

It's time for football.

We stand for the anthem, which Liam sings beautifully. After, he hugs Noah, which brings tears to my eyes. When Julius goes out for the coin toss, Reggie and I cross our fingers. I close my eyes and listen for the call. When I hear that the Pioneers have won the toss, I feel relieved.

Reggie tugs on my shirt, and I bend toward him. "We're going to win," he says. "I can feel it in my bones."

"Me too, bud."

The kick-off happens, and the Pioneers return it for a touchdown. Within seconds, it's seven to nothing. Four downs later, Noah and the team he's led to the Super Bowl take the field. My man lines up on Noah's left—a position I've been told is very significant to Liam, and Peyton's father, Mason. I made the mistake of asking Julius, in front of Peyton and Noah, why he's never on the right side of his quarterback. Once Noah shared Liam and Mason's story, I understood.

Noah's first attempt goes to the running back, Brandon Garrison. He picks up six yards, according to the announcer. Not that we can hear much of what they're saying because this stadium is loud. People are yelling, chanting, and stomping their feet. I've never been in the middle of something like this. It's both exhilarating and terrifying.

In the next play, Noah takes the ball and steps back. He looks left and then right and fires a pass downfield. I lean forward and see Julius running toward the end zone. A guy is trailing him. I have no choice but to watch everything unfold on the massive screen hanging in the center of the stadium. There are too many people, and they're standing, blocking my vantage point. The guy in pursuit of Julius is waving his arms in the air, but none of this affects Julius. He holds his hands out, and the ball lands perfectly in his arms. Another player comes at Julius and tackles him, but not before the ball breaks the plane. Every Pioneer on the sideline puts their arms up.

Touchdown!

"Mom, did you see that?" Reggie says as he pulls on my arm. I glance at him and smile. "I mean, Autumn. Did you see that?"

It doesn't hurt that he changed what he called me. Reggie has to move at his own pace. If he wants to call me mom, he can. If not, Autumn is perfect too. "Your dad scored a touchdown in the Super Bowl!" Reggie and I high-five each other, plus everyone around us, and then we cheer for Julius as he reaches the sideline.

Julius comes over to the railing and holds the ball up. He points at Reggie, who scrambles to get down to his dad.

When Reggie comes back, he shows me the ball. "Dad says it's mine to keep!"

"We'll get a stand for it, and you can put it in your bedroom."

"Awesome," he says. He shows his grandfather and my dad before showing everyone else in our group. Roxy comes to me and tells me she's sad and then screams to her dad that she wants a ball.

The other team scores a field goal next, and then Noah runs for a touchdown after taking the team from the thirty-yard line to the end zone. I fully expect him to give the football to Peyton, but he comes over to the stands and points at his dad. They hug, and when I look over at Josie, she has tears in her eyes.

"That's another true love story," Nola says to me. "Ask Noah or even Josie about it sometime."

"I will, thank you."

After halftime, the following two scores put the other guys up. Reggie is stressing but keeps telling me that he knows we are going to win. The Pioneers call a time-out, which my dad says is smart because they need to regroup. All around me, everyone talks about football, and I realize I need to learn a lot before next season starts. I've got the basics down, but that's about it.

When Noah is at the line of scrimmage, he calls an audible. Everyone shifts, even Julius. Noah steps back and hands the ball to Chase Montgomery, who rears back and throws a bomb toward Julius.

"Catch it," I mutter. He does and runs the last ten yards into the endzone without being touched. Before I can alert Roxy, she's made her way to the railing and holds her hands out. She brings the ball back to me and asks me to hold it while she goes back to sitting with Noah's sister.

"Dad has two touchdowns! I told you we are going to win."

"Let's hope, Reggie."

The game is back and forth. The Pioneers go up. The other team catches us. The other team moves ahead. The Pioneers take the lead. My anxiety level is off the charts. There is under two minutes left in the game, and it's tied. I'm biting my knuckles. My heart is racing. And my knees are weak.

It's fourth down.

And we have the ball.

Noah puts the play in motion.

Bodies are flying everywhere.

I'm praying.

His arm rears back to throw and then drops down.

Liam yells for his son to throw the ball.

Bianca Westbury tells the referee to pull his head out of his ass because the other team did something illegal.

Noah throws the brown leather odd-shaped ball. It flies through the air—bodies jump. Hands fight for control.

One person comes down with the ball, and the stadium erupts.

Everyone around me screams.

Julius has it, and he's crossed the plane.

"Touchdown!" the announcer screams.

Everything is a blur until Julius stands at the railing, yelling my name. I go to him and kiss him, thankful he's removed his helmet. He hands me the ball. "Read it," he says.

Read it?

I look at the ball with its black writing, '*Will you marry me, Weather Girl?*'

"Julius?"

Someone on the sideline hands him a box. He opens it and shows me a ring nestled in a black cushion. "Autumn LaRosa, will you do me the honor of being my wife?"

I nod and cover my mouth. "Yes. Yes. Holy crap, Julius."

"Hold this. Don't put it on yet. I'll do that after we win this game!" He kisses me and sets the box in my hand. When reality sets in, the clock is at zero, and confetti is raining down from the sky. It takes me a moment to grasp the situation until Reggie is at my side, jumping up and down.

The Portland Pioneers have won the Superbowl.

ACKNOWLEDGMENTS

I have to say I never thought I'd get to the acknowledgments for this book. It feels like I've been writing it forever, and for me, it has been. Writer's block is no joke, but I'm thankful for my friends. They encouraged the creative side, held my hand (virtually), and promised me they would stick with me until the end, and they did.

Reggie—I want to thank you for taking my concepts and producing the images I needed to get these covers done. You knew the models to use, sent me great footage, made me FaceTime while I was in my pajamas, and kept me in the loop the entire time. I enjoy working with you so much.

Sarah—it's hard to believe we've been together for nine years! I've lost count of how many covers we've done, but you always know what my stories need. Thank you!

Amy & Traci—I'm lumping you both together because my passages will be redundant, and you'll pick on me. I miss you terribly. We had plans in 2020 and again this year. Now it won't be until 2022 when we can be together. The best part, you girls don't know each other, but you're going to become besties! Bring on Texas!!

Trudy—I'm thankful for you & all the help you've given me over the past couple of years. You're a breath of fresh air and a great sounding board.

Debra & Drue—best team ever. I'd be lost without you in my life.

The Beaumont Daily—you ladies crack me up. I appreciate all the love you give me, my characters, and the stories.

To the readers—I appreciate you. I love all the teasers you make on your own, the posts you make about whatever book of mine you're reading, and when you tell me how much a story moved you. If you're following me on Facebook, Instagram, Twitter, or TikTok – please know that I see you.

And if you've read through this—you're the real VIP in all of this.

Much love,

Heidi

ALSO BY HEIDI MCLAUGHLIN

THE BEAUMONT SERIES

Forever My Girl

My Everything

My Unexpected Forever

Finding My Forever

Finding My Way

12 Days of Forever

My Kind of Forever

Forever Our Boys

The Beaumont Boxed Set - #1

THE BEAUMONT SERIES: NEXT GENERATION

Holding Onto Forever

My Unexpected Love

Chasing My Forever

Peyton & Noah

Fighting For Our Forever

A Beaumont Family Christmas

THE PORTLAND PIONEERS:
A BEAUMONT SERIES NEXT GENERATION
SPIN-OFF

Fourth Down

Fair Catch

False Start

CAPE HARBOR SERIES

After All

Until Then

THE ARCHER BROTHERS

Here with Me

Choose Me

Save Me

LOST IN YOU SERIES

Lost in You

Lost in Us

THE BOYS OF SUMMER

Third Base

Home Run

Grand Slam

Hawk

THE REALITY DUET

Blind Reality

Twisted Reality

SOCIETY X

Dark Room

Viewing Room

Play Room

THE CLUTCH SERIES

Roman

STANDALONE NOVELS

Stripped Bare

Blow

Sexcation

HOLIDAY NOVELS

Santa's Secret

It's a Wonderful Holiday

THE DATING SERIES

A Date for Midnight

A Date with an Admirer

A Date for Good Luck

A Date for the Hunt

A Date for the Derby

A Date to Play Fore

A Date with a Foodie

A Date for the Fair

A Date for the Regatta

A Date for the Masquerade

A Date with a Turkey

A Date with an Elf

ABOUT HEIDI MCLAUGHLIN

Heidi McLaughlin is a New York Times, Wall Street Journal, and USA Today Bestselling author of The Beaumont Series, The Boys of Summer, and The Archers.

Originally, from the Pacific Northwest, she now lives in picturesque Vermont, with her husband, two daughters, and their three dogs.

In 2012, Heidi turned her passion for reading into a full-fledged literary career, writing over twenty novels, including the acclaimed Forever My Girl.

Heidi's first novel, Forever My Girl, has been adapted into a motion picture with LD Entertainment and Roadside Attractions, starring Alex Roe and Jessica Rothe, and opened in theaters on January 19, 2018.

Don't miss more books by Heidi McLaughlin! Sign up for her newsletter, or join the fun in her fan group!

Connect with Heidi!
www.heidimclaughlin.com

Made in United States
North Haven, CT
03 September 2023

41089575R00200